Checkmate. Copyright © 2012 by Melodrama Publishing. All rights reserved. Printed in the United States of America. No part of this book may be used or reproduced in any manner whatsoever without written permission except in the case of brief quotations embodied in critical articles or reviews. For information, address Melodrama Publishing, P.O. Box 522, Bellport, NY 11713.

www.melodramapublishing.com

Library of Congress Control Number: 2011927249
ISBN-13: 978-1-934157-65-7
Mass Market Edition: March 2013
10 9 8 7 6 5 4 3 2

Interior Design: Candace K. Cottrell
Cover Design: Marion Designs
Cover Model: Vanessa

Checkmate

THE BADDEST CHICK

NISA SANTIAGO

Buy

for Melodrama

Prologue

The days and nights since her capture were an agonizing nightmare for Apple. She no longer knew, nor understood, what time it was—minutes seemed like hours for her. She felt pieces of her soul being torn from her daily, and her dignity was buried in the filthy soil of some poor, faraway, forgotten town tucked away in Mexico, miles away from the border.

The rape was continuous. Men of all shapes and ages would walk into Apple's forsaken and vile room with stares of lust, their cocks swelling in their jeans. The reek of previous customers who'd had their way with Apple didn't deter them from being with her. They didn't care that one side of her face was badly disfigured. Some men even relished that she was badly disfigured and would touch and caress her burned face passionately, falling in love with what she was—beautiful, but monstrous at the same time.

The men who frequented Shaun's whorehouse paid for a service, and to most of them, pussy was still pussy, no matter who spread their legs. They were all looking for sexual relief, and Apple was still a young, shapely, American woman who had become a fantasy for them.

"Come get yourself a piece of the American Dream," Shaun would say to the men. "Look how shapely and young she still is. Her pussy still runs wet with paradise."

Apple was doped up most of the time, but was no longer physically handcuffed; only in her mind did the chains still exist. She didn't know if it had been days, maybe months, maybe a year since her arrival.

She was almost always naked; her tattered clothes were nothing but decorations for the floor. In one hour, she would find herself being fucked by as many as four men. Most were quick on top of her—in and out like fast food. Others wanted to take their time with her, savoring every moment, taking advantage of her condition and her youth.

Apple lay on her back and felt the tremendous pressure. The man sprawled out on top of her, with his protruding gut, flabby arms and bad hygiene, weighed about three hundred pounds, and she was sinking down into the soiled, flimsy mattress like it was quicksand. He grunted with each thrust into Apple, while her legs dangled off the side of the small bed like a leaf blowing to the wind. She had no control. For a few pesos, she was his. No arguments. It was business.

"So good, mami, so good. You so good, mami," he chanted.

Apple just lay there; her body was present, but her

mind was somewhere else. The dope helped with the sex. It took her away from the hell she was experiencing.

The man ravaged Apple's nipples with his long tongue. He held her thin body captive on the mattress with the force of his weight, and had her legs spread so far apart, they were ready to snap like a wishbone.

His grunts became louder. "Ugh! Ugh! Ugh! So good, mami, so good! Ugh!" he cried out.

Moments later, he shook on top of Apple like he was having a seizure, bursting inside of her. When he was done, he rolled off Apple and lay flat on his back, the sweat from his body dripping onto the mattress. He was breathing heavily. He then looked at Apple's disfigured face and bluntly asked, "What happened to yo' face?"

Apple ignored the question. She continued to lie there next to him on the dirty mattress, but her mind was still absent. She didn't even realize that the man was done.

"You don't answer me? You speak English, right?" he asked.

Apple remained lifeless on the mattress. She didn't care to have any conversation with the man. He wasn't the only one who had questioned her burns, but she always ignored them. Her disfigurement was her secret to keep. He was only there to do his business with her and leave.

The man got up, leaning his weight onto the floor, and began collecting his clothing. He looked a little irritated with Apple. He spoke in Spanish as he pulled up his pants and began buttoning his shirt.

"¡Puta con retraso!" he exclaimed.

He threw on his shoes and glared at Apple. "You is one *ugly* bitch!" he exclaimed before making his exit for the door.

Apple was relieved that he didn't get violent with her, like some men had done previously.

The room fell quiet for a moment. But it wouldn't be lasting.

Before Apple could remove herself from off the unclean mattress, the dilapidated door flew open and Shaun rushed in carrying a bucket of cold water. He immediately grabbed her up off of the bed and dowsed her with it, causing her to screech from the sudden attack.

"Shut up!" he roared. "You need to clean yourself up! You stink!"

Apple stood dripping wet from the water thrown on her and wanted to burst into tears. Shaun was nothing but unkind and cruel to her. He abused and insulted her every chance he got. His cruelty had nothing to do with her keeping up with her hygiene and everything to do with his murdered sister.

"You ain't in fuckin' Kansas anymore, you dumb bitch! Go clean yourself up and get right! You got another customer in twenty minutes. I don't want him complaining about how stank you are!"

Shaun exited the room, leaving Apple to dry herself off and pick up her things. Inside, she was seething. In Harlem, he would have been a dead man.

Though Shaun had the upper hand momentarily, Apple was certain there was a way to escape the madness she was living in. Every day, her rage kept building. She played the docile role because, in her mind, it was the only way of survival. And she constantly fought the depression of missing home and who she used to be. Apple needed that one break in the chain, and she would be gone. But she needed help.

She donned the dingy, teal robe that hung from the back of a chair and exited out into the narrow, ramshackle hallway. The place was flooded with Mexican whores, some of the girls as young as thirteen. And most of them shunned Apple because of her looks and ethnicity.

"Stupid American girl," some of the girls would say to her.

She tried to make friends with some of the other whores, telling them that she had lots of money back in the States, and that she could make them wealthy if they aided in her escape. But they only laughed.

"You is a whore, just like us. You have no money. Shoot away from us wit' your lies," one of the girls had exclaimed.

"I have money, lots of money, and connections. Believe me."

They constantly taunted her. Some even tried to pick fights with her, but she proved to them that she wasn't a pushover. A few fights ensued because of the constant verbal abuse, but they were quickly broken up by a few of Shaun's goons.

Apple made her way down the hall, toward the bathroom that was shared by all the girls in the building.

She had steadily gotten used to the overflowing toilet with broken seats and duct-taped repairs, the overflowing trashcan filled with used tampons and sanitary napkins, peeling paint, stained mirrors, and the mold and mildew that had infested the two showers.

Apple entered the bathroom as two whores were walking out; they exchanged hard stares at each other, but no words were said. She walked over to the mirror and peered at her reflection for a moment. She had gotten used to her disfigurement, but her mind didn't want to get used to her imprisonment. Every day she fought with herself to keep her sanity. Every day she thought about home. She thought about Chico. She was full of regrets.

She turned on the water and splashed some on her face. She soon heard the toilet flush behind her, indicating that someone was in the makeshift stall. She turned to see Mary.

Mary was in her late fifties and hadn't aged too well. Her face was wrinkled, she had missing front teeth due to violent abuse, and her tits sagged into her stomach. Only a few still paid for her services. She had been a whore since she was fifteen years old, forced into the business because of dire circumstances and the poor family she came from. It was the only trade she knew.

Mary was kidnapped and raped in her village and held for two weeks by the pastor of the local church. She was only fourteen. When he finally let her go, no one believed her story. The locals ridiculed her family, so they turned their backs on her, proclaiming that she lied about the rape and abuse. She had nowhere to go and no one to turn to. Within two days of living on the streets without food or water, she turned to the only thing that could sustain her: prostitution.

Apple and Mary locked eyes for a moment, both carrying sad gazes. Mary was one of the few women who spoke English well. She had no problems with Apple. She understood her hardship, but at the same time, she wasn't too quick to make friends with Apple.

Apple stared at herself in the mirror and then fixated her eyes on Mary.

"You have a problem?" Mary asked calmly.

Apple shook her head. "No."

"You need to stop telling lies about how wealthy you are," Mary said. "It only upsets the girls even more."

"I have plenty of money, Mary."

"Then where is it? Why hasn't your money or your connections freed you from this place?"

Apple wanted to make everyone believe that Chico would come for her; that he would either buy the town or shoot it out, whichever would lead to her return. In her heart of hearts, she knew he would. And if all else failed, there was a small glimmer of hope that Kola would search for her. Although they had their differences, they were still blood. But right now, standing before Mary, Apple couldn't muster the strength to retell the story she'd been spewing since day one of her capture.

Mary stood next to Apple, both women silent. The whorehouse they lived in was becoming a burden to both women.

Mary was sick, but healthcare was non-existent in her country and in her line of work. She'd gradually accepted the fate that cancer would be the death of her. She thought that dying would be the only way to be free.

Apple continued to wash her face and other areas of her body and then walked out the bathroom. She went back into her room and shut the door. She looked around her nasty, barren, run-down room with peeling paint and black mold and sighed heavily. This couldn't be her life.

Before Apple could attempt to get comfortable, there was a knock at the door. She instantly knew what it meant. Her next appointment had arrived too early. Apple didn't even have a moment to gather her thoughts after her last trick.

The door swung open, and Shaun marched in first, with a crew of men behind him who looked to be in their early twenties.

"This is her: The American Dream," Shaun said, auctioning off Apple with great pride. "The pussy is to die for."

The young men smiled. The first crewmember quickly handed Shaun a few hundred pesos.

Shaun counted the money quickly. "Enjoy. You got a half hour, each. Make it worth ya while."

The men nodded.

"Homes, we gonna have more than fun."

The minute Shaun was out the door, a stranger with a teardrop tattoo began unbuckling his pants and charged for Apple, who was still sore from her last session. He forced himself on top of her, placing his hand around her neck, and almost choking the life out of her. He thrust his erection so deep into her, she couldn't help but cry out from the size and girth that penetrated her.

The young kid on top of her was vibrant and rough. But he was quick. He came in a matter of minutes, jumped off Apple, and quickly allowed the next in line to have his turn.

The young gang members treated her more like she was a toilet, than a teenage girl being held against her will.

Chapter 1

Kola sat in the bedroom of her plush home clad in a flirtatious pink baby doll chemise trimmed with a delicate sequined Venice appliqué. She was giving herself a pedicure to the sounds of Maxwell, but even his soothing words couldn't erase the troubles in her head. Her mind couldn't escape Cross and his infidelity. Then there was trying to cope with him having a newborn son.

Then she had Edge on her mind. She knew she had to watch her back with that snake.

Then there was Eduardo. The sexual tension between the two of them was undeniable. Kola knew it wasn't good to mix business with pleasure, but it was one pleasure she thought about constantly. Eduardo was so tempting, just the thought of him had her pussy dripping wet with passion.

Business was good for Kola. Her product was profitable, her name was buzzing in the streets, and her team was strong. Candace was fierce when it came to the streets, and her murder game was on point. Candace proved that women could kill and be as ruthless as any man.

But Kola's love life was in shambles. She didn't want anything to do with Cross at the moment. His betrayal had really hurt her. One thought of that bitch Cynthia and her son by Cross would have her shedding tears, and she'd never cried over any man.

Cross had gotten word about what had transpired between Kola and Cynthia, and it sent him into a small panic. His two worlds had now collided in a violent way. He tried to figure out how Kola had found out about his Brooklyn chick. Who could have told? But he figured, since he still took care of her, it would be a small issue that would resolve itself in a few days.

He wanted to get back to business. Money needed to be made. He felt that Kola was acting childish. His rationalization was, "So what, I fucked her? It was just pussy, but I love you, Kola. It ain't gotta change what we do. We a team, baby."

But weeks had passed, and Kola wasn't budging.

Cross had arrived home one day to find all the locks had been changed. He rang the bell continuously, but to no avail.

"Kola, what the fuck is wrong wit' you? Are you stupid? Why the fuck you changing the locks?"

Kola rejected his calls and left him standing outside his lavish home to ponder on his regret for cheating on her. Cross soon got the hint. He left, feeling Kola needed more time to cool down and collect herself.

Kola nodded to her favorite tracks by Trey Songz, who had replaced Maxwell in the CD changer. She planned on meeting up with Candace and her girls.

As Kola continued to paint her nails, the doorbell sounded. She stopped what she was doing for the moment and scurried downstairs toward the front door. She glanced out the window, only to notice a flower truck parked outside.

"Who?" she shouted.

"I have a delivery for a Kola," the man said.

"From who, or where?"

"Um, from a Cross."

Kola sighed, shaking her head in disbelief. She didn't want anything from Cross, but the deliveryman was adamant.

"Ma'am, I have over two dozen roses and flowers that need to be dropped off," the deliveryman stated. "They're already paid for, and I can't take them back with me."

"Just leave them out there and go," she replied sharply.

The man shrugged and did what he was told. He left the assortment of flowers and roses outside her door and drove away.

Kola opened her front door soon after his departure and stared at the flowers. "What, is he crazy?"

Cross had purchased everything from lilies, tulips, daisies, and sunflowers, with two-dozen roses. Kola was never big on flowers, but she had to admit, the arrangement and delivery was nice. The idyllic moment was temporary, though, because soon after, she had a nearby lawn worker toss everything on the street for the trash to pick up. Kola didn't have time for bullshit. She had work to do and a business to run. Cross needed to learn that she wasn't the bitch to be played with or manipulated.

Kola slammed her front door and went back upstairs to her bedroom to get herself ready. Kola got dressed in a pair of tight, shimmering gold pants that accentuated her curvy figure, a stylish halter-top, and a pair of chic heels. She looked stunning, with her long, silky hair reaching down her back. Kola put the right touches on her face with makeup, exited her home, and jumped into her pearl-white convertible Benz with the vertical doors and bright red interior.

She sped out of her driveway on her way to meet up with Candace and her ruthless crew of girls. She placed a Lil Wayne CD in the stereo and began jamming to "Lollipop."

It was a quarter to midnight when Kola pulled up to The Red Spot, a vibrant and popular club on the West Side of Manhattan. She stepped out of her Benz looking like a superstar and passed her keys to the valet attendant.

The Red Spot was a plush, high-end, all-in-one chic spot near the West Side Highway. It was a dance club, restaurant, pool hall, and had an indoor smoking lounge with polished décor. Celebrities, music moguls, and the city's elite frequented the club, and Kola was a regular. It was one of the places she did her business; extracting clientele for her parties and services. She was subtle with her business, passing out her cards and whispering in ears about her events. But mostly, she was profiling the males, and even a few females, in the club.

Kola strutted toward the entrance like the boss bitch she was. She was instantly recognized by the security and bouncers, and was able to bypass the long wait to get inside and escape the cover charge.

A beefy bouncer greeted her with a warm smile. "Hey, Kola."

"Hey, Bobby," she replied.

The velvet rope was unlatched, and Kola entered the 10,000-square-foot space, where the caramel hues and warm earth tones dressed the interior, and the dimly lit chandeliers set off a sensual vibe.

The DJ had Rick Ross blaring throughout the club, and the place was alive and jumping with partygoers, drinking, and beautiful women.

Kola didn't care for the party. She had to meet with Candace and her girls, who were also regulars at the club, and had connections with the owner.

She moved through the large crowd and headed toward the VIP area. She received stares from men and women as she passed. Her beauty and style were captivating, and her presence was intimidating. She didn't smile or pay the attention any mind. They weren't worth her time.

Kola reached the stairway that went up to the glass-enclosed smoking lounge, for VIP guests only, and two strapping male bouncers made sure only the elite passed through.

Both bouncers acknowledged her as she approached, smiling and stepping to the side, allowing her up the stairway and into the room. But they quickly turned their heads, admiring her plump backside as she walked up the stairs.

"Damn, that's nice!" one of the men said.

Kola entered the glass-enclosed lounge and was right away greeted by the manager of the club, Pablo, a short, round, Dominican man, with bronze skin and thinning black hair. He was sharply dressed in a grey pinstripe suit and a gold Rolex.

"Kola, it's good to see you," he greeted joyfully.

"Hey, Pablo."

"Candace is already in the office. They're waiting for you."

She nodded.

Pablo allowed the girls to conduct business in his establishment. He was always paranoid about being watched or indicted. He had cameras watching every angle of his club. He always swept his place for bugs on the daily, so it was hard for any law enforcement to wiretap his club or office. And he screened his employees thoroughly, via his brother having a background in computers and knowing how to hack into any secure account. If someone was fraudulent, then Pablo's brother, Joseph, had the means to find out.

It was always business with Pablo and Kola. He was a regular at Kola's sex parties, and Pablo showed her the same hospitality at The Red Spot that she'd always shown him. She was always on the list, and always invited into VIP.

Kola nodded and walked toward the backroom, where the main office was located. Beyond that was the balcony area with a phenomenal view overlooking the West Side Highway and Hudson River.

Kola entered Pablo's office to find Candace and Patrice seated in one of the swanky chairs, laughing and drinking martinis.

Meeting at Pablo's club made it look like they were a trio of ladies only out to have a good time, in case cops or the feds were watching. Both Candace and Patrice were dressed seductively in tight, leather skirts that exposed their thick thighs, revealing tops, and six-inch wedge heels. Candace and Patrice may have looked like promiscuous, partying chicks, but they were skilled killers on Kola's payroll—and their portfolio was displayed throughout the streets of New York.

"Look at y'all bitches," Kola greeted with a smile.

"We waitin' for you, boss lady," Candace said.

The ladies hugged each other, and it was all smiles, but Kola wanted to shift things to important business. She had a lot of things to discuss with her top enforcer, Candace.

"What you drinking?" Kola asked Candace.

"One strong martini."

"I'll take one too." Kola walked over to Pablo's private assistant and asked her to get her the same thing that her girls were drinking.

The young woman nodded and rushed to fill her order.

It didn't take long for Kola to get her drink. Any orders coming from the VIP section or Pablo's office were handled ASAP. She served Kola her martini and exited the room so the girls could talk business in private.

"Come, let's talk on the balcony. The air and view is better out there," Kola said.

Candace and Patrice followed behind Kola. Kola slid the glass sliding door shut, peered around, and took a few sips from her martini.

"What you need to talk about, Kola?" Candace asked.

Kola didn't respond right away. She walked toward the edge of the balcony and peered over. They were only two stories up, but it was a steep fall. Kola took a sip from her martini, stared at the New Jersey skyline for a moment, and then turned to lock eyes with her girl.

"Some muthafuckas don't have an ounce of respect for us, just because we bitches. I mean, look at us. We got shit on lock. But these haters, they ain't gonna never learn that what any man can do, a fuckin' woman can do twice as good."

"I hear that," Patrice chimed with a smile.

"But check this," Kola continued. "We gonna prove these bitch-ass niggas wrong, starting with Edge."

"He always been hating on you, Kola. It's about time you made something happen to his triflin' ass. I'm ready to put in work on that nigga," Candace said.

"You will, baby girl. You will. His jealousy of me is starting to rage out of control, and I ain't giving him any more free passes just because he's Cross' right-hand man. I'm sick of his shit!"

"When you want it to go down?" Candace asked.

"Soon."

Candace nodded.

"I got a lot of shit to prove, y'all feel me?"

"Hells yeah," Patrice and Candace said simultaneously.

"But what about Cross? He's still in the picture or what?" Patrice asked.

Kola was silent for a moment, hesitating to answer. She thought about Cross. She still loved him, but love and emotions for any man was a problem when it came to handling her business. Cross had fucked up. He had a gun charge hanging over his head, and a snake friend in his corner that he failed to recognize. Kola felt that Cross was slipping, and she didn't need his mistakes interfering with her business. She already had his connect, and her name was starting to ring out more than his. In the streets everyone had heard of *Coca Kola*—the name given to her by the Columbians because she was moving so much weight. In her mind, she didn't need a man for shit.

She wanted to make Cross pay for his infidelity. He had a son with some Brooklyn bitch, and Kola disapproved of it. Kola felt that she was too fine and good of a woman to be cheated on. It would be Cross' loss, not hers.

"You know, with Edge out the way, then Cross would have to fall solo on that gun charge," Kola stated.

Candace nodded.

Kola continued with, "Cross fucked up. He's lucky

that a short bid is all he's gonna get for fuckin' cheating on me."

Patrice took another sip of her Martini. "If you ask me, a couple years away in a State pen is hardly payback. Shit, that's a mini vacation."

Kola shrugged. She knew she wasn't going hard on Cross and she knew why. She still loved him despite the betrayal. Her mind said to dead him, but her heart said no. She spoke, "Patrice, that's the plan for now. But like the weather, shit could change."

The girls stood under the canopy of night and towering buildings, excited about their future.

Kola raised her glass in the air for a toast. Patrice and Candace followed, and then Kola said, "This is our time . . . our fuckin' moment, and ain't no muthafucka taking it away from us. Here's to makin' paper hand over fist!"

They clinked glasses together and downed what was left of their drinks. "Here's to makin' paper!"

"Now, let's go out there and make it happen," Kola stated. "Show these clown-ass niggas just how good a bitch can do it."

Chapter 2

C hico sat snug in his brand-new, gleaming XJ Jaguar in front of the Pink Houses on Linden Boulevard. The luxurious car caught attention and turned heads from many passers-by as it sat parked on Linden Boulevard, with Chico the sole occupant.

Chico had felt uncomfortable and apprehensive being in the Brooklyn hood as he waited. He had the chromed Desert Eagle concealed in a stash box and a .380 under his seat. He nodded to a 50 Cent track, and was dressed like a don, looking suave and clean in a dark-gray YSL suit and sporting a pair of David Chu Bespoke Italian wingtips, and a Presidential watch on his wrist. He screamed ghetto wealth.

※

Since Chico's return from North Carolina, his name had started ringing out again on the streets. He had established a strong, but temporary connect with the Johnson brothers, who had him supplied for a few months. But he needed a firm cartel connection. The Haitians' product was unreliable and weak. Chico was also willing to invest his money into anything profitable, but with the continuing war with Cross and Kola, he knew that he needed a crew of killers in his corner to maintain his stronghold over the neighborhood. He got that from a young, wild kid named Two-Face.

Two-Face was a sixteen-year-old assassin from a small town in Mexico called Ahome. He'd migrated to the States when he was eleven years old. Two-Face came from a family of thugs and assassins that murdered anybody that got in their way—government officials, diplomats—and extorted drug dealers and raped women. His father was in the corrupt Mexican military, which was nothing but assassins with badges, and Two-Face's family was associated with Los Zetas, a notorious Mexican cartel.

When Two-Face had turned twelve, he joined a ruthless Mexican gang and passed initiation by pumping two bullets into a schoolteacher's head. He followed the petite and well-liked school teacher coming from school one afternoon, and rushed up on her, raised the loaded .45 he carried and pressed the gun to the back of her head.

Before she could react or scream, Two-Face shot her in the back of the head twice. He had received his first symbolic trophy—a tiny tattoo teardrop under his right eye that indicated how many people he'd killed.

The sixteen-year-old kid had gotten the name Two-Face for many reasons, but one particular reason was because he had the ability to become your friend, have you trust him with his boyish features and catching smile. But then with the blink of an eye, he was easily able to betray you and set you up, and kill you without hesitation. Two-Face was feared anywhere he went. In his hometown, they gave him another nickname, Body-Count. Killing was a skill for Two-Face. He had learned it through his father, his older brothers and uncles, who were all notorious in violence and warfare. They knew how to torture and steal, and wreak havoc wherever they rested their heads.

Chico had come across Two-Face during his short stay in D.C. He was conducting business out there with a few locals and kept hearing the name, Two-Face, in passing. It was like a constant tune in his ear wherever he went. Two-Face this, and Two-Face that. The name was notorious wherever he went in D.C., and it caught his interest.

Many figures in the underworld didn't like or want to deal with Two-Face because he was young, too deadly, and out of order. The major heads in the city feared him, and so many of the young locals looked up to him. But Chico saw an opportunity, especially when he got word that Two-Face had two murder warrants out for his arrest.

Chico began asking around about him, and after a few days of searching, he finally came face to face with the young killer at a downtown bar in Capitol Hill.

"Yo, you the nigga lookin' for me?" Two-Face had asked, his face full of scorn, and eyes narrowed at Chico.

"Yeah, I've been hearing about you," Chico replied coolly.

"Why the fuck you lookin' for me? You know what I'm about?"

Chico was far from intimidated by the young thug, having seen his fair share of killers over the years, including himself.

"Yeah, I know what you're about. I can use a nigga like you."

"What the fuck you mean?"

Chico figured it was better to show him than tell him. He reached into his jacket, pulled out a wad of bills totaling ten thousand, and tossed it to the young killer.

Two-Face caught the rolled-up stack of money in his hands. "What the fuck is this for, homes?"

"Call it a down payment for your services."

"How about I just kill you and take whatever else you got on you." Two-Face lifted his shirt and revealed the butt of a 9 mm tucked in his waistband.

"And then what? I'll be just another body under your belt instead of a golden opportunity for you. And then you'll be ignorant."

"Homes, who the fuck is you? You in my nest, yo. I run these streets."

"And you're a wanted man out here. I guarantee if you don't leave here soon, you'll be locked up."

"And go where, homes? You know where I'm from, what I'm about?"

"New York. Come work for me. And believe me, I have plenty of work for you. That ten thousand in your hands, it's only a start."

Two-Face stood, thinking about the opportunity.

"My name's Chico."

"If you ain't serious about this, or playin' game wit' me, homes, I'll fuckin' kill you."

"Oh, I'm serious as ever. Do I look like the type of nigga to play games, especially when it comes to money? Who else would be willing to just hand over ten stacks to a kid?"

Two-Face nodded.

It was the beginning of a sweet and deadly business arrangement. The next day, Chico and Two-Face were on I-95 headed toward New York. After Two-Face's first month in New York, he was already implicated in three homicides. And like in D.C., his name was becoming notorious in Harlem and the Washington Heights areas.

Chico glanced at the time as he continued to sit in his XJ Jaguar. "What the fuck is takin' this bitch so long?"

It was getting late, and he didn't like lingering in Brooklyn too long. He was unknown in that part of town, the Pink Houses, where Brooklyn held the reputation for being one of the grimmest boroughs. He picked up his phone and was about to make a heated phone call, until he noticed Blythe exiting the lobby.

She strutted toward the gleaming Jaguar with her sultry looks, wearing a pair of tight-fitting Seven jeans with pink stitching, a snug-fitting baby pink Benetton shirt that highlighted her ample breasts, and a pair of pink-bowed peep-toe ankle strap wedges.

Blythe had full lips, round hips, butter-like complexion and almond-shaped, cinnamon eyes that captivated any man with one stare. She was a queen in her hood—wanted and envied by so many people.

*

Chico had been dealing with Blythe for a month, and she'd become his new flavor. It was rumored that she used to fuck with the rapper Fabolous on the down low for a moment, and she was a high-end woman with an appetite for expensive things and having a good time.

The two met in downtown Manhattan, at an industry event and listening party for an upcoming rapper who was coming out under the Def Jam label. Chico was there with his friends, showing his presence and looking intimidating with this thuggish posture. But he was at the listening party only for pleasure. He was friends with one of the producers that he grew up with in the Heights, and had a personal invite.

Chico and Blythe locked eyes, and Blythe showed that she was interested in him with her pleasant stare and inviting smile. Chico casually made his move on her, spoke a few nice words in her ear, and things took off from there. Soon after, Chico began sporting his young, beautiful prize all throughout Harlem. He flaunted her in his new Jaguar, and bought her nice things, taking her shopping on Fifth Avenue and downtown. They were starting to look like the "it" couple in the hood. Blythe was a good look under Chico's arm, and she was falling in love with her newfound boyfriend.

But unbeknownst to Blythe, Chico had simply started dealing with Blythe only to try and bring Apple out of hiding, have her come out from whatever rock she was hiding under. He was missing her, and she was still in his heart. It had been months since her disappearance, and no one knew or didn't have a clue where she was.

Chico had gotten tired looking or asking around about her, especially with Denise, Apple's mother, being so resistant and uncaring. Denise had tried to drill into Chico's head that Apple had left on her own accord.

"Look, Chico, I don't know where that bitch went off to. She just ain't been around lately. Fuck her anyway! Bitch gonna kick me outta her swanky crib, like her own shit don't stink. Nigga, just stop lookin' for that tramp! 'Cuz I ain't fuckin' worrying! And neither should you."

Chico's plan was to be with Blythe and flaunt her around Harlem in an attempt to bring Apple back to him maybe because of jealousy. But days became weeks, and soon after, Chico found himself having feelings for the girl.

And she was more than just a pretty face with a terrific figure. She was enrolled in New York City Technical College for Legal Assistant Studies. When she told Chico that she wanted to become a lawyer, he knew that she could be just the type of chick he needed on his arm. If Blythe got her law degree she could very well be an asset to his empire. It was small details such as that which started to chip away at his feeling for Apple. Apple was street-smart and had the heart of a lion. But with Blythe, there was a full package. She was book and street smart; it was an unbeatable combination.

Blythe proved herself to be worthy when, one day, she was willing to conceal a loaded gun in her Prada purse when she and Chico got pulled over during a routine traffic stop. The officers became suspicious of Chico, but Chico kept his cool. He was riding dirty; something he had to do in his line of work although he knew it could cost him his freedom.

While one of the officers was ready to ask for Chico to step out of his pricey car so they could conduct a search of the vehicle, Blythe politely intervened in the conversation by saying, "Officer, we're so sorry to have been speeding, but my fiancé and I are running so late for my doctor's appointment. You see, I'm two months pregnant."

"Congratulations," the officer replied.

Blythe added, "But we just wanna be on our way, with no problems. Feel free to search us, or the car, anything if it will speed things up."

Chico thought Blythe had lost her mind, but he kept an impassive look and went along with the plan.

Both officers glanced at each other briefly. Blythe looked so calm and collected, giving the officers a hearty smile.

The cop handed back Chico his license and said, "Just get there safe and slow things down."

"Will do, officer," Chico replied.

When the cops were back in their patrol car, Chico wanted to hug Blythe. But he looked at her and said, "You took a risk wit' that shit. What if they decided to search the vehicle?"

"They weren't going to," she replied.

"And why not?"

"Because . . . it's mind control, baby. I learned that in class. When you volunteer and give them the go-ahead to search your shit without them saying so, they already are thinking that it might be a waste of their time. Yeah, it's a risk, but it worked, right, baby?"

Chico saw something different in Blythe from that day. She was gradually becoming something more to him than a temporary replacement for Apple. She proved that she was about something.

Blythe fucked Chico like the king he felt he was, grinding her sweet pussy into his erection, hugging his body close, and panting in his ear. She loved when Chico would suck on her nipples and finger-fuck her ass, simultaneously. She was a freak. When she was naked, her body was something great to see, thick and shapely in all the right places, ample and bouncy tits, and shaved pubic hair. Her pussy protruded from between her thighs like it was in 3D. The sex was phenomenal, and Chico couldn't fight the love that started developing between him and her.

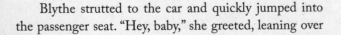

Blythe strutted to the car and quickly jumped into the passenger seat. "Hey, baby," she greeted, leaning over and giving Chico a kiss on the lips.

Chico admired her stylish attire for a short moment. Then his face turned into a scowl. "Why you take so fuckin' long?"

"'Cuz I gotta look nice. I'm a fly bitch, and it takes a while for me to get right. I can't be rushin' out my crib lookin' like some bum bitch. You know that ain't even my style, baby." Blythe pulled down the visor mirror to admire herself. "But look at me and tell me it wasn't worth the wait."

Chico sighed. "You know I don't fuckin' like waiting for you out here too long. It ain't my scene."

"And who gonna step to you? Please. You always packin', and your name ring bells."

"Not out here like that."

"Well, they know me, and niggas know I don't fuck with nobody that can't handle themselves or me when it comes to the streets and in their pockets. I don't fuck wit' weak niggas, Chico, so when they see me with you out here, these niggas know you about something serious. So you ain't even gotta worry, baby. It's all good."

"Ain't nobody worried," he corrected, Blythe. "Just carry your narrow ass downstairs quicker when I fuckin' pull up. When I was with Apple she knew a nigga didn't play that shit. She never kept me waiting!"

Blythe rolled her eyes. "Well, I ain't Apple!"

Chico didn't say anything back. He shifted the car in drive and sped out the parking spot, and made a sudden U-turn on Linden Boulevard, heading toward Harlem.

The sooner he was out of Brooklyn, the better.

An hour later, Chico was back uptown where he belonged. He pulled up to Shannon's, the popular Bronx club on Fordham Road, a few blocks from the Major Deegan Expressway.

Chico and Blythe strutted toward the front entrance of the place. There wasn't a line outside, but security had a heavy presence. Shannon's was a place known to have gang members and thugs around. The west side of the Bronx was a battleground for drugs, and on some nights, Shannon's was a place where many gang members and drug dealers came to unwind, drink, and look for bitches to fuck with. But the majority of them didn't leave their attitudes and beef on the block. In fact a few gunfights had ensued outside of the club because of tension between a few groups.

But Chico wasn't worried about bringing his lady to a troubled spot. His authority and connection went everywhere with him. Tonight, it was personal and business.

Two-Face came in handy for Chico in more ways than one. And Chico was proud that he'd tracked him down in D.C. It didn't take long to find out that Two-Face had a cocaine connection down in Mexico. His father was big time, and twice a year, Two-Face would travel down to Mexico to visit his family, especially his elderly mother, who he loved dearly. Two-Face had eight siblings, mostly brothers, and all of them had inducted themselves into the violence and drug trade that plagued Mexico.

Chico was barely hanging on to his corners with what the Haitians were providing him, and with Cross and Kola having that straight Colombian connect, he needed to upgrade. But what he lacked in potent product, he made up for heavily in muscle. Chico's crew was deadly like a terrorist organization, striking fear wherever they went. And Two-Face held it down in places where some felt Chico was weak.

Chico and Blythe walked by security without acknowledging them. Security knew his name and reputation, and allowed Chico to slide through without any searches or cover charges.

Shannon's was packed, and even Jim Jones and his fiancé Chrissy were in the crowd. The DJ had Dipset blaring and everyone was dressed in mostly jeans, Timberlands, sneakers, Yankees fitted caps, and tons of jewelry. It was a place and time to show off wealth and money. The ballers popped bottles in the corners and kept the young ladies entertained with their antics, and the dance floor was crammed with sweaty revelers and scantily clad hood rats.

Chico didn't have time to mingle with any partygoers. He was recognized by a few goons he passed, and everyone admired Blythe. But they knew she was off limits. Chico looked around for Two-Face. It was his kind of atmosphere—lions within the den. Within his short time in New York, Two-Face had already put together a crew of young, reckless shooters with the same crazy mentality as himself. Instantly, everybody in the place knew not to fuck with them by their thuggish demeanor and through word of mouth on the streets.

Chico spotted Two-Face seated in one of the elevated VIP booths above the crowded dance floor. He was surrounded by women and young goons, and popping bottles like it was soda. Blythe followed behind Chico closely, not wanting to get lost and separated with the thick, growing crowd around them. She clinched onto his arm, and played Chico close.

Chico walked up to the booth and looked at his young enforcer.

"Chico!" Two-Face shouted with a twisted smile.

Chico looked around. It was too crazy. He only focused his attention on Two-Face, wanting to discuss brief business with him.

"Two-Face, let me holla at you for a moment," Chico said.

"You wanna drink, homes?"

Chico waved him off. He knew Two-Face was tipsy. Two-Face removed himself from his crowd of friends and the ladies and walked up to Chico.

"What's up, homes? What we need to talk about?"

Chico looked at Blythe and said, "Go have a drink and chill for a moment, baby. I'll be right back."

Blythe didn't look too comfortable being alone, but she knew being Chico's woman, no one would dare disrespect her. She nodded.

Chico and Two-Face walked away to speak in private. They entered the men's bathroom. Chico made sure that there weren't any listening ears inside any of the stalls. He then looked at Two-Face and asked, "You got word on your peoples about that thing across the borders?"

Two-Face smiled. "Yeah, spoke to my old man, and he's interested, homes. I told him good things about you."

Chico nodded. "Cool."

"We meet though—"

"When?"

"Next week."

"A'ight."

"Like I said, you take care of me, and I'll take care of you, homes. ¿Comprende?"

"Comprende," Chico replied. "But I need another thing taken care of, ASAP."

"What's that?"

Chico walked out the bathroom, and Two-Face followed. They went back into the club area. Two-Face stood next to Chico. Chico looked around and then subtly pointed out to someone across the room, who was seated in another VIP section opposite of Two-Face's. The man was tall and slender, sporting heavy jewelry and a silk shirt. He was flanked by women, and was very boisterous.

"Who he, homes?" Two-Face asked.

"A problem."

Two-Face locked his attention on the man, as Chico continued to talk.

"I need him taken care of."

Two-Face nodded. He didn't need to know why or what was the problem with him and Chico. The only thing

Two-Face understood was that Chico had pointed him out and he needed to be killed. Two-Face didn't care for questions; he only craved for murder, money, and bitches—in that order.

"Consider it already done, homes," Two-Face assured him.

Chico nodded and headed over back to Blythe, who was seated by the bar, nursing a drink. Chico walked over to her, placed his arm around her waist and said, "We're leaving."

Blythe was pleased. The crowd wasn't her scene anymore. She was used to industry parties and more classy events, not a room full of thugs, hood rats and killers. She had been there and done that.

The couple made their quick exit, while Two-Face was left behind to ponder and scheme on the man Chico wanted taken out.

✳

It wasn't until three in the morning that the crowd from Shannon's began to dissipate slowly into the street. The one-way street was flooded with cars blaring their loud systems and people mingling about, walking to their cars or some other location. The horde of people just about made it look like a block party.

Trevor was flanked by two scantily clad ladies in tight, booty-hugging shorts and low, revealing tops. He was the attention-grabber, with his long, bulky chain, extravagant diamond cross pendant, the pinky rings, the loud talk and looking like a rap mogul. He had his arms around both women as they walked toward his big-body Benz sitting on 22-inch chrome rims.

It was obvious what Trevor was—a drug dealer/pimp. He flaunted his lifestyle and riches like it was legal. He made it known all over town that he was a playboy and womanizer, and some of his raunchy ways with the ladies had gotten him into hot water with some of the men around town. Boyfriends, brothers, and fathers to some of the women he'd used and abused weren't happy with him after he got their loved ones hooked on drugs or pregnant. But Trevor denied being a father to any child.

Trevor walked around the hood like he was untouchable. He had guns and he had a reputation, being connected to "the Juice crew," a powerful and deadly organization coming out of Yonkers, New York.

"I'm sayin', though," Trevor said to his lady companions, "I love ya both. Y'all both would die for me, right?"

Both ladies chuckled.

Trevor hugged them close, his smile wide. He was ready to share a night of pleasure at his Harlem apartment on 155th Street. They were a few steps away from the car. Trevor reached for his keys and pressed the button to deactivate his alarm system.

"There goes my chariot. Nice, right, I paid eighty grand for it. Came fully loaded. Niggas ain't fuckin' wit' me out here. This is how I always roll, so y'all bitches better get used to it."

"I see. I like, I like," one of the girls said, smiling.

As Trevor continued his approach to his car, he wasn't aware of the young hooded teenager slowly creeping up behind him with a loaded .45 gripped in his hand, and down by his side. He had his eyes on Trevor like a hawk, watching everything he did.

He quickly lurched closer, and was ready to strike, not caring about the crowd around him. When Two-Face was within arm's distance of Trevor, he swiftly raised the gun, had it aimed at the back of Trevor's head and fired without an ounce of hesitation.

Bak! Bak! Bak!

Trevor suddenly dropped to the pavement, sprawled out face down against the concrete pavement, blood pooling around his shattered skull. The ladies he was with started to scream out in sheer horror. Panic erupted everywhere, as the crowd around started to scamper on hearing the gunshots.

Two-Face wasn't finished with his victim yet. He stood over the body and fired three more rounds into his head. After the shooting, he casually walked away and got into the backseat of an idling truck, which sped away, leaving the carnage behind for the cops to pick up and the locals to talk about another deadly shooting at the club.

"Damn! I fuckin' love what I do!" Two-Face exclaimed.

Chapter 3

Cross sat in the Yonkers strip club looking detached from the activities going on around him. He was nursing a beer and looked spaced out. The thunderous sound of a Plies' track blared throughout the underground club, as swarms of naked and scantily clad strippers moved throughout the place, grinding, giving out lap dances, and even a little something extra if the price was right. The dim, erotic atmosphere with the curves, tits and ass exposed was a haven for the male customers, but Cross sat there, his mind elsewhere. He caught a few of the ladies' attention with his mysterious demeanor and handsome look, but he didn't even give them a second thought.

"What's on ya mind, playa?" Edge asked, taking a seat next to his long-time friend at the table. "You got all this ass around you and you actin' like you in an empty room right now."

"I just got a lot on my mind, that's all," Cross replied.

"You thinkin' about Kola?"

"Thinkin' about everything, my nigga—her, this gun charge, Cynthia. What the fuck is goin' on? This bitch ain't even tryin' to accept my apology. Sent her a fortune in flowers the other day, and she had the nerve to toss them to the curb. You fuckin' believe that shit?"

"I'll tell you what's goin' on. You lettin' these bitches and all this dumb shit get in your head. You slippin', nigga. That's what's the fuck up! You need to wake the fuck up, Cross, and see what the fuck is really goin' on."

"What the fuck you talkin' about, Edge?"

"I'm talkin' about, Kola. You givin' her too much slack. I know she ya shorty and all, but get ya head out ya ass and really see what the fuck is goin' on."

Cross was listening intently. He wanted to know where Edge was going with the conversation. But Edge looked a little hesitant in continuing with the conversation about Kola. He saw in Cross' eyes that he was uneasy.

"Nigga, stop fuckin' double-talking, and just fuckin' come out with what you gotta say to me."

Edge moved in closer to Cross. "Yo, she tryin' to take over and move us the fuck out."

"What the fuck you talkin' about, Edge?"

"What I'm sayin' to you is, I don't trust her! No disrespect to you, my nigga, but look at the way she fuckin' moves, and how she's suddenly treating you. You don't see it, nigga? She already got ya connect, and you the nigga under her wing, running her fuckin' errands. It's like she's the boss and you're now her second in command. The streets aren't calling out your name, man. All I fuckin' hear is *Cocà Kola*. When did you suddenly become her bitch?"

"I ain't anybody's bitch," Cross retorted.

"Yeah. Where you stayin' at now? With me. Who ya sudden supplier been for the past few months? Kola. Look how fast and dramatic shit done changed with us since that bitch came in the picture. She is playin' you, my nigga. And Eduardo, funny how all of a sudden he wants you out of the picture and her in. He so easily don't want nothin' to do wit' you, after you been doin' business with him for how long now?"

Cross was forced to think about how things had changed rapidly between him and Kola. After the incident with Cynthia—Kola finding out about his son—she kicked him out and he'd been staying at Edge's crib ever since. Although he tried to give her space to get over his cheating, he felt she was taking too long to completely forgive him. Kola still hit them off with work she got through Eduardo, but for the most part, Edge was speaking truth. He was giving Kola too much slack because he loved her.

"What the fuck you implying, Edge?" Cross said through clenched teeth.

"Nigga, do I gotta spell it out for you—She fuckin' that nigga!"

Cross remained quiet and calm for a brief moment, but the rage was bubbling inside of him. Just the thought of Eduardo betraying him and fucking the woman he loved was eating him up inside. Cross knew Edge had some good points, but he didn't want to admit it. It had been a passing thought of his the past few weeks. He wanted to deny it, but the truth was in his face.

Abruptly, Cross shouted, "I'ma kill that muthafucka!" and violently tossed the bottle he had been nursing in his hand across the room, shattering it against a wall and catching the attention of everyone in the room.

"Just chill, Cross," Edge said.

"Fuck that! If Eduardo wants a war, I'll give him a fuckin' war!"

"Nigga, why not just rob that muthafucka and then kill him? Do it right. You know he gotta be sittin' on a few hundred ki's and a lump sum of cash in that spot."

Cross nodded.

A bouncer walked over to their table with a stern look. He focused on Edge and Cross, towering over them with his bulging muscles. "Is everything OK over here?"

"Yeah, we good, big man," Edge said. "It ain't no problem. My dude just had to let off some steam, that's all."

"Well, next time, tell him to take that shit outside, not in here."

"A'ight," Edge said.

Cross glared at the bouncer and felt like cutting him down with gunfire. But he had other matters to take care of.

Edge continued with, "I'm sayin', we gotta make this shit happen fast, my nigga. They might be making a move on us. We don't know that. But shit ain't right, Cross."

"I feel you."

Edge wanted payback for so many things. He was still salty about Kola's constant rejections. And, like Cross, the thought of her fucking Eduardo and not him was one he couldn't deal with.

But Cross had to be officially done with Kola for Edge to take his leftovers. Edge didn't want any repercussions coming his way. His plan was simple. Kill two birds with one stone—Set up Kola and Eduardo. It seemed to be easy pickings.

Both men tried coming up with the perfect plan to rob and kill Eduardo while they sat and continued to drink. Cross had it in his heart to do the unthinkable. Even though Eduardo was an international kingpin, Cross felt that he had crossed the line and disrespected him, when it came to messing around with his heart. Love had Cross thinking insanely.

The men exited the strip club at two in the morning, both slightly tipsy. Edge held his car keys in his hand and looked for his truck.

"What you about to do, Cross?"

"I need to go see my son and hit his moms off with a couple stacks."

"Yo, you go do that, and holla at me tomorrow. But we gonna do this. We gonna take care of this problem. But, you know, we might have to take out Kola too. If she fuckin' around wit' this nigga, then she can't be trusted."

"I need accurate proof."

"And we'll get it." Edge smiled.

The two men gave each other dap and went their

separate ways.

Cross got into his dark-colored Lexus and sped to Brooklyn in the late hours of the night. It had been weeks since he'd last seen his son. He pulled up and parked his Lexus in front of the project building on Myrtle Avenue. It was almost three in the morning when he stepped out of the car and walked toward Cynthia's building.

Cynthia was still traumatized from the beat-down she'd received from Kola and Candace. Her wounds had healed, but her heart was still torn. Cynthia was more upset to find out that she wasn't the only woman in Cross' life. She tried ignoring him, and refused to see him or accept any of his phone calls. But Cross was relentless, always calling or stopping by unexpectedly. Cynthia was ready to move on, but for the past two years, the only man she knew was Cross.

Cynthia's sister vowed revenge on Kola and Candace. Her family was enraged when they found out about the home invasion and pistol-whipping. They wanted to see justice done, either via courts or in the streets. They held Cross accountable for what had happened to Cynthia, and the three days she had spent in the hospital.

When the detectives came to question Cynthia, she refused to snitch, with some persuasion from Cross, who had promised to take care of the situation and make things right by her. Cynthia and her family were still waiting on that promise. They wanted Kola and Candace badly, but Cross warned Cynthia and her family that the two ladies were nothing nice and not to be messed with.

Cross rushed into the project building and took the stairs to the fourth floor. The building was quiet. People were asleep. But he was ready to change all of that. He entered the hallway and went straight to Cynthia's door. Like Kola, she also had changed her locks, and it infuriated Cross. He wanted to see Cynthia and his son. And he refused to leave until he got what he wanted.

He began banging on the door, shouting, "Cynthia, open the fuckin' door! Cynthia!" The banging went on for a minute.

"Go away! I don't wanna see you!"

"I wanna see him. I wanna see my son. Please."

"No, Cross. I hate you! I fuckin' hate you!"

"Baby, open the door, please. It's been weeks. I just wanna talk. I just wanna see you and make things right. I promise."

"You're always making me promises. I'm tired, Cross, I'm tired," Cynthia cried out.

"I'm not fuckin' leaving here until you open this door and I get to see my son. Don't have me knock this muthafucka down!"

"He's not here. He's with my sister in Queens."

"Then open the door, and let's talk. Please, baby, I need you right now. I'm sorry," he said, sounding sincere.

"You played me, Cross. You played me."

"I just wanna talk!"

Cross began banging on the apartment door aggressively, waking up a few neighbors. He was making Cynthia very nervous. She knew he wouldn't leave unless he got to see her.

"Cynthia, just give me a minute with you face to face. That's all I'm asking right now."

Cynthia was quiet, thinking about it. She sighed. "Five minutes, Cross," she said.

"That's all I'm asking."

Cynthia began turning the locks and slowly opened the door. She was nervous. But she still loved him. She stood before him in a long, blue T-shirt that she always wore to bed, and a pair of slippers. Her hair was wrapped up under a yellow scarf, and the bruises she suffered from the assault were becoming less visible.

She peered at what seemed to be a distraught Cross standing in the hallway clad in a wrinkled T-shirt and jeans, his gleaming long chain and diamond pendant dangling.

"What you want from me, Cross?"

Cross rushed into the apartment and grabbed Cynthia in his arms and began hugging her. "I need you, baby. I fuckin' need you right now."

Cynthia pushed him off. "Now you fuckin' need me? Your crazy side bitch and her friend jump me, and you don't do shit. And, come to find out, you got that bitch living the good life in some mansion upstate somewhere, while you got the mother of your son and your son living in the fuckin' projects and you fuckin' need me! Nigga, is you fuckin' serious?"

The tears began trickling down Cynthia's face as she stared at Cross. She put some distance between them in the living room.

Cross stood there for a moment, looking speechless, but then rebutted with, "I told you, I'm gonna take care of it. You definitely got my word on it, baby."

"How?" Cynthia demanded to know.

"That bitch is dead to me right now, you hear me? Right now, it's only you and my son that matter to me. Nobody else."

"But she's still gonna be in the picture, right?"

"Not for too long."

"What you mean?" Cynthia said, confused. She wanted to hear him say that he had cut Kola out of his life for good. No ambiguities or ominous statements.

Cross walked up to her. His vulnerable demeanor had suddenly disappeared, and he focused on Cynthia like a lion on its prey.

Cynthia noticed the change and took a few steps back, nearing the window.

"It's just you and me, Cynthia. You don't need to know the details about that. You ain't gotta worry about her for too long."

Cynthia quickly read into what he was saying, and straightaway Cross felt like he'd said too much. He approached Cynthia with conviction. They locked eyes. Cross suddenly grabbed her into his arms again, this time with more passion and strength. He embraced her tightly, feeling the softness of her petite figure.

Cynthia gasped. "Cross!"

"I miss you, baby."

Cross pressed his lips against hers. He had her pinned against the wall. He then slid his hands underneath her T-shirt and began feeling on her booty. He fondled every inch of Cynthia, whose body seemed to go in a sudden trance from his touch.

"Cross, I can't," she said feebly.

Cross pulled up her T-shirt, exposing her tight, lace pink panties, and dug his hand inside her front, feeling on her shaved pussy and wet lips.

Cynthia moaned, feeling the tip of Cross' fingers digging into her cookie jar, her lips trembling and her body yearning. She didn't understand it. One minute he was at her door screaming and yelling about seeing her and his son, and she was reluctant to let him inside. But somehow, Cross talked his way into her apartment, and then into her panties. He had such a hold over her; it was almost pathetic.

Slowly, the panties came down, and the T-shirt she wore to bed came off and was tossed across the room. Cynthia found herself up against the living room wall in his grip, her legs straddled around Cross, his jeans lying around his ankles.

Cynthia suddenly felt a hard thrust.

"Ugh! Shit!" she panted in his ear, as he moved between her raised legs.

Cynthia's body lit up with pleasure as Cross kissed the side of her neck and fucked her passionately. His deep strokes lingered inside of her like a lasting thunderstorm. He cupped her breasts with his fist, and her thighs vibrated against him. Cynthia's nipples were hard like pebbles, the heat building up inside of her. She could feel her juices leaking out and running down her legs.

Cross quickly switched positions and suddenly had Cynthia on her back against the thick carpet, cooing beneath him.

Cynthia showed her strength, her arms and legs tightened in a grip around him as she felt the deep penetration, her pussy pulsating nonstop around his thick size.

When they were done, Cynthia lay next to her baby's father looking spent. She stared up at the ceiling, trying to catch her breath, and asked herself, *What happened?*

Cross, sweaty and looking exhausted, leaned over onto his side, gazed at Cynthia's naked figure. "I'm moving in wit' you, baby. I need to lay low here for a while and think about things. And I need to see my son."

Cynthia didn't respond to Cross' statement. She continued to look away from him, and the tears started to trickle down her face slowly. She was still in love with him. But how long could she live like this? Her sisters wanted her to leave Cross alone. They felt he was too dangerous to be around her and her son, especially after the incident with Kola and Candace.

Cynthia wanted Cross to be a father to his son, but the risk with him in the streets and warring with a rival crew always had her on edge. But she allowed him to move in with her because she loved him.

He thought it was because he was already paying the rent.

Chapter 4

Apple floated her face over the dirty toilet for the umpteenth time in one day. Constantly nauseated, she was throwing up chunks in the toilet. She had stomach cramps and was getting headaches on the regular. Between turning tricks and being drugged up on dope, she didn't know what was going on with her body. Sometimes, she would go for days without eating, or go for long periods of time without sleep.

There were moments when she would be sick while a trick was on top of her doing his business. She would have the urge to throw up, and a few times, unable to hold the sickness in, she had thrown up on a few of her dates. This ended up upsetting the client and made Shaun to go into a rage. The clients would demand their money back, and Shaun would only give them half, since they didn't finish but still got half the pleasure. When the men left, Shaun would unleash his wrath on Apple, berating her and sometimes becoming physical.

Apple's sickness went on for weeks, but none of the

whores or Shaun paid her any attention. Some of the whores even thought she was faking illness to stop from turning tricks or to get sympathy.

When she threw up on her tenth date within the month, Shaun screamed out, "What the fuck is wrong wit' you? Are you fuckin' retarded? I'm losing money because of you!"

Apple sat there naked, cleaning the puke from her face and looking sorry for herself. She was sore and feeling nauseous again. She just realized she had stopped menstruating months ago.

Mary was in the room during Shaun's outburst. She looked at Shaun and blurted out, "I think she's pregnant."

Shaun stood there looking dumbfounded. "What the fuck you say?"

"She's pregnant, Shaun—look at her!"

Shaun looked over at Apple, who was hunched over a bucket next to her bed and holding her stomach. The thought wasn't farfetched to him, knowing how many tricks had been inside of her, and not knowing which one probably pulled off the condom, or if they even used one. Shaun had a strict rule inside his whorehouse and that was no raw-dogging it. He was furious that one of the tricks had played him. He would have charged a fortune to a trick if they wanted to go raw dog. When Apple got sick he thought she'd contracted some sort of virus that runs rampart around Mexico; like H1N1.

"Fuck me!" Shaun shouted.

Mary's eyes showed concern for Apple, knowing that

she was now carrying a life inside of her.

Shaun marched around the room, trying to come up with a plan. He glared at Apple and shouted, "She ain't goin' to no fuckin' hospital. Y'all fuckin' hear me? It ain't happening. That bitch is gettin' a fuckin' abortion. I ain't having no daycare up in here. This is my fuckin' place of business."

Mary cut her eyes at Shaun, but she didn't say a word to him. She remained silent and watched Shaun storm out of the room, slamming the door behind him. She walked over to Apple and crouched next to her. She was now trying to console and comfort Apple.

"Just try and breathe easy, relax," she told Apple calmly.

Mary understood Apple's condition. She had been pregnant a few times over the years. Her last pregnancy ended in a miscarriage fifteen years earlier. But Mary gave birth to four children, and after giving birth, she never saw her babies again. She was distraught about her kids being snatched away from her by the men she worked for. But afterwards, the depression would fade, and it would be back to business for her. Mary understood that because of where she lived, and what she did, she wasn't fit to raise a child anyway. So soon after, she came to terms with giving birth, kissing her newborn lovingly for one last time and then departing from them. It was the life she was used to.

"I'm not pregnant, Mary," Apple said.

"I think you are. I know the signs. I've been there, Apple, too many times," Mary stated, sadness in her tone.

Apple looked at Mary. She suddenly became confused why Mary became so caring for her all of a sudden. Mary wasn't difficult or cruel to her, like the majority of the whores in the place, but she always made sure to keep her distance from Apple. Mary showed a different look in her eyes. She rubbed Apple's back gently, and only soothing words came out of her mouth.

Apple continued to float her face over the bucket. She wiped her mouth and said to Mary, "He's gonna come for me, you'll see."

"Who?"

"Chico. He's gonna find me... kill Shaun, and take me away from here," Apple said almost convincingly.

"Oh...sí...Chico..." Mary replied.

"Y'all have no idea who the fuck I am or what I'm capable of doing," Apple exclaimed.

Mary stared at Apple. She noticed the fire and hopes that the young girl had in her eyes about freedom and revenge, believing that her Chico would find her soon. Mary once had that same fire so many years ago. She remembered when she thought her knight in shining armor would come rescue her. She had faith and believed that her life as a whore wouldn't be forever. But as every year passed, gradually, that same fire and hope began to fade from her eyes and she began to accept the situation.

Mary sighed. "They always promise, they always say they come, rescue you from this place, but soon those promises become nothing but empty words, and echoed in your mind."

"Chico is different," Apple replied.

"Is he? I remember when I thought that way about someone. I was young, so naïve. He made me feel good, like a woman, even though he was a trick. I was the only girl he would come to see, and he would spend money on me. He taught me how to speak English. He used to tell me about his trips to America. And he promised that one day I would go with him. Promised that he would take me away from such a vile place and we would be together. I believed in him for two years, until one day he just stopped coming. I used to yearn for his visits, but he just disappeared from my life, but he left me with a child. My first. My son was taken away from me right after I gave birth to him. See, in this place, there is no room for children."

Apple looked at Mary with an impassive stare. She didn't want to hear anything Mary had to say to her. She believed in Chico. They loved each other, and Apple felt that even though she had been harsh with Chico before her capture, Chico wouldn't forget about her. He had made a promise to always look out for her and take care of her, no matter where she was.

Apple's stomach started churning again, and she quickly lowered her face into the bucket and begun puking once more. She couldn't take being sick any longer and being held captive against her will. She was ready to go home.

A week after Apple's pregnancy was confirmed. Shaun refused to take her to the local hospital and hired a quack

Mexican doctor with a questionable medical background to perform an abortion on Apple. She was twelve weeks pregnant, and she was scared.

Mary was by Apple's side as she was forced onto a cold, long table butt-naked. Her feet were placed into a pair of stirrups, and her legs were widely spread. Shaun stood a distance from the procedure with a scowl on his face. The room door was locked, and the atmosphere was tense at this illegal abortion.

The man performing the procedure on Apple was Dr. Skiff, a short, round forty-year-old American/Caucasian man from Houston, Texas. He came to Mexico to continue with his practice after his medical license was revoked after a slew of suits for malpractice and negligence. Mexico became his home, and Dr. Skiff became Shaun's go-to guy when there were any medical or emergency problems with any of the girls.

"Doc, let's just get this shit over wit' already," Shaun said. "Time is fuckin' money."

Dr. Skiff, clad in dark blue scrubs and wearing thick, rimmed glasses with a small light attached to them, nodded.

"I want that fuckin' baby outta her!"

Dr. Skiff nodded and replied, "It takes time."

"I'm paying you good money, Doc. Don't fuck this shit up!"

The doctor positioned a tall stool between Apple's spread legs. Apple lay there and was extremely nervous, until Shaun injected a good portion of dope into her system to help her relax.

Apple laid her head back, and soon became loopy from the heroin seeping into her system.

Dr. Skiff removed the tools he needed for the procedure from his leather handbag and placed them on a wooden table next to him—forceps; uterine curette; cervical dilator; syringe with spinal needle; and a pair of embryotomy scissors.

Dr. Skiff took a deep breath, put on a pair of latex gloves, and leaned forward between Apple's spread legs and started with the method.

Mary stood next to Apple, holding her hand and watching. She had seen the practice done many times, so she was used to it. Many of the whores were quick to get an abortion done; sometimes Dr. Skiff was at the whorehouse five or six times a month.

Apple felt numbness below as she was poked and prod with the cold instruments digging inside of her, and the tools weren't sterilized properly. There was blood everywhere. The doctor had to dilate Apple's cervix just enough for a small tube to be inserted that would be able to remove the fetal tissue. Apple felt a little cramping, but the drug soon had her feeling far-off somewhere.

Dr. Skiff continued with the procedure, roughly removing the baby and breaking it apart. No one in the room cringed or showed any remorse.

Soon, the abortion was completed, and the still fetus was pulled from Apple's wound and laid on the cold table. Apple was still loopy from the drugs and medication.

Dr. Skiff rose up from off the stool, removed his bloody latex gloves, looked over at Shaun and said, "She's done. No more baby."

Shaun nodded and tossed the doctor a lumpy envelope filled with cash. The doctor snatched it from the air, quickly opened it, and counted the hundreds and fifties. He was satisfied with his payment.

"She needs rest," he told Shaun.

"She needs to start making me some money again."

"She'll be no good to you, if she doesn't get a few days rest and begin healing."

Dr. Skiff quickly gathered his tools, stuffed them into his leather handbag, and made his exit from the room.

Shaun looked over at Mary and said, "Make sure she is able to start working again in three days. I ain't fuckin' playin wit' her. And that bitch better not get pregnant again. I can't afford to have this doctor take away all my money 'cause y'all bitches are slippin' wit' these tricks."

Shaun left the room, slamming the door behind him. Shaun thought about Apple and the pain she caused his family. She didn't know it but she had an expiration date. He planned on selling her pussy to get his paper up and once he was done with her, he planned on beating her within a half inch of her life, putting her in a coffin and burying her alive where no one could ever find her body. Then he planned on going back to the states and murdering Denise and Kola. He vowed to wipe out the whole family.

Mary turned to Apple, who was sweating and

delirious. She cleaned up the blood and put a wet rag against Apple's forehead.

"You'll be all right," Mary said.

＊

A few weeks after the abortion, everything seemed to be back to normal with Apple. She was taking antibiotics and turning tricks again, still hoping that Chico would find her and rescue her from her hell.

Apple was being fucked by a trick, as his hairy chest pressed against her.

"Oh my God! Your pussy is so good. Ooooh, it's so good! So damn good!" the trick chanted, looking like he was in a trance.

Apple felt a sharp, sudden kick inside of her. She quickly pushed him off of her and clutched her stomach.

What the fuck! she thought.

"Why you stop?" the man asked.

Apple wasn't worried about his questions. The sharp kicking continued. She sat hunched over, holding her stomach. "Oh shit!"

"Mami, you OK?"

Apple didn't realize that her small belly was still growing. The world around her was so fucked up and unpleasant, she didn't have time to notice too many things. Her eyes grew wider as she thought about the possibility.

"Mami, you okay? What's wrong?" the man said. "I need to finish." He approached her, placing his hand on her shoulder gently.

Apple went berserk. She yanked away from his touch and screamed out, "Get away from me!"

The man jumped back.

Apple ran toward the wall and coiled up into the fetal position.

The man she was fucking became nervous. He grabbed for his pants and started to dress quickly. "You crazy!" he shouted. *"Locà."*

Apple remained in the corner looking paranoid.

Soon, Shaun came rushing into the room. He looked around, saw the trick getting dressed, and Apple in the corner looking shocked.

"What the fuck?"

"That whore is crazy," the man said. "I want my money back!"

"You ain't finish?"

"She just suddenly stopped."

Shaun's face turned into a scowl. He marched over to Apple, grabbed her by her hair, and began pulling her toward the mattress.

"Bitch, you gonna finish fuckin' him!"

Apple screamed and kicked. "I'm still pregnant!"

Shaun suddenly stopped. He let go of Apple's hair and looked down at her unpleasantly. "What the fuck did you say?"

Apple peered up at Shaun with watery eyes.

The trick said, "Forget the money. You people is crazy. Crazy!" He rushed for the door, leaving Apple alone in the room with Shaun.

Shaun stared at her slightly round belly in astonishment. "Impossible! I paid that muthafuckin' doctor enough money to get rid of the fuckin' baby. How the fuck you still pregnant?"

Apple remained silent.

Shaun looked like he was ready to strike her out of pure frustration. His fist was clenched and his eyes were narrowed in annoyance at Apple's belly. He had the urge to kick the baby out of her himself.

Mary suddenly walked into the room and saw Shaun towering over Apple with a posture that said he was ready to hit her. She stared down at the naked Apple, holding her pregnant belly.

The two women locked eyes. Apple had tears streaming down her grief-stricken face.

Mary instantly understood the predicament. "She was carrying twins."

"What?"

"Your doctor messed up. He didn't know. He got rid of one, but not the other,"

Mary said.

"This stupid muthafucka!" Shaun screamed out. "What the fuck am I gonna do with this bitch now?"

But then Shaun gazed down at Apple with a different look. "Fuck it! Niggas will pay for anything nowadays . . . even for some pregnant pussy. You gonna still make your ends in this house, pregnant or not! I can even charge muthafuckas more for it."

Apple didn't respond. She stayed on the cold floor

near Shaun's feet thinking about what she'd have Chico do to him once he found her. Visions of cutting off each finger and toe were running through her mind.

Mary didn't respond to his statement, knowing that men would flock to have sex with a pregnant woman, raving about how different and more pleasurable the experience was. She had been in the predicament many times herself. Apple was in for one whirlwind of a ride.

Apple found out that she was almost five months pregnant—she was carrying small, and that gave Shaun a four-month time span to profit from her condition. It didn't take long until word started to spread about Apple's condition and about the botched abortion. Some of the girls in the house started to name Apple's baby, "Miracle Child." They started proclaiming that Apple's botched abortion and continuing pregnancy was only a clear sign from God saying that she was meant to have this baby.

Some of the whores started to warm up to her more, and the tension of her being an outsider, an American, slowly started to fade, but with the help of Mary also, who took to caring for Apple.

But Shaun was relentless. His attitude toward Apple didn't change at all. He was still money-hungry. He had Apple turning twice as many tricks, because the men in Mexico came in droves, and were willing to pay top dollar to have sex with Apple and experience the pleasure of fucking a pregnant American woman. Apple became the American Dream for so many men in the small Mexican town.

Chapter 5

Kola stepped out of her stately home looking like she was ready to strut down the red carpet of some award-winning Hollywood event. She was wearing a form-fitting black satin dress with a plunging neckline, and sporting a pair of Dolce & Gabbana sunglasses, expensive jewelry, and a pair of stylish six-inch heels. Her long, sensuous hair framed her face perfectly and her attitude was about business, but her look spoke pleasure.

She strutted toward her pearl-white convertible Benz, carrying a small duffel bag filled with cash for her re-up from Eduardo. She tossed the brown bag into the trunk, got into her high-end ride, placed a mixed R&B CD in the changer, threw the top back and sped out the driveway for the one-hour ride to Jersey City.

Kola's business with Eduardo had increased significantly, and things between the two of them were good. Money was being made, and the two individuals had no complaints. Eduardo had been back and forth between Colombia and New Jersey on several occasions, and was also conducting additional business ventures in several countries. He rarely saw Kola, but when he did, there was always a strong attraction between them, along with flirting and conversation.

When Eduardo would be away in Colombia or another country, Kola was always in and out of the penthouse, not having a legitimate reason to stick around. But when he was in town, she would linger around in his penthouse suite drinking champagne with him, having dinner on some occasions, or mingling with his other guests from time to time and talking about everything from business, to love, and even Cross.

It had been two months since she'd seen Eduardo. Colombia had been taking up most of his time lately. He had a few prior engagements in different cities and a situation at home that he needed to handle personally.

Eduardo had called Kola on her phone, informing her that he would be around during their next business transaction. Kola couldn't help feeling a little excited about seeing him again. Her heart fluttered hearing his voice via phone, and her panties became moist just thinking about his sexy body. Kola made sure to look her best when they met up again.

Kola sped across the G.W. Bridge with a lead foot. The traffic was light. It was late in the evening, the rapidly graying sky above the city indicating a thunderstorm looming with heavy rain.

Kola, rushing to see Eduardo, was unaware of a dark Chevy Impala following her closely. Three cars behind her, the Impala had been on her since she'd pulled out of her driveway and kept a watchful eye out to every lane change and turn she did on the highway.

"Keep up wit' that bitch," the passenger said harshly.

The car matched Kola's speed as she crossed into New Jersey and merged onto the New Jersey Turnpike. But it kept a safe distance to remain unnoticed.

Twenty minutes later, Kola was in Jersey City and parked in front of the towering high-rise building. She stepped out of her convertible like the diva she was, popped the trunk, removed the duffel bag, and strutted toward the entrance with a beaming smile. Her outfit and sex appeal could entice any man. Kola disappeared into the lobby.

"You see that shit! That bitch ain't goin' in to meet wit' that nigga Eduardo just to do some quick transaction, lookin' and smilin' like that. She is playin' you, nigga!" Edge exclaimed. "She goin' in there lookin' like that to fuck that nigga, thinkin' we stupid, my nigga!"

Cross was scowling like he'd just sucked on a sour lemon. He had his fist clenched so tightly, his nails were digging into his skin. Every wicked thought about Kola being with Eduardo was running through his head. It was driving Cross insane just thinking about how Eduardo could be sliding his dick into his girl, and the freak nasty shit that was probably going on inside that building, with him just parked outside.

Cross looked at Edge, his face twisted with jealousy. "Make that call, Edge. Fuck that bitch! Let's fuckin' do this shit!"

Edge smiled and pulled out his cell phone.

✳

Kola gave the doorman a nod and strutted through the lobby with her heels click-clacking against the marble floors like she owned the place. The doorman watched her for a lingering moment, admiring her backside and curves in the tight-fitting dress. He smiled, and then picked up the phone to call upstairs.

"Yeah, it's me . . . she's coming up now," he said to his employer on the top floor.

Kola stepped into the waiting elevator and pushed for her floor. She dropped the bag at her feet, and the sharp upward take-off astounded her, as always. She was on the top floor of the penthouse suite instantly. The doors opened, and Kola stepped out, greeting the three-man security team in the hallway by the door.

"Hey, boys," she greeted with a smile.

Only one nodded. She had become a regular, but Eduardo was always a cautious man. The men weren't there to make friends, but to do their job and protect their boss and his assets. Behind the thick doors, was a mass fortune of money and drugs totaling into the millions. The guard quickly searched Kola, even though her outfit was far too tight and revealing to conceal any weapons, his touch lasting against her longer than necessary.

"I know that always makes your day, Sandro," Kola said to him with a teasing smile.

"Just doing my job," he replied coolly.

"I bet you are."

Once they were confident she wasn't a threat, she was let inside. Kola pranced inside with the duffel bag in hand. She smiled and looked around for Eduardo. She dropped the bag on the sprawling black-and-white marble floors and walked over to Eduardo's private stocked bar. She took the initiative to prepare her own drink, since Eduardo would always offer her one when she showed up. Kola mixed herself a Long Island Ice tea, and walked over to the floor-to-ceiling windows and peered at Manhattan's skyline. She never got tired of the sweeping view. It was always breathtaking.

Kola took a sip from her drink and just stood by the windows, enjoying the view.

"I see you already started without me."

Kola turned. She saw Eduardo coming down the spiral stairway with a gentle smile. He was styling in a pair of Armani white silk pants with an open matching white silk shirt, exposing his defined pecs and firm abs. He was barefoot, and a thick gold chain with a small cross pendant adorned his neck and complemented his gold Rolex. His dark hair and chiseled features made him look like a male model. Eduardo didn't look like a murderous Colombian drug kingpin, but had the deceiving image of a gentle middle-aged man.

"I got thirsty," Kola replied with a smile.

"Not a problem, *mi casa* your *casa*," he returned, stepping closer to Kola.

"It's good to have you back," Kola said.

"It's good to be back in this city, and in the presence of such a beautiful and striking woman as yourself. You, my queen, are the perfect image for a very lasting thought."

Kola blushed, which she rarely did.

Eduardo gently took Kola's free hand and had her spin around slowly to capture the full length of her figure and the outfit she wore. He lusted after the way her curvy figure and backside filled out the satin dress. It definitely held his attention.

"You like it?" she asked.

"I love it, my dear."

Kola nodded and smiled.

Eduardo released her hand and walked over to his bar to make himself a drink. He mixed himself a cocktail. He walked over to Kola, glanced at the duffel bag on his floor, and stood mere inches from her.

"So, you came here for business or pleasure?"

Kola smiled. "Always business."

"Business, huh. For some reason, dressed the way you are, I hardly believe that."

"I have somewhere else important to be after I leave here."

"So you do, huh? What's more important than making money and myself?"

"Prior engagements."

Eduardo took a sip of his drink and moved closer to Kola. He almost had her pinned between the window and himself. He couldn't take his eyes off her. He neared his lips to hers, touched her side, and then shifted his fingers up to her breast and pinched her nipple against the fabric.

Kola gasped.

Eduardo smiled. He then placed his hand between her smooth thighs, tickling her with affection. "And do these prior engagements have something to do with Cross?"

Kola remained silent. She felt Eduardo's touch between her legs shift upwards, nearing her pussy. They exchanged an intense look. Kola could see Eduardo's package growing inside his silk pants as he touched her in places that made them both tingle and itch for more. Eduardo wanted to press his lips against hers and shove his tongue down her throat. He craved to journey into her glorious insides. Kola was a forbidden pleasure that had been on his mind since the day they'd met.

Eduardo placed his lips near Kola's ear and whispered, "I can give you whatever you want. The world could be yours."

He tried to kiss her, but she pushed him away.

Eduardo didn't look pleased. "Do you reject me because of him?"

Kola didn't answer him immediately. She knew Eduardo had a serious thing for her. She understood that Eduardo always got what he wanted. And if there was something in his way that he wanted greatly, then he had the power and force to have it removed. Kola feared that if she said yes, then somehow, Cross would end up missing.

"No, it's not him. I hate him right now."

Eduardo looked surprised by this. "You do, yes. Why?"

"He's an asshole. I thought I knew him, but I don't."

"Talk to me, my queen. I'm here to listen."

The two moved into another room that was more comfortable to get situated in. Two giant crystal chandeliers hung high in the room, and the warm walnut and cherry furnishings with a few high-end paintings hanging about complemented the area.

Kola took another sip from her drink and stared at Eduardo. "That bastard was cheating on me with some side bitch and had a baby by her, so we ain't together right now. He fucked it up!"

"His loss," Eduardo uttered.

"It is," Kola spat.

"But men will be men, Kola, and that alone shouldn't take away your love."

"Well it has. I didn't deserve disloyalty. Not from him..."

"You are a beautiful woman. You deserve the best that any man has to offer."

"I know. That's why I can't be with him. He betrayed me. After everything I did for him, the loving I gave him, this empire that I helped him maintain, and he does this shit to me. I'm more woman than he'll ever have. He didn't have to cheat on me. I was faithful and loyal to that man."

"What do you desire now, Kola?" Eduardo asked her.

"Fuck men!" she hissed.

Her mood had changed as soon as Cross' name came up. She was crushed by his infidelity. Kola had switched into a bitter and betrayed woman.

"Including me?" Eduardo asked softly.

Kola gave off a deadpan gaze at Eduardo. Suddenly, Eduardo had gone from a seductive and beautiful specimen of a man to just a man—someone like Cross.

"I can't be with you, Eduardo," she uttered.

"And why not?"

"Because I want to be special. I don't want to share you. You have two sisters that you're intimate with at your mansion in Colombia, from your words exactly, and I don't want to become number three. I'm too much a good woman to be shared like I'm some basic bitch."

"I so agree. And you will be my one and only, Kola," Eduardo said. "Those sisters, they are no longer a priority in my life. Both of them . . . gone like the wind."

"Why?"

"Because they are not you," he returned.

Kola blushed a little by his comment. He was saying everything she wanted to hear. Her ego had been bruised by Cross' infidelity, so Eduardo's reassurances that she could be his main chick were tempting.

Eduardo had caught the sisters stealing from his home, and they had betrayed him by bringing men to sleep in his mansion. Eduardo had heard about it and rapidly had the sisters disposed of execution-style—shot in the back of their heads and buried in the jungle.

"I will do anything for you, Kola. Just ask me."

Kola looked at him. The attraction she had for Eduardo clearly showed in her body language.

Eduardo stood up and took Kola by her hand. He

lifted her out of her seat and brought her close to him.

"The reason why I like you is because I never met a woman quite like you before. You see, the sisters, they were only leeches, sucking the blood out of me. But you, Kola, you have something special. You're a businesswoman along with being beautiful, and what man can't respect that? You are the one woman that made me contradict myself," he stated. "And I never contradict myself."

"How?" she asked.

"You remember when we first met? What did I tell you?"

Kola chuckled at remembering his words to her. "You never do business with women. You only fuck them, or they fuck you, but never business with a bitch."

"And look at us, months later. We built chemistry, something beautiful between us. And any woman that can make me go against what I believe in so strongly is a woman well worth having around."

His words melted Kola away. She became open like a good book.

Eduardo tenderly took Kola's chin into his hand and gazed into her eyes. "Your eyes still show the soul of a lion."

"I know they do," she replied.

Eduardo's hazel eyes penetrated Kola. He leaned into her and pressed his lips against hers. Kola didn't resist. They began kissing passionately as she became wrapped into his hold. His tongue swam around inside of her mouth; he savored the taste and touch of her like she would be extinct the minute he let her go.

Kola fell backwards against the wide, cushioned chair with Eduardo on top of her. Her legs parted with Eduardo positioned in between. He reached underneath her dress and grabbed for her moist panties with his touch brushing against her throbbing pussy. Kola moaned into his ear, feeling this moment was inevitable. She could feel Eduardo's thick, hard dick pressing against her, ready for some activity inside of her.

"I want you so fuckin' bad," Eduardo cried out, slowly removing Kola's panties.

He had gotten them mid-thigh, ready to drop them around her ankles, when Kola suddenly stopped him.

"Eduardo, stop. I can't," she said faintly.

"Yes, yes, you can."

"I can't. Not now. It ain't right."

"I usually don't ask, Kola. I usually don't express myself to any woman, you understand me? Are you teasing me, Kola?"

Kola heard the frustration in his voice. She knew she was in a vulnerable situation, and if Eduardo decided to take it and rape her, there wasn't anything she could do about it. She had to play it cool. She had to re-think her situation.

"No, I'm not teasing you. In fact, I'm falling in love with you, Eduardo. The things you say to me, and who you are, I know I would be a fortunate woman. I just need some time to myself to think about things. Cross really hurt me. And no man has ever gotten that close to me to hurt me the way he did."

"So I'll hurt him," he responded harshly.

"No, I don't want that," she snapped back.

Eduardo rose up and stared at her. "I think about you every day. I'll do anything to have you, Kola. Anything."

"I just wanna continue doing business with you for now, and then when Cross is out of my system, we'll see what happens."

Eduardo wasn't thrilled about her reply, but he had enough respect for Kola to let her be. If it was any other woman, he would have had his way with her and there wouldn't have been a thing she could've done about it. He stood up and regained his composure.

Kola did the same, fixing her panties and her dress, and the two continued on with their business. Kola got what she came for and gave Eduardo a long, passionate kiss before leaving with several ki's of cocaine.

Kola exited the building and strutted back to her car casually like the way she walked in. She was smiling and seemed to be excited. She tossed the bag into her trunk, stared up at the towering building, and thought about Eduardo. She then jumped into the driver's seat and started the ignition.

Kola was flabbergasted that Eduardo was ready to kill for her. Having that kind of power at her beck and call excited her. She pulled out of her parking spot and headed for the New Jersey Turnpike, unaware that Cross and Edge had been watching her the entire time.

Chapter 6

"Yo, you should have let me body that bitch, Cross. She been in that fuckin' building for over an hour wit' that nigga," Edge exclaimed.

Cross thought about it, and every inch of his body ached with rage and vengeance. He wanted to run across the street and put a bullet in Kola's head and just watch her bleed out on the street. He clutched a loaded 9 mm in his hand as he glared at Kola getting into her car with a big smile, looking like she'd just gotten dicked down. Cross' imagination went wild about the freak-nasty shit that Eduardo was doing to his girl to have her smiling so hard.

"I'ma get at that bitch later. I thought we were focused on gettin' this money," Cross reminded Edge.

Edge nodded in agreement.

As they watched Kola pull off, the two noticed a dark Tahoe come to a stop beside them.

The driver's window came rolling down and the driver stared at Cross. "What's good?" the driver spoke.

"Just park and get out," Cross said.

The driver nodded. He was clad in all black and wore dark shades. He was with two men seated in the Tahoe, part of Cross' deadly Harlem crew, and each one of them had the same deadly mentality—They were ready to kill for the wealth. They had arrived just in time and were heavily armed with submachine guns concealed under camouflage raincoats.

Cross and Edge stepped out of the Impala. It started to rain and the sky crackled with loud thunder, leaving the Jersey City street free and clear of any pedestrians or witnesses. They cautiously made their way toward the building—a five-man team ready to provoke war with a deadly kingpin.

The doorman stood behind the giant oak counter near the front entrance. His attention was on a *People* magazine and sipping on a bottle of water. It was a quiet evening, and with the rain and thunder pouring outside, the residents decided to stay indoors. He turned the pages and then looked up to see a hooded black male abruptly entering into the lobby wearing an army camouflage raincoat. He walked by the doorman without saying a word or giving him any acknowledgment.

"Excuse me, sir, you just can't go up there. I need to announce you. Who are you here to see?" the doorman spat quickly.

"Fuck you!" the boy exclaimed.

"If you don't comply with the rules and regulations of this building, I'll call the cops."

Before he could reach and pick up the phone, four more men swiftly burst into the lobby and rapidly attacked him, punching him in the face, knocking him down, and holding him at gunpoint.

"Don't fuckin' move, muthafucka!" one of his attackers exclaimed, masked up, a .50-cal. Desert Eagle trained at the man's head.

The doorman lay on the floor, wide-eyed and terrified, surrounded by five masked men.

"I swear to god, if you fuckin' move one damn inch and don't listen, ya fuckin' brains is gonna decorate this lobby floor. You fuckin' understand me?"

He nodded nervously.

The alpha male of the pack spoke. He crouched down near the man, roughed him up by pulling at his suit jacket and smacking him around violently, and then said, "This is easy for you. I want you to get on that phone, call up the top floor and say to them, Kola's coming back up. She needs to speak to Eduardo about something."

The doorman looked reluctant to comply.

"You understand?"

"They'll kill me."

"Nigga, you think we ain't, if you don't do what we say? Nigga, get ya ass on that phone and make the call." Cross clutched the doorman by his collar jacket tightly, pulling him up harshly and pushing him toward the counter. He pressed the gun to his head and cocked back the pistol. "I'ma count to five. One . . . two . . . three—"

"OK!"

"Do it now!"

The doorman slowly picked up the phone and pushed a button that directly connected to the top floor. His call was quickly answered. Cross and his goons listened in closely. The doorman swallowed hard.

"She's coming back up, Kola . . . . OK, very well."

He hung up. Cross nodded and smiled. "You did good."

Cross then looked at his goons and asked, "Y'all ready to do this?"

"Nigga, we ready! I'm hungry, nigga," one young boy replied eagerly.

Cross nodded to one of his young goons and said, "You stay and watch him. He moves wrong, you know what to do."

The boy nodded.

Cross, Edge, and the other two shooters approached the elevator. They knew that they had the element of surprise—especially with no cameras. They stepped into the lift and pushed for the penthouse floor. The men were slightly caught off guard as they were shot up toward the sky. Silencers were placed onto the barrels of the guns, which were cocked back, ready and loaded to cause havoc.

They approached the top floor instantly, and the bell chimed and the doors began to open. Eduardo's men weren't on high alert, thinking that it was Kola coming back to see Eduardo about something. They sat back relaxed, with only one of them moving toward the elevator to greet her.

Sandro moved closer and caught the shock of his life. Four masked gunmen rushed out onto the floor and began firing, with the silencers suppressing the gunshots.

Poot! Poot! Poot! Poot! Poot!

Sandro caught three slugs directly into his chest, and got pushed back, falling dead. The other two scrambled to react.

Cross didn't want the sound of gunshots to alert Eduardo and his other men. But before they got to mow down all three guards, one of them was lucky enough to squeeze off a few rounds from the Uzi he carried, alerting whoever was waiting behind the door.

The hallway erupted with chaotic gunfire, and the last guard caught a bullet to his head, pushing him violently back into the door with a loud thud.

Cross knew he had lost the element of surprise. "Go! Go! Go!" he shouted.

Edge and the others quickly rushed for the door and tried to kick it in, and then a shotgun blast took the door completely off the hinges. The four masked men rushed into the room blazing, gunfire erupting between both camps in the posh-looking room.

Eduardo was startled by the sound of gunfire. His right-hand security, Andrea, rushed into the room screaming, "We're being hit!"

Eduardo scrambled to get his gun and some other belongings, while Andrea was posted by the door keeping a watchful eye out with a .50-cal. clutched tightly in his hands. Eduardo hurriedly got dressed.

"Who got balls to come at me?" he shouted.

Andrea pushed his boss into the next room, while the intense gunfire scattered all about. Men were heard screaming and it sounded like a small war in the next room.

Cross and his goons had killed three of Eduardo's men who'd tried holding down the fort. Now their bloody, bullet-riddled bodies lay sprawled across the gleaming black-and-white marble floors.

"Let's do these niggas and get this fuckin' money," one thug shouted.

The men ran amok across the penthouse floor, shooting their weapons off and destroying priceless artifacts. "Find Eduardo," Cross shouted.

Eduardo and Andrea raced to the next room that had a secret doorway leading into an adjacent apartment room and toward an escape route. Eduardo clutched a heavy duffel bag, his bodyguard following right behind him. But as they turned the corner, just a few feet from the room, they were met with heavy gunfire.

Tat! Tat! Tat! Tat! Tat! Tat!

"They right here, son! They over here!" a young thug shouted.

Cross ran up, and more gunfire was exchanged between Andrea and Cross and his goons. The hallway lit up like a Christmas tree. Cross was relentless.

Edge returned fire with the submachine gun gripped in his hand. The deadly tool let loose a barrage of bullets like a firehouse hose. The walls were coming apart with bullets.

"Go, Eduardo, go!" Andrea shouted, pushing Eduardo forcefully into the adjacent room and covering him with gunfire from his .50-cal.

Eduardo kept his head low and sprinted across the hall and dove into the next room. He looked back for Andrea, but his right-hand guard was pinned down by heavy gunfire.

Bak! Bak! Bak! Bak! Bak!
Boom! Boom! Boom! Boom!

Cross and his goons moved in closer, pushing Andrea back. He was outnumbered and outgunned. The rage in the men's eyes was evident that they came to kill and take.

Andrea tried to hold them off as long as he could, giving his boss ample time to make his escape. He glanced back and saw Eduardo gone. His only job was to protect Eduardo. He nodded. Andrea rushed from behind the wall that he was taking cover and quickly fired a stream of shots at his assailants. They fell back, giving Andrea a split second to make his escape behind Eduardo. He rushed for the room feeling and hearing the bullets whiz by his ear. They missed him my mere inches. When he ran into the room, he right away shut the door and reloaded his weapon.

Eduardo had pushed a mechanism that opened into a downward, short tunnel. He tossed the duffel bag back into the tunnel, removed a pistol, and yelled to Andrea, "Let's go!"

Andrea nodded. He was locked and loaded again. Eduardo had made his escape through the tunnel. Andrea had one foot in and one foot out.

The door came crashing open, and the gunfire erupted again. Andrea quickly fired back, but before he could make it all the way inside, he was shot, catching a slug in his lower abdomen. He went berserk, shooting erratically and fell backwards into the escape route, with the door closing tight behind him.

"Fuck!" Cross shouted.

Once the doorway to the escape route had shut, Cross and his men didn't know how to re-open it. He was fuming.

"Fuck them!" Edge shouted. "Let's get this money."

The team quickly ransacked the penthouse, taking whatever they could before the police showed up. They took money and drugs, and quickly made their exit, via elevator. Once they hit the lobby floor again, the men ran out with their guns exposed.

The young boy left behind to watch the doorman was smiling. "What y'all got?" he asked.

"We out!"

But before they made their complete exit, Edge glared at the doorman. He pushed the man to the floor and pumped four shots into his chest and stomach. "Now we out!" he said.

They bolted from the building and ran to their vehicles. The rain and thunder was still coming down, giving less visibility of Cross and his goons to any witnesses that happened to be around. Cross knew that they'd made off like bandits. It was the heist of all heists for them.

*

Eduardo made his escape via the service elevator on the other side of the building and rushed out the back door carrying the duffel bag. Andrea was seriously wounded. He grasped his gunshot wound and stumbled behind Eduardo toward a parked SUV. He barely could hold onto his gun. Andrea collapsed into the backseat, bleeding profusely.

Eduardo got behind the wheel and started the ignition. "I'm going to get you to a hospital. Just hold on, Andrea. Hold on," Eduardo shouted.

Eduardo was fuming. He began wondering how his place was easily penetrated. *What the fuck happened?* he thought. He raced out of the alleyway and headed for the nearest hospital.

Eduardo halted the SUV in front of Christ Hospital. He jumped out and ran toward the emergency room screaming out, "My friend's been shot!"

The staff immediately came rushing out pushing a gurney toward the truck. They speedily removed Eduardo's bodyguard from the backseat and placed him onto the gurney and rushed him inside.

Eduardo didn't follow. He stood outside the hospital with a scowl on his face. He was upset. His mind was spinning with revenge. He wouldn't rest until he found out who was responsible for the invasion.

One emergency staff member lingered behind and wanted to ask Eduardo some questions. But Eduardo didn't have time to answer silly questions about his business. He pulled out wads of hundred-dollar bills and subtly gave the man five thousand dollars in cash.

The man was shocked. "Sir, I don't understand."

"My business is hush. You just make sure he doesn't die in your hospital," Eduardo explained to him coolly.

The man was still shocked. He gripped the cash in his hand with a bewildered look. "I'm not a doctor."

"Find him and make sure he lives!" Eduardo said and then walked away.

He got back into the truck and sped away. When he was a good distance from the hospital, it finally came to him. Eduardo uttered, "That fuckin' bitch!"

Eduardo was parked by the waters overlooking downtown Manhattan and puffing on a cigar. His operation in Jersey City had been breached, and he wasn't too happy about it. He pulled out his cell phone and decided to make an urgent call.

On the other end, Kola picked up. "Hey," she answered excitedly. "What's this about, Eduardo? You miss me?"

"You're a dead bitch!" he spat and then hung up abruptly, leaving Kola stunned.

Chapter 7

Chico was to meet up with Two-Face's connection in a small, remote town a few miles outside of Austin, Texas. It was a tiring trip for Chico and Two-Face, first by flight and then by car. Two-Face peoples didn't feel comfortable traveling to New York, so they had requested that Chico meet with them in Texas, someplace near Mexico, where they had the advantage. Chico reluctantly agreed.

His beef with Cross and Edge was becoming costly, and being with a woman like Blythe cost money. So Chico was ready to take risks to solidify his presence in the streets, and conquer the domains of Harlem with pure force and power. Two-Face was his gateway to having that strong connection. The young killer turned out to be a better investment than Chico thought, in more ways than one.

Chico and Two-Face had landed in Austin-Bergstrom International Airport early that afternoon, and then the two rented a car and drove about eighty miles south-east into Bandera, population a little over 1,500; a boring, isolated white Christian town, where two individuals like Chico and Two-Face would stand out.

Chico wasn't worried about being seen or judged. He wanted to be in and out of Texas as quickly as possible. But he felt vulnerable. He'd hardly known Two-Face a few months, though the young Mexican teen had boosted Chico's fierce reputation in Harlem.

Chico drove around in the rented white Chevy Malibu. It was inconspicuous for him and cheap. He drove down Main Street, where he and Two-Face seemed to be the center of attention. They were new faces in town, and the locals quickly turned to get a look at the two minorities slowly creeping into their town.

Chico pulled up to a Silver Dollar on the dusty Main Street, where some of the stone buildings and old saloon-looking businesses recalled the set of a Western movie. Chico noticed the several dusty old pickup trucks that lined the streets, and the residents that walked Main Street were average-looking citizens in dusty Wrangler blue jeans, cowboy hats, cowboy boots, and simple T-shirts.

"Fuckin' twilight zone, homes," Two-Face uttered.

Chico didn't respond to the joke. He shut off the engine, looked around his surroundings for a moment, and then stepped out of the car. Chico hated that he wasn't carrying a gun on him. He felt naked, especially being miles away from home and in a strange town.

"You sure they said here?"

Two-Face nodded. "My uncle is always accurate."

The two walked toward The Silver Dollar. They stepped into the business and suddenly got stares from a few patrons minding their afternoon beverages. Then they just went back to drinking. The jukebox was playing some really dated country music that the men knew nothing about. The place smelled of history, where you could see a few bullet holes in the ceiling. Chico and Two-Face looked around; the place was decorated with old posters on the walls, with its ample dance floor and good sound system. And plenty of ice cold beers were scattered throughout the place.

"Where is he?" Chico asked.

"They be here soon, homes."

Chico and Two-Face took a seat at one of the round wooden tables. They both ordered two beers and quickly quenched their thirst after coming out of the Texas heat.

A half-hour later, a well-established-looking man walked into The Silver Dollar wearing a dark, three-piece suit in the Texas heat. Dark shakes covered his eyes, and he sported a thick goatee with a diamond pinky ring. He was average height with brown skin and had dark black hair. He was flanked by a tattooed, muscular man in loose khakis and a wife-beater.

The two men instantly caught the attention of the patrons when they walked into the bar. Chico knew it was Two-Face's peoples.

Two-Face stood and smiled. "*Cholo*, over here," he greeted loudly, waving them over.

Chico remained seated.

The men walked over, and Two-Face greeted his

uncle in Spanish. It was a brief family reunion, with Two-Face giving his uncle a hug, and then everyone took a seat at the table.

"Chico, this is my uncle, Roman, a serious *vato* in my old town, homes," Two-Face stated excitedly.

They ordered a few more beers.

Chico locked eyes with Roman across the table, as Roman removed his dark shades and nodded at him.

"I've been hearing a lot of good things about you," Roman said.

"Likewise," Chico returned with an expressionless gaze.

"My nephew speaks highly of you, and knowing Two-Face, he doesn't speak highly about anyone. You left an impression on him, so you a man about your shit."

"I'm a businessman first."

"So, what do you have in mind with us?" Roman didn't have an accent or speak in slang like Two-Face. His posture and power might have been intimidating to many, but not to Chico.

"I came to talk business, you know, expand my horizon."

"The sun doesn't rise here," replied Roman.

"So, where can I see it rise?"

Roman looked at his bodyguard and nodded. The man in the wife-beater slid a piece of paper across the table to Chico.

Chico picked it up and looked at it. It had an address and directions on it.

Roman put back on his shades and said to Chico, "There is where the sun rises. You come tomorrow morning, nine o'clock sharp."

Chico agreed. He placed the paper in his pocket.

Roman stood up. "If you like what you see, then we can be in business. But you remember this, the only reason you were able to meet with me today is because of this boy right here." He nodded toward Two-Face. "You look out for him, and then we look out for you."

"It's not a problem," Chico returned calmly.

Roman exited The Silver Dollar.

Two-Face smiled. "You in, homes. My uncle likes you."

Chico just held his nonchalant attitude. But he had confidence in doing business with the Mexicans. He knew that their product would be superior to the Haitians'. Chico wanted to make the business transaction and get back to Harlem. He didn't like Texas at all.

✳

Early the next morning, Chico and Two-Face met with Roman at a small, shabby log home right off Route 173, Ranch Road. The home was sheathed with thick shrubbery, trees, and uncut grass. It looked abandoned and run-down, but it was one of many stash houses for the Mexican cartels.

Chico pulled the Chevy into the dirt driveway and got out. He looked around. It was definitely the perfect place to do business. It was far out in the boondocks; no neighbors, so nobody in your business.

Chico and Two-Face walked toward the cabin and was greeted by one of Roman's goons standing outside the front door carrying an M-16. He nodded at the two men and allowed them entry. Chico walked into a full-blown drug operation. Every drug imaginable was being processed, from black tar heroin, ecstasy, to pure uncut cocaine. The home was well furnished, with half a dozen men processing hundreds of kilos on the inside. There were money-counting machines, scales, drug paraphernalia, and many guns displayed.

Chico was impressed. He wanted to get straight to business.

Roman stepped out of a backroom flanked by his bodyguard. He looked more relaxed in a red and white velour sweatsuit. He acknowledged Chico and Two-Face and gestured for them to follow him into the next room.

Chico walked into a smaller room, and displayed on a small table was an open kilo of cocaine, a few white lines spread out, a razor, and a rolled-up banknote.

Roman took a seat at the table and quickly did a line. His nose was like a vacuum, with the banknote shoved into his nose on one end and inhaling the quick line on the other. The line he snorted was exhilarating.

He looked up at Chico. "You care to try the product?"

Chico wasn't a big coke user. He rarely got high on his own supply. But this time, it was reasonable. If he was to get into business with the Mexicans, he had to know how potent their product was.

Roman held out the banknote for him to use. Chico

took it from Roman's hand, leaned closer to the table with the banknote slightly pushed into his nostrils, and quickly inhaled a white line. He soon experienced a high like he'd never experienced. He felt his body suddenly becoming numb. His pupils then became large, and his heart started to beat rapidly. Chico had to take a seat.

Roman smiled. "I assume that you like the product," he said.

It was exactly what Chico was looking for. He loved it.

"Shit, I want a taste too, homes," Two-Face said, stepping up to the table and grabbing the banknote from Chico. He didn't hesitate to do a line or two. He snorted the lines like a professional user and then stood tall with a large smile. He stared at his uncle and stated, "Some good shit."

Roman looked at Chico and asked, "So, are we in business together or what?"

Chico quickly got his mind right. "Yeah, we definitely are."

"Then we'll arrange for a transaction. We want eighteen a ki," Roman stated. "And for a man of your status, that price shouldn't be a problem for you."

Chico wasn't too sure about the asking price, but business was business and he knew that everything could be negotiated.

The two men talked everything out, and a few hours later, Chico and Two-Face were on a plane back to New York with a new connect.

As they sat in their first-class seats, Chico couldn't

help but ask a few questions that were nagging him.

He leaned in and asked, "Yo, so you never wanted more for yourself?"

"What the fuck you talkin''bout, homes?"

"More, nigga. Paper. Bread."

Two-Face looked puzzled. "If you got a way I could come up on some paper, holla at ya boy."

Chico shook his head. "You got the pot of gold in your family tree, muthafucka."

Two-Face finally understood where Chico was trying to go with the conversation.

"I ain't never been wit' huggin' the block, selling hand-to-hand. Roman wanted me to start at the bottom and work my way up." Two-Face shook his head. "And I ain't never been no chef in the kitchen cookin' up rock. I'm a triggerman. I kill people. That's all I'm good at. My uncle gave me plenty of product on consignment throughout the years and I'd fuck it up every time. It came down to either I step off and find my own way to make money or force my uncle's hand to put me six feet deep."

Chico understood, but still shook his head at the kid's naiveté. For the rest of the flight the two men remained silent, both deep in their own thoughts.

Chapter 8

Apple woke up in the early hours of the morning and felt a sudden gush of fluid between her legs. The thin mattress she slept on was wet.

"Oh my God!" she uttered with panic.

The fluid was clear and odorless. Apple knew she was about to go into labor very soon. She picked herself up out of the bed and clutched her stomach. She needed to call for help. She moved to the door, swung it open and shouted, "Somebody help me!"

A moment later, Mary came running into the room. She grabbed Apple into her arms and led her back toward the bed to lie her down. She told Apple to try to relax and breathe easy. Mary knew there weren't going to be any doctors coming to aid with her birth. The only one Apple could count on for help was Mary and hopefully a few of the girls who'd warmed up to her.

Mary rushed out into the hallway to wake some of the whores up that were still asleep. She needed quick assistance. Moments later, a few of the women came rushing into the room to assist her. She instructed some of the girls to get a wet rag and warm bucket of water. Everybody went into action.

Apple quickly went into labor. She was into her first stage—with the shortening and dilation of her cervix. The contractions were intense and prolonged; her loud screams pierced the halls, and had Shaun rushing into the room.

"What the fuck is goin' on?" he yelled.

"She gonna have the baby!" Mary shouted.

"Now?"

"*Sí.*"

A few whores held Apple down onto the mattress as she squirmed and screamed. Apple was scared. It was her first time giving birth, so she didn't know what to expect without the assistance of proper medical care. Mary had to become the midwife. She was the only experienced woman in the room. She looked at Apple's condition and knew that she was only dilated by 3 cm. Mary remained at Apple's side and tried to comfort her, and also watching her cervix progressively dilate.

Shaun couldn't stay in the room to watch the birth. The whole thing disgusted him. The situation made him cringe. He left the room to make a phone call.

Mary glanced at him leaving while Apple was having her contractions, and she was relieved.

Hours passed, and each contraction grew stronger and stronger. Apple had nothing to take for the pain. Her first birth would come naturally in a whorehouse on Mexican soil. Her legs were spread far apart, her head was propped up against a few pillows, and she clutched two whores' hands, squeezing tight with every strong contraction.

Apple finally reached her second stage of the birth, and the pain grew worse. Her cervix had fully dilated.

Mary shouted, "You gotta push, Apple! Push!"

"Aaaahhh, it hurts! Oh my God! Fuck! Fuck!" Apple screamed out. She was exhausted, sweaty, and disoriented.

"Push, Apple! Push!"

The pressure on Apple's cervix increased. Apple twisted her face in a scowl of agony, squeezing the girls' hands.

"It hurts! Aaaahhh! It fuckin' hurts!"

After hours of intense labor and continuing pushing, the baby's head was finally visible. Apple started to feel a burning and tingling sensation below. She was almost done.

"I see it! I see it! Keep pushing, Apple, keep pushing!" Mary shouted.

Apple continued to do so.

Shaun suddenly re-entered the room after his absence for hours. He stared at Apple with no words. He hated that she had gone into labor already. He still had many willing customers to pay for sex with her. He had never imagined that a pregnant American woman could bring in the type of profit that she had.

Apple was his goldmine. But with her pregnancy about to be done with, he thought of other ways to profit. Then it hit him. *Just get her pregnant again.* He thought of the idea with a cunning smile.

Soon, there was the sound of a crying infant filling the room. The miracle of birth had everyone smiling and in awe.

"It's a girl!" Mary announced.

Mary had the tiny infant wrapped snugly in a sheet in her arms. She knew the procedure with the umbilical cord. She had one of the girls get a pair of sharp scissors. Nothing was sterilized; only washed with soap and water. Mary clamped and cut the cord, and then she handed the infant over to Apple.

Apple was spent. She didn't know what to do. She looked hesitant and reluctant in taking her own child into her arms. "I can't."

"Just hold her gently. A baby needs to feel her mother's touch," Mary said.

Apple slowly reached up to pull the infant into her arms. Anxiety washed over her.

Mary gently placed the infant girl into Apple's arms, and Apple took a tender hold of her baby. She gazed at her daughter and couldn't help but smile, weep, and then feel remorseful.

Giving birth was rough for Apple, but looking into the infant's innocent eyes and feeling her fragile frame against her own made her feel like she was something from heaven. "Oh my God!" Apple uttered. "She's beautiful."

In some way for Apple, the child was a blessing and a curse. She didn't know who the father was. It had to be some Mexican trick she'd fucked. But it was hers. It was the only thing Apple had felt proud of in a long while. The other whores who stood around her watching smiled also. They spoke in Spanish, which Apple vaguely understood. But she knew the word *primorosa* meant *beautiful* or *exquisite*. She still had a lot to learn with her Spanish.

"You need to name her," Mary said.

Apple looked at her child and decided to name her daughter Peaches. She felt it was the perfect fit.

Shaun was in the room with an emotionless gaze glued on Apple. He was just happy that everything was over with. He wanted his house back in order and his whores back to making money. He stared at the infant for a moment and walked out the room.

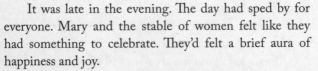

It was late in the evening. The day had sped by for everyone. Mary and the stable of women felt like they had something to celebrate. They'd felt a brief aura of happiness and joy.

"You need your rest, Apple," Mary said.

Apple nodded. She felt that her baby was in good hands with Mary. She rested against the pillows and slowly dozed off.

Hours passed. It was after midnight, and the whorehouse was booming with activity. But in Apple's room, there was silence and a momentary peace that Apple felt while having her daughter in her arms. She gave life, and it was an overwhelming feeling that she would never forget.

"Peaches," she said softly.

Her room door unexpectedly split open, and Shaun stormed into the room shouting, "Wake the fuck up!" A stranger in a dark three-piece suit accompanied him.

Apple clutched her baby tightly. She fixed her stare at Shaun and shouted, "What you want, Shaun?"

"That baby! You need to give her up to this gentleman here," Shaun said.

Apple was confused. "What?! No!"

"Listen, you dumb bitch, what the fuck you think was goin' to happen? That you was goin' to be a mother to that little brat in this house? Bitch, please. I run a whorehouse here, not some fuckin' daycare. And, besides, this is business. You see, my friend here paid fifteen thousand pesos for your daughter. That's five thousand dollars." Shaun stepped forward.

Apple clutched her child securely in the sheet.

Shaun reached for the baby girl.

Apple flinched with the infant in her arms. "Nooooo!" she screamed hysterically.

"Give that child here!" Shaun screamed.

Apple continued to draw back and shouted out, "Nooo! She's mine! She belongs to me."

The stranger in the suit stood in the shadows and only watched. Shaun punched Apple in the face and quickly grabbed the baby from her arms.

"I told you, don't fight wit' me," he exclaimed. "This baby is already sold."

Shaun passed the crying infant over to the stranger in the suit. He took the newborn infant in his arms, and then gave a nod of approval to Shaun.

"Nice doing business with you," Shaun said.

The stranger made his exit.

Apple started to cry, hysterically. The tears flooded her face. The anguish she felt had her paralyzed. She was too weak to fight back and didn't know if she could endure the pain she felt. *How is this happening to me? How is this even possible?* She felt trapped in a bad dream and just wanted it to end. She made up her mind that if someone didn't come to rescue her soon, she'd end her life on her own accord.

Shaun stood over her and proclaimed, "Don't worry about that one, 'cuz we gonna get you pregnant again very soon."

Apple looked up, with swollen, puffy eyes, her voice barely a whisper. "I'm going to see you dead...I put that on my child's life."

The ominous threat spooked Shaun, but only momentarily. He left the room, slamming the door behind him. Apple's piercing crying could be heard from the hallway.

Mary stood not too far from the room. She sighed heavily, understanding Apple's grief. She had been through the same grief plenty of times. Mary agreed with Shaun. A whorehouse was no place to raise a child, and Apple had to understand that.

Chapter 9

The sprawling five-bedroom mansion in Great Neck, Long Island was perfect for Chico and Blythe. The place was Chico's speed and taste.

Blythe fell in love with her new home. It was far removed from the ghetto trenches of Harlem and the drug-ridden Pink Houses in Brooklyn. Blythe felt like she was in a different world—this was the good life for her.

She explored her new home with a huge smile and took in everything slowly—the dual fireplaces, French-chalked wood paneling, Brazilian wood floors, and magnificent floor-to-ceiling windows.

The backyard had an in-ground pool and Jacuzzi with a patio. The bedrooms were tricked out with plasma TV's mounted on the walls, thick, rich carpeting, and the master bedroom had a massive custom bed that could fit five adults comfortably. The bathroom featured marble-tiled floors, a deep-sunken jetted tub, glass shower, and granite countertops, with mirrors everywhere.

Blythe felt like a queen in her new home. She hugged and kissed Chico passionately and exclaimed, "Baby, I freakin' love it!"

Chico smiled.

It was only one of many fruits of his hard labor. The Mexican connect was working out better than ever for him.

It had been a month since his meeting with Roman, and afterward he'd flooded the hood with his new product—pure cocaine cooked up and cut into crack for his customers uptown, cocaine for his midtown and downtown clientele, and then the black-tar heroin he was distributing.

He was making a boatload of money, and business was good, but his problems with Cross and Kola were escalating.

The streets were on fire with bloodshed. The war was costing Chico soldiers and workers. And the NYPD were trying to crack down on his turf.

Two-Face was doing his job on the streets a little too well. He had a few of Cross' men shook and running with his ruthless killing tactics. Chico's name was heavy from corner to corner.

Chico stood in the center of the living room and looked around. *Blythe deserves it,* he thought to himself. His girl already had plans for their new home. She moved from room to room and already had decorators on the phone.

He walked out to the patio area and peered at the grassy yard, the trees, and his in-ground pool. He could remember growing up poor in the ghetto, enduring harsh conditions, and dreaming about a place like this. He was a child birthed into a world of destruction. His life was the same old cliché like many young men from the hood— no father figure around, abandonment issues, detention centers, violence, and yearning to get rich quick.

By the time Chico was thirteen, he was a hardcore gang member and violent repeater in and out of the justice system on a continuous basis. He knew guns and selling crack. He knew the streets, and that the only way to handle a problem was through gunplay.

Chico committed his first murder when he was sixteen. He shot a rival dealer in the head over a corner. Chico was panicky afterwards, but it was a fleeting feeling. He had gotten away with it, and he soon knew that he was capable of doing anything. His reputation grew fast in the hood, and in due time, he was making tons of money and ordering hits against his rivals.

The streets were a hard and cold place. At first, the only thing Chico knew was the projects and violence. His first love, his girlfriend back then, Nikki, taught him about diversity and expanding into more positive things with his money. But after Nikki's violent death, all that she tried to teach him went out the door, and Chico became more of a brutal gangster. Now, he had the money to buy three homes if he wanted to. He'd come a long way from the gangs and the corner shootouts.

Chico became lost in his own thoughts as he stood in the backyard of his lavish home. He thought about his cousin, Dante. He was truly missed. He thought about Nikki, his mother, and a few friends and homeboys he'd lost over the years.

Chico started to think about Apple. He had never forgotten about her. He couldn't comprehend how Apple could just vanish without a trace so easily. He knew she was upset—maybe damaged goods with the incident with her face—but he was willing to look past everything.

Chico was upset about Apple's disappearance, but he kept it in and moved on with his life. Blythe had his attention now. And it was Apple's loss. He had business to take care of, a woman to support, and a war to win.

"Baby, why you just standing out here? Come inside and let's enjoy our new home together," Blythe said cheerfully. She walked up to Chico and wrapped her arms around him. They nestled together for a moment and both took in their backyard view. "It is lovely out here," she said.

Chico remained quiet.

Blythe began to pull up his shirt and slowly massaged his abs. As she touched him, her hand brushed against the butt of his gun, which was tucked in his waistband. "You don't need that tonight, baby. Nobody knows us out here," Blythe said.

"I feel safe wit' it on me."

"But I'm with you. I have something safe for you to be in, baby." She gripped the gun and began to pull it out of his waistband.

Chico was hesitant, but he allowed her to remove it.

Blythe gripped the gun in her hand and placed it on

the table. She wasn't a stranger to the deadly tool. She was from the Pink Houses. She could recall her brothers always having a collection of guns in their mother's apartment. Growing up with three older brothers, with them all being in the streets, Blythe knew how to aim and shoot a gun like the best of them.

Blythe wrapped her arms around Chico again. She reached around his waist, fumbled with his zipper for a moment, and began stroking his dick with the softest caresses he'd ever felt from a woman. Chico moaned from her seductive touch.

"You like it, baby?" she whispered in his ear.

Chico's moaning gave her the answer. He turned to face his beautiful woman.

Blythe smiled. She felt that he was the sexiest, most thuggish man around. And she wanted to please him to the fullest. Especially after the marvelous new home he had bought her.

Blythe took Chico by his hands and began pulling him into their new home. As they entered the kitchen, Chico took in her sexy attire from head to toe—she was barefoot in a pair of coochie-cutting shorts that exposed her camel toe, and a lace bra.

"C'mon, baby, let's just enjoy this house together," she said with a smile.

Chico pulled her into his arms, groped her ass, and the two began kissing fervently. He then lifted Blythe onto the granite countertop.

Blythe straddled her long, toned legs around him and

felt his erection pressing against her. She wanted Chico inside of her. She moaned in Chico's ear as his fingers undid her shorts and he reached for her treasure.

Chico fingered her, setting off a reaction inside of her, as she squirmed and panted like a winded runner from the stroke of his touch.

Blythe's shorts came off and were tossed to the floor, followed by Chico's jeans. He then slammed himself into her love box. She cringed and clutched Chico to her frame, feeling his large erection tunnel into her. Her legs trembled against him.

"Aaah! Aaah! Shit, baby!" she cried out.

Chico pumped in rhythm into Blythe. He felt her juices trickling, and her lips tasted his ear.

The two soon repositioned onto the cold, tiled floor. They were tangled in the missionary position.

Her manicured nails traveled down Chico's sweaty back and rested against his moving ass between her thighs. "Fuck me, baby! Ooooh, fuck me, baby!" she chanted.

A moment for a quickie turned into an hour, and soon they both were lost in the rapturous haze of mind-numbing orgasms.

When Chico was done, he got up and walked outside into the backyard buck naked, leaving Blythe spent on the leather sofa, her hair disheveled and feeling very satisfied. He lit up a cigarette, took a few drags, and looked around.

Chico felt peace for a moment. He wasn't known in Great Neck, which was a high-class, Long Island neighborhood many miles from his hood. This was what life was about for Chico—having his own and having respect, along with power, in the streets. The new product from the Mexicans had taken off like a rocket, and he wasn't trying to come down from the high of his success anytime soon.

Chico started thinking about ways to get rid of Cross and Kola, his main competition in the streets. He clearly understood that, with them out of the way, he would be finally able to corner the market.

Chico and Blythe's names were buzzing in the streets of Harlem. They were the talk of the town—the couple doing it big. The men in the hood envied Chico, and the women wanted to be with him. But some were disturbed and highly upset that Chico had the audacity to bring a Brooklyn girl into their mix and have her in his circle. The local ladies in the hood felt that it was the ultimate betrayal.

But Blythe moved through the streets of Harlem unfazed by the hate and negativity aimed at her. She drove around Harlem like she owned the place in her fully loaded powder blue Lexus IS with moon roof and cream leather seats; a gift from Chico. Blythe loved the car and often stunted in it with her Brooklyn friends.

Blythe drove down Seventh Avenue profiling, the windows down and her music system blaring Drake and Nikki Minaj. She had her best friend Vanessa riding shotgun, and her cousin TT was seated in the back. The girls were enjoying the warm, summer day in uptown. The streets were filled with people, and a few turned their heads to take notice at the young, pretty girls cruising in the high-end car.

Blythe smiled. She felt like she was on top of the world. It was her day out with her friends, and they chose to spend it chilling in Harlem. Her man ran the streets, so Blythe wasn't worried about running into any trouble. And the haters thought twice about messing with her, because of Chico and Two-Face. The girls had gotten a pedicure and manicure at a popular Korean spot in midtown then went shopping on Fifth Avenue and decided to get something to eat at one of Blythe's favorite spots uptown, Mamma's Take Out & Stay soul food restaurant on Lenox Avenue.

Blythe pulled up to the restaurant where there was already a crowd of people waiting inside and out. Mamma's was famous for their fried catfish, smoked salmon, rib dinners, peach cobbler, sweet potato pies, and macaroni and cheese. People from every borough and even out-of-towners flocked to the low-key, modest-looking storefront location restaurant with the weathered black-and-white awning and fading sign that read, "Mamma's, We Feed and Please."

Blythe stepped out of her car with a smile as she peered at the sign. It'd been a while since she'd eaten from there, and she was craving to taste her some fried catfish and a piece of peach cobbler.

The three ladies walked toward the place looking fresh. Blythe had on a pair of tight-fitting Citizen jeans, stylish high heels, and a form-fitting shirt that accentuated her ample breasts and curvy waistline. Blythe's friend and cousin had on similar attire, but different color jeans and shirts. Each of the girls had their long hair flowing down to their backs, looking like video vixens.

As they strutted toward the entrance to Mamma's, the ladies turned heads and caught hard stares, and the catcalls came from every direction.

"Damn! What's good, ma? Can a nigga holla?"

"Yo, shorty, let me holla at you fo' a minute."

"Yo, ma, what's up? The one wit' the phat ass!"

"Damn, y'all fine!"

Blythe and her Brooklyn crew didn't even break their stride or a smile as they walked toward the soul food restaurant. The men calling out to them were a waste of their time. None of them were Blythe or her friends' taste. Blythe just wanted to get something to eat from her favorite spot and head back to midtown and party at her favorite club.

The ladies walked into the crowded eatery and couldn't make up their minds if they wanted to stay and dine in or take their food to go. TT wanted to stay, but Blythe didn't feel comfortable lingering around the place longer than she needed to. She was starting to get bad vibes. There were too many eyes focused on them, and some were looking at Blythe and her friends for all the wrong reasons. She felt the hate coming from a few of the ladies in the place. She knew that some of the girls already knew who she was and who she was affiliated with.

"Let's just get our shit to go and leave. We can eat at Chico's place on the West Side," Blythe said.

"A'ight, I'm down," TT said.

Vanessa went along with them. The girls waited on line and couldn't help but to roll their eyes and glare back at the men and women constantly checking them out. Blythe heard the snickering and noticed the dirty looks.

TT also took notice. She was the most hood of the trio. She carried a small blade on her at all times.

As the girls waited, a group of young girls walked by Blythe and her friends and one of them uttered, "Bitches think they fuckin' cute!" as they started to exit the place.

Blythe tried to keep her cool, but TT responded, "What the fuck you said?"

"Bitch, what?" one of the young girls quipped back, halting her exit.

TT was ready for a confrontation.

Blythe sighed and said to her friend, "TT, just chill."

"Nah, fuck them bitches!" TT shouted.

"Fuck you, bitch! Y'all bitches think y'all cute. Y'all dumb Brooklyn bitches better not get it twisted. Don't come up to Harlem and get fucked up!"

"Bitch, we ain't scared!" TT retorted, stepping closer to the group of girls.

By now, the confrontation had captured everyone's attention in the restaurant. Everybody just looked on, wondering what was about to go down.

Blythe wasn't in the mood to fight. She was looking too cute to scrap and wanted to leave with her weave intact.

TT jumped into the girl's face and was ready to throw down with all four of her friends. But before things got heated, a security guard came between the two groups of ladies and broke it up. He had the Harlem clique moved to outside and allowed Blythe and her friends to continue standing on line for their food.

But Blythe had a funny feeling and was ready to leave. "Let's just go," she said to her friends.

"But I'm hungry, Blythe," Vanessa complained.

"We can go somewhere else and snatch something up," Blythe said.

Blythe continued to keep her eyes on the group of girls who had left and saw that they were lingering outside of the establishment. She already knew what they were waiting for. It was about to become a problem. She tapped TT and pointed outside.

"Fuck them bitches!" TT marched outside and began approaching the threat.

Blythe sighed heavily and followed her friend outside. Vanessa was right behind them, along with a few patrons from the eatery who were excited about seeing a fight outside.

TT marched up to one of the girls with her sharp blade in hand and was ready for any confrontation. "What you gotta say now, bitch?" she shouted.

The Harlem girls approached TT and quickly had her surrounded. Blythe and Vanessa had TT's back. They clenched their fists and were ready to show Harlem how Brooklyn got down.

"Yeah, ya man Chico ain't here to have ya back now, huh, bitch," one girl shouted. "You Apple wannabe bitch!"

"Fuck you!" Blythe screamed out. "And fuck Apple. My man don't want her raggedy ass!"

"I bet you won't say that shit in her face!" another girl shouted.

"Ain't no shook hands from Brook-land. Apple and I can toss it up whenever, however," Blythe yelled. She was so heated that they kept taunting her about Apple. It was bad enough that deep down inside she wondered what would happen if Apple showed back up. Where did she really stand with Chico?

As the group of girls screamed back and forth at each other, Blythe quickly took off her diamond earrings and removed her jewelry. She was ready to show them how Brooklyn threw down. But the sudden presence of a blue-and-white patrol car in the street and the blaring of sirens quickly halted any violence that was about to happen.

The girls turned to stare at police. Two white male uniformed officers stepped out and approached the crowd.

"Is there something wrong here?" one officer asked.

"Nah, we good, officer," a girl from the Harlem crew said.

The officers quickly scanned the crowd and studied faces. A few people rushed back into the restaurant, while some just strolled away casually.

"We got a disturbance call," his partner stated.

"It's no disturbance here. We were just about to be on our way home," Blythe said.

"I think that's a good idea . . . for both groups to part ways right now before everyone sees Central Booking tonight."

The girls didn't argue back. TT hid the blade, and Blythe began walking to her car. Vanessa and TT were right behind her. Blythe was relieved though, knowing that if the cops didn't show up, things would've gotten really ugly.

The mob outside of Mamma's was quickly dispersed, and things went back to normal.

Blythe got behind the wheel of her Lexus and sped away. She cursed at TT for putting them in danger, but TT let it be known that she wasn't about to be disrespected, no matter where they were at. Blythe knew that they were targeted because of jealousy. She had what every girl or hood rat in Harlem wanted, Chico. She was flooded with jewelry, clothes, cars, and money, and a few Harlem girls couldn't tolerate that a Brooklyn girl had Chico's heart.

Blythe jumped on the West Side Highway and headed to one of her favorite clubs in midtown, Club Foreplay. She needed a drink, to dance and wanted to chill. Blythe just wanted to escape the quick madness that she almost gotten into.

The girls did it big with bottle service while sitting in VIP and enjoying the fruits of Chico's hard labor. For Blythe, it was the only way to live.

Chico sat in his new custom black Range Rover with the 22-inch black rims, blacked-out windows, with black and chrome side vents and custom paint on all the trim panels, door handles, and the front grill. The Range Rover was fitted with bulletproof windows and doors, run-flat tires, and secret compartments, and was capable of protecting the president. It was a necessary measure for Chico. He needed to ride around protected in a lavish ride that was built like a tank. He had enemies everywhere and couldn't take the risk of being hit while he was mobile. And with Cross and Kola still out there, an attack was able to come at him from any direction.

Chico sat parked on the corner of Riverside Drive and 145th Street. He was in the passenger seat, with Two-Face seated behind the wheel. The sun had set hours ago, and darkness covered the Harlem streets. Both men were heavily armed, with guns concealed in secret compartments hidden inside of the truck.

Chico took a few pulls from his Newport and peered out at the park across the street. He then looked at Two-Face. "So, give me the status."

"I'm on it, homes. I've been all over this hood tryin' to get at them clowns, but they secure wit' their business, Chico. Cross hasn't been around like that, and Edge be in the cut, and that bitch, Kola, she ain't been out. But I'm gettin' they attention. I cut down a few close associates of theirs. They saw the end of my gun, homes, and you should have seen how I had these clowns beggin' for their lives. They came across a true *vato*, and lost, homes."

"I need results, Two-Face," Chico explained loudly. "I need shit done out there. I can't have that nigga and that bitch stepping on my business."

"I feel you, homes, and you know, soon as they come out they fuckin' holes, homes, I'ma be there to push 'em back in, permanently."

"Just do what you do best. Make their end happen quickly."

Two-Face nodded.

As the two talked, Chico's cell phone began to ring. He didn't recognize the number but decided to answer it anyway. But before he picked up the call, he instructed Two-Face to drive him to the Bronx for a meeting.

Two-Face started the ignition and headed north toward the highway.

"Who this?" Chico answered.

A female shouted out, "You fuckin' bastard!"

"Who the fuck is this?"

"Where's my daughter, muthafucka?"

"What?"

"Where is she? I know you did something to her!"

Chico was confused. But he soon recognized the voice on the other end. "What the fuck you talkin' about, Denise? I have no idea where Apple is."

"Yes, you do. You're a fuckin' liar, Chico! You did something to her. You think I'm stupid? Don't fuckin' play wit' me, you fuckin' bastard!"

"Bitch, you better chill out and remember who ya talkin' to."

"I don't give a fuck who you are. I'm not scared of ya bitch ass, Chico!" Denise shouted hysterically.

Chico's face twisted into a scowl. He tried to keep his cool, but Denise's constant ranting was making his blood boil. He wanted to know how she had gotten his new number.

"I know you did something to her, you bastard. You coming around asking about my daughter like you cared was nothing but a front. Apple didn't just suddenly leave. You did something to her so you could flaunt your new bitch around Harlem. You think I don't fuckin' know— You stunting wit' that new bitch, while you did something to my daughter. Nigga, you better tell me where she at or what you did to her."

"Bitch, you tripping!"

"I'm trippin'? I'll show you how I'm trippin' when I go to the police and tell 'em all ya fuckin' business, muthafucka! I ain't that bitch to fuckin' play with! I want my fuckin' daughter back, and you better find her. You think you can play my daughter for that new bitch you got stunting around Harlem? Nigga, it ain't happening."

Chico looked at Two-Face and was ready to tell him to make a U-turn and head over to the East Side to pay Denise a visit. He was ready to give her a severe beatdown. She was talking reckless, and Chico couldn't tolerate that. He knew that he had nothing to do with Apple's disappearance, but he figured Denise was drunk and talking shit. So Chico thought against it and played it off as the alcohol talking.

"What you need me to do, homes?" Two-Face asked, ready for some action.

Chico looked at his lethal soldier for a moment, with Denise still on the phone. He only had to give the order and Denise could easily become a memory to him and the hood, but he said to Two-Face, "Just drive me to the BX."

Two-Face nodded.

"You better find her, muthafucka!" Denise shouted. "You better find my daughter." She then hung up.

Chico rolled down his window and tossed his cell phone out the window, saying, "Fuck that bitch! I'll get a new one." He then rolled up his window and reclined in his seat. He then said to Two-Face, "If that bitch continues to act up, then next time I won't be so fuckin' nice."

Chico gave Denise a pass for her insult, only because she was Apple's mother. But it would only be one time. And if she decided to force his hand, then he was ready to show her how a bitch can truly disappear.

Chapter 10

Kola was doing seventy miles per hour headed north on the Major Deegan Expressway, on her way to Yonkers to meet with Candace and her girls at one of the stash houses. It had been a moment since her meeting with Eduardo, and she was still puzzled by the phone call she'd received from him. It didn't make sense to her and disturbed her more than she wanted to admit.

Kola needed to re-up soon with Eduardo and figured he was probably upset because she didn't give him any pussy. She knew how bad he craved her, and their sexual cat-and-mouse game was becoming somewhat tedious. So she decided that the next time they met, she would give him some, knowing that sex with him would be truly worth it and would strengthen their relationship.

It was almost midnight when she got the phone call from her mother. She was hesitant to answer the call, but took it anyway. "What the fuck you want?"

"I want that muthafucka dead, Kola!" Denise shouted.

"What the fuck you talkin' about!"

"Chico. You need to take care of him, Kola! He did something to Apple."

Kola wasn't in the mood to hear from her mother or about Apple. She hadn't heard from her sister in months, and she didn't care. Apple had been nothing but a headache for her and the sole reason Nichols was dead. The less she heard from her, the better. And she felt that the hood was better off without her around. For her it was out of sight, out of mind.

Denise continued to rant about the false run-in. "You need to fuck him up, Kola. Get some niggas to do that muthafucka! That muthafucka threatened me. He put his fuckin' hands on me, Kola. He disrespected this family. You hear me, Kola? He needs to fuckin' go! I'm your fuckin' mother!"

Kola couldn't care less about what her mother had to say, but she was right about one thing—Chico had to go. He had been a thorn in Kola's side for too long. Chico was in her way with business, and he was starting to spread like a virus. And she had been hearing the name Two-Face on the streets plenty of times. The young killer's name was starting to give her a headache, and he was becoming more of a nuisance. She knew he was helping Chico try and take over what Kola considered to be her town. Harlem. They were laying down niggas like Dominos, and from what Kola could see, Cross and Edge weren't doing shit.

Kola got tired of hearing her mother's ranting about Chico and Apple on the phone and just hung up the call. "Fuck that stupid bitch!"

Kola needed to relax, but her mind was spinning with so many problems as she approached Yonkers. One being Edge. The contempt that Kola had for him showed clearly. She couldn't even be around him without biting down on her lip and wanting to kill him. There were a few disputes between them, but Cross had broken it up and was always defending Edge. And she was getting sick and tired of it. Edge was putting a strain on their business. She didn't trust him, and felt that Edge and Cross were plotting against her.

The only place that Kola found trust was with Candace and her ruthless crew of bitches. They were ready to ride or die for Kola, and Kola had much respect for them. She felt that they needed to make the first move on Edge, and if Cross was stupid enough to follow him, then she was ready to put down her ex-lover too. Things were changing, and Kola knew that she had the upper hand. She had Eduardo—she had the drug connect— she had reputation, and power. And she had muscle, with Candace.

Kola arrived at the stash house in Yonkers. She had her operation set up in many places, but the place in Yonkers was her main location. It was secure and discreet and away from the city, and not too many people knew about the four-bedroom home. Kola wanted to expand and move her business into Yonkers, and she planned on doing it slowly. She already had her hands full in Harlem.

She parked in front of the three-story, Victorian-style, four-bedroom home with the wraparound porch, small chain fence, and dying, brown grass out front. Two security cameras watched the front. She stepped out of her Benz and strutted toward the front entrance. She was already caught on the security cameras and was buzzed into the place by Candace before she walked to the door.

The home was sparsely furnished with hardwood floors stretching out from room to room and the windows blacked out with dark curtains and rusted, old folding furniture. In the back room was where the action took place.

Kola strutted through the house and walked into the den area, where there was a few ki's of cocaine displayed alongside a few guns and assault rifles. The girls were heavily armed and ready for anything that came their way. They had a counting machine and security monitor mounted on the wall that showed all four corners of the house. Kola and Candace didn't want any surprises. Yonkers was a high-risk area with crime, but the girls came and went discreetly, not wanting to attract attention of their neighbors.

Kola greeted her crew and looked around. "What we got?"

"We about to run low and gonna need a re-up soon," Candace said. "You spoke to your connect?"

"I haven't been able to get him on the phone yet," Kola said. "But he always comes through."

Kola didn't want to worry about why she wasn't able to reach Eduardo. She understood that he was a busy man, but she had been trying to call him for a week and was unsuccessful in reaching him. His primary number had been disconnected, but she tried other numbers that she was able to reach him by, but they were all going straight to voice mail.

"We gonna need to re-up soon, Kola. I mean, this shit pretty much sells itself, and out here, they loving it," Candace said.

"I'll get at him soon."

"We got a problem though," Candace stated.

"I told you, don't worry about my connect. He always comes through."

"It's not that, Kola."

"What is it then?"

"We got hit last night," Candace said.

"What the fuck you mean?"

"Our spot in Harlem, the apartment . . . it got shot up, and we got taken for fifty stacks. And we lost two of ours."

"And I'm just now hearing about this shit?" Kola barked.

"I tried to call you, but I kept getting your voice mail."

"By who?"

Candace looked reluctant to say the name responsible because he had been a new problem for Kola for too long. "That kid, Two-Face."

"How the fuck did he know where to hit us?"

"People are talking and running scared of that little Mexican!"

"Fuck me!" Kola shouted and knocked over a nearby lamp, shattering it against the floor. "I don't need this shit right now, Candace."

The other girls just stood around silently, but kept at their work, producing cocaine into crack or counting money.

Kola was seething. She had to step into action and take care of a growing problem. Chico was already a headache, but the constant ringing of the name Two-Face in her head had her ready to go out there and go gunning for the kid on her own. She'd had enough of Two-Face and Chico.

"He hunt us, then we can hunt him too," Candace said. "We can put that fuckin' *puta* into the dirt and spit on him."

Kola looked at her right-hand with a deadpan expression. The war was costing her money, time, and soldiers. She felt that her back was against the wall, because not only did she have enemies in the streets, but close men were plotting for her downfall in her own organization.

Kola sighed. The frustration was starting to show on her face. She walked over to the table that was cluttered with handguns and picked up a chrome 9 mm Beretta. She removed the clip, checked the ammo, and nodded. She took the gun and stuffed it into her purse. "I'll handle it," was the only thing she said to Candace before leaving the Yonkers stash house.

Candace shrugged at Kola's unorthodox reply and continued with her business in the home. Money never stopped.

Kola got into her convertible Benz and sped back into the city.

New York City was buzzing with nightly activity as Kola cruised through the city with the top to her Benz down and feeling the warm breeze blow through. From block to block, the streets were flooded with ladies in tight skirts, jeans, and tight-fitting dresses, strutting in their high heels and revealing club outfits, and the men dressed in their best attire to impress the ladies about.

The balmy night was the perfect night for driving, and Kola needed to clear her head and think about her next chess move. She tried endlessly to reach Eduardo, but to no avail. She didn't want to panic, but without Eduardo, then her grind on the streets would soon come to a stop. Kola was ready to drive to New Jersey and make a personal trip to his penthouse suite unannounced.

It was well into the early hours of the morning when Kola found herself driving uptown, past the Apollo Theater on 125th Street and making a right onto Eighth Avenue/Frederick Douglass Boulevard.

Kola was ready to drive back to her Yonkers stash house and talk to Candace. She hated that she left the place abruptly, but she was upset, and for once, she didn't know what to do. Now, she was ready to put as many guns out on the streets and have them be on a constant hunt for Chico, Two-Face, or anyone associated with that crew. Kola needed to turn the tides, and one problem had to go away, starting with Chico. Then she would go after Edge and handle her business with Eduardo.

Kola continued to sail down Eighth Avenue, and like midtown Manhattan, uptown Harlem was buzzing with people and the nightlife. She slowly approached 145th Street and was ready to make a left, heading toward the Henry Hudson Parkway, when something immediately caught her eye.

"Muthafuckas!" she exclaimed.

She stopped her Benz and looked closely. It was definitely them. She wasn't mistaken at all. Kola sat parked on the corner and watched Chico, Two-Face, Blythe, and one of Chico's low-level enforcers walk toward a parked pearl-white Bentley. For Kola, it was a beautiful moment, the perfect opportunity. Instantly, death entered her mind. Kola wished she had Candace with her, but at that moment, she didn't give a fuck.

Kola spun her car around, put up the rag-top for cover, and slowly drove in their direction. She removed the 9 mm she took from the Yonkers crib from her purse, cocked it back, and kept a keen eye on all of her foes.

Chico and Blythe were hugged up on each other as they walked, but Two-Face and the other supposed gunmen were looking around, watching everything that moved. The block was thick with activity. The only thing open was a shabby bodega and a low-key lounge.

Kola turned the block slowly and was ready to take action. She didn't want to miss. She wanted to shoot Chico in his head and push his wig back, and then take out Two-Face, who had become her primary problem in the streets. Chico and Blythe were about to step into the

Bentley, his two enforcers only steps behind them.

Kola didn't give a fuck who was around.

Bak! Bak! Bak! Bak! Bak! Bak!

Glass in nearby cars shattered abruptly and Kola was seen poised only a few feet away near her Benz with the gun gripped in her hand and shooting wildly at her enemies.

Chico and Blythe instantly took cover, but Two-Face and the thug went into reaction. Two-Face pulled two .45s from his waistband and crouched behind the Bentley. The second thug followed suit, pulling out a .380.

The firing continued, and Kola stepped closer with a fiery gaze of agitation. She didn't speak a word, but aimed to kill. The shots echoed into the night.

Blythe was screaming and taking cover, Chico yelling at her, "Stay the fuck down! Stay the fuck down!"

Two-Face stood up rapidly and returned fire strongly. Bullets went whizzing by Kola's ear, and she stumbled back toward her car, suddenly becoming overwhelmed with chaos. Two-Face rushed from behind the Bentley where he was crouched and started gunning for Kola. She was quickly outgunned and outnumbered.

She rushed into her idling Benz while the shots at her continued. Two-Face was aiming to kill. Shots penetrated Kola's Benz as she sped away, with her ducking in the driver's seat from shattering glass.

Two-Face chased behind the car for half a block, firing intensely and making Kola's car look like Swiss cheese, but she was able to get away. "Fuck! Fuck! Fuck, that bitch!" he yelled.

Two-Face looked back at his boss and his woman and saw they were OK. But he was furious that Kola had gotten away. He gripped the twin .45s in his hands tightly and knew it was time to make an exit. He'd already heard the police sirens in the distance.

Kola sped away in her bullet-riddled Benz for blocks, making sharp turns, blowing through red lights, and trying to collect herself. She didn't know what she was thinking when she attacked Chico and his peoples. It was a bold move, but she also knew it was stupid.

Kola finally slowed down her ride when she got near the highway. She came to a stop and stepped out of her car on a quiet street. She needed to relax and calm herself. She knew her Benz was hot, with the bullet holes and having a 9 mm on her. She took a deep breath, peered around her surroundings, and then got on her cell phone to call Candace for a ride back to Yonkers. She decided to take what she needed and scrap the Benz.

When Candace heard about what happened, she knew her boss had heart and wasn't just about talk. It was one of the reasons why Candace had so much respect for Kola. She was gangster.

The two rode back to Yonkers in Candace's Escalade. Kola needed to regroup, get her mind right, and think about her next move. She knew that, after tonight's action, Chico and Two-Face would come gunning for her and her crew even harder. So she put everyone on alert, telling her girls and her soldiers to be extra careful on the streets and to always stay armed.

Kola finally arrived home after handling business in Yonkers with the sun peeking in the sky. Candace had dropped her off, and she wanted to stay around and protect her, but Kola assured her that she was safe. No one knew about her residence, and she had enough guns in her home to supply a small army. Candace lingered around for a moment and then headed back to Yonkers.

Kola was home for no less than an hour when she heard a car racing into her driveway and coming to a screeching stop at her front door. Kola didn't know what to expect, so she grabbed a sawed-off, double-barrel shotgun and ran to the window. She narrowed her eyes to see who it was and was shocked to see Cross and Edge. She sighed heavily, but didn't lower her gun or her guard.

Cross ran to the door and started knocking on it hard, shouting, "Kola, open the fuckin' door!"

Kola stood poised by the front door with the shotgun gripped firmly in her hands. She peered out the window once again and shouted, "Go away, Cross. I don't want you here."

"Well, I'm fuckin' here now. What happened last night? Those muthafuckas came at you? You OK, baby?" Cross shouted.

"I'm fine. Just fuckin' leave!"

"I'm not goin' nowhere, baby. I still fuckin' love you!

And, believe me, Chico and that new young nigga of his is goin' to get got! I promise you that, Kola. We gonna kill 'em all!"

"You should have done that a long time ago. Now I'm the one left handling business."

"What the fuck you talkin' about? Just open the fuckin' door so we can talk. I ain't gonna hurt you, baby."

"I know you won't 'cuz, one, I'm not opening this door, and two, I got the sawed-off in my hands just for insurance."

Cross twisted his face in anger and looked at Edge.

"Fuck her, Cross!" Edge said to him. "She always gotta be extra with her Queenpin attitude!"

Kola heard his words clearly and was ready to shoot him through the door. But she held her anger and shouted once again to Cross, "Get the fuck away from my door! I don't need you here!"

Cross kicked the door violently and shouted back, "Bitch, you always gonna need me! Sooner than you think."

Kola readied the shotgun, indicating that she was ready to shoot first if either one of them tried to rush inside her home. Cross quickly got the hint and slowly backed away from the door, but Edge lingered at the front door for a moment. It made Kola extremely nervous.

"You stupid fuckin' bitch! I don't know why the fuck Cross got wit' ya triflin' ass!"

Kola swung open the front door and aimed the sawed-off shot gun at his face.

Edge was quickly taken aback. But then he calmly spoke the words, "You got balls, bitch."

"Call me a bitch again, and Cross will be picking your brains up wit' a shovel." Kola threatened.

Edge glared at her and then chuckled. "You still don't get it. You're all alone, baby, all fuckin' alone."

Kola stared at Cross, who stood by his car and only looked on, while Edge disrespected her in front of their home. She'd had enough of them both.

"Y'all niggas want a war wit' me, then fuckin' bring it!"

"Nah, no war," Edge said to her. "You know what I want."

"And you, Cross, you disappoint me. You gonna stand there and let him talk to your woman like that?"

"My woman? Then you need to start fuckin' acting like it. You won't fuck me! You won't let me come home even after I told you I don't fuck wit' no Cynthia. You do all that grimy shit to me, and you're my woman? Edge, c'mon, let's get the fuck outta here. We fuckin' done."

Edge grinned and secretly blew Kola a kiss. "I'll be back, and next time, we ain't asking to come in—well, me, anyway."

Edge took a few steps backwards, his eyes still focused on Kola. He gave her the creeps.

Kola looked over at Cross, and their eyes locked for a moment. She didn't see that street hustler or gangster anymore; the man she fell in love with. She only saw a punk. Cross had changed. He had slipped greatly and allowed Edge to get into his head.

Kola watched both men get back into the car and peel out. She sighed with relief and went back inside.

Something was troubling her about what Edge had said to her, about her being alone. She didn't know what he meant by it, and she wasn't ready to find out. She placed the shotgun back in its location and sprawled out on her sofa. They kept saying it was a man's world, but Kola was ready to show and prove that a woman could play it better.

Chapter 11

Chico and his crew were ready to tool up and go head-hunting, starting with Kola. Chico was furious—especially because Blythe was in the line of attack, and they almost killed his girl. He wanted blood to spill at any cost. He gathered many of his soldiers and held a restricted meeting in a basement. There were guns everywhere and willing young men ready to use them to kill anyone.

Two-Face stood behind his boss and looked troubled about something as Chico held court in the room.

Chico stood tall amongst his men clad in a velour sweatsuit and holding a Desert Eagle in his hand. He had everyone's attention in the room. Chico looked into every man's face and studied their expressions as he spoke. He didn't want any weakness or doubt in his crew. He gave out orders and told everyone that their main goal was to hunt and kill Cross, Edge, Kola, and everyone close to them. The goons nodded and were ready to go into action.

"It's a new fuckin' day, ya muthafuckas hear me? A new fuckin' day!" Chico exclaimed.

His thugs nodded.

The meeting went on for a half-hour, and then Chico made everyone leave the basement, leaving him alone to talk to Two-Face. Chico noticed the troubled look on his top enforcer's face. He turned to face his soldier and asked, "What the fuck is bothering you?"

"That bitch," he uttered.

"She's gonna get got," Chico said.

"Nah, there was something else about her."

"Like what?"

"I can't pinpoint it, homes, but I know that bitch from somewhere," Two-Face said.

"From where?"

"I'm thinkin', homes, but I know that face."

It had been gnawing at Two-Face about knowing Kola's face from someplace different. He thought about it night and day. Chico didn't think anything about it, until Two-Face finally remembered where he had seen Kola's face before.

"Homes, she ain't look like that when I saw her. She different," Two-Face explained.

"Different? What the fuck you mean, different? Just say what the fuck you gotta say Two-Face, and don't fuckin' sugarcoat it."

"I mean, me and my *vatos*, we seen that face at a Mexican whorehouse. We ran the train on her something nice, but her face, her face was badly burned in some way, but her body was something nice to play with. I swear to you, homes, that bitch Kola could be her twin because they looked so much alike. You know they say we all got a twin," Two-Face stated.

Chico was quiet for a moment, taking in everything Two-Face was saying to him. He knew it *had* to be Apple that Two-Face was talking about. There was no mistaking it. But Chico wondered how she ended up in Mexico selling pussy. He looked at Two-Face and asked, "This girl, how long ago was it when you saw her?"

"Don't know, homes. I go back home like three or four times a year. It was less than six months ago."

"And you sure this bitch you saw was whoring?"

"I'm positive, homes."

"And what side of the face was her burn on?"

Two-Face laughed. "I was too busy into that pussy to care about any scars." He gyrated and thrust his hips jokingly, mimicking his sexual act with the whore. "But why you ask, homes?"

"I'm just curious, that's all," Chico stated, impatiently. "But what city was this girl in?"

Two-Face shrugged. He wasn't sure of the exact location where he saw the girl. He stared at Chico and asked, "Homes, why you asking so many questions about this bitch? Is she important to us?"

Chico didn't respond. He had a stone-cold look about him. He locked eyes with Two-Face and the look instantly said to Two-Face that he had revealed too much.

"Why you ask so many details about this one whore, homes? She special to you or something? You know this whore?"

"Nah, I was just asking."

"But you asking way too many questions."

"It's nothing, Two-Face. Just asking you some questions, a'ight! Just fuckin' dead it!" Chico barked.

"A'ight, homes, I feel you."

But the tension in the room and the uncomfortable stares put both men on edge with each other. Two-Face wanted to know why a Mexican whore was bringing up questions with Chico.

And Chico figured out that he finally had a line on Apple's whereabouts, but he wasn't a hundred percent sure that it was her. He was determined to find out the truth, though.

Several days had passed since Chico and Two-Face talked. It was bothering Chico that there was a strong possibility that Apple was kidnapped and forced to sell pussy in Mexico. It was the only explanation he could come up with.

Chico remembered waiting around at the motel for several days, but she never showed up to collect her things. He remembered the motel room in New Jersey. Apple's things were still there, but she was gone. He remembered her being upset with him and the trouble she was enduring. She had plenty of enemies, and anyone could have been responsible for her disappearance.

Chico figured Kola and Cross had the means and reason to have Apple kidnapped and suffer a humiliating fate in a different country. It would have been a slow death for Apple—to be stripped away of her dignity and respect. Chico was now determined more than ever to hunt and kill everyone in Kola's crew, from the bottom up. The war with them became even much more personal.

It was after midnight when Chico parked his truck near an open area not too far from the shimmering lights coming from the long, soaring G.W. Bridge. He sat alone in the driver's seat, a .50-cal. concealed underneath, and waited while smoking a Newport. He listened to nothing but silence around him. There was no radio playing or loud traffic anywhere around him. The area was isolated, shaded with many trees and shrubbery all around.

An hour later, a car began pulling up slowly. Chico glanced at the approaching headlights and knew it was the person he was waiting for. He wanted the meeting in private, so he came alone. He didn't feel threatened by the car's approach. The single occupant in the burgundy Cadillac CTS was well known to Chico and vice versa. They had done business with each other before.

The CTS came to a stop near Chico's truck. The headlights shut off, and the door to the Cadillac opened slowly. Chico took one last pull from his cancer stick and tossed it out the window, and then he proceeded to step out of his vehicle.

The man approaching Chico was tall, six three, with a trimmed goatee. He was dressed nicely in a charcoal three-piece suit and sported a pair of wingtip shoes. He wore an expensive Cartier watch and wore shades even though it was night. He looked cool, but also menacing with his mysterious demeanor.

Chico walked closer to him. Both men were expressionless. Chico was familiar with his style of work. He was expensive, but always worth the pay. Chico somewhat trusted him, and only used the man's services when there was no one else to do the job correctly.

"It's been a long time, Chico," the man spoke, his voice raspy and deep.

"I know. But I have a job for you, Dario."

Dario nodded.

"I need someone wit'ya skills in tracking and hunting. I need someone found ASAP."

"My fee will be the same," Dario stated. "Twenty-five thousand plus expenses."

Chico nodded.

"Who is it that you need found?"

"A girl, and last I heard, she might be in Mexico whoring."

"Rough place. You have her picture?"

Chico reached into his jacket and handed Dario a small photo of Apple, before the damage to her face.

"Pretty girl."

"She's scarred, carries a burn on the side of her face, and she's young."

Dario stared at the photo, taking in Apple's features.

"I need her found."

"I will. And when she's found, you want her to disappear silently or harsh?" Dario asked, gravity in his voice.

"No. I need her brought back to New York. I need her alive."

Dario nodded.

Chico then tossed Dario a sealed, lumpy white envelope filled with cash. Dario caught it in his grip.

"That's fifteen thousand in there. You get the rest when she's back in New York."

Dario nodded. "I'm on it."

Business was done, and Chico walked back to his truck.

Dario went through the green bills in his hands and was satisfied. Chico always paid him well, even though he rarely used his services. Dario was a former CIA agent. He had been with the CIA for fifteen years until he went rogue and became a mercenary for hire. Dario knew how to hunt and track people globally. He had an expert network system of computers and toys, had connects in every region of the globe, and was a skilled killer.

Chico last used his services several years ago when trying to locate a snitch that fled New York and went into hiding. The snitch turned state's witness against Chico and his crew, and was willing to testify in court. His testimony was about to propel Chico into a life sentence in prison or the death penalty. The DA had moved the snitch out of New York for his protection, but Dario found him in less than two weeks and dealt with the problem accordingly— Two shots to his head and dismemberment, with pieces of him dumped miles apart, in eight different states. Chico was acquitted of all charges.

Dario watched Chico pull off and was ready to implement his tracking technique right away. He got on his cell phone and booked the next flight into Mexico and would start his search from the border.

Chapter 12

It had been two weeks since Shaun took the newborn baby from Apple. Apple had dried her tears, but her heart was still torn from the sudden removal of her baby. In fact, Apple sunk into a quick depression. She'd never thought about having any kids, but when she gave birth to a girl, she instantly had a connection with her daughter, even though it was short-lived.

"Peaches," Apple would whisper. "Peaches. Peaches."

Apple thought about her daughter day and night. Mary was there for her, and a few Mexican whores began to feel sorry for what was happening to her. They started coming around and taking better care of her when Shaun wasn't around. They soon started to see Apple as one of their own. They brought Apple extra food to help get her strength back and gave her prescription antibiotics to help ward off any infections. Gradually, the girls were becoming a family to Apple.

Mary would always talk to Apple, telling stories of her past, about her family. She even talked about men to

Apple, tricks that she'd fucked or that had fucked her.

"Some were nice, and some were assholes. Coldhearted bastards," Mary said. "Sometimes, they would do these cruel things to me when I was only so young, and it would hurt so bad. I would drown myself in my own tears night after night, praying for it to stop. But it never did, and soon you just get used to it."

Apple was listening, but she was silent. Mary became her unexpected comfort, like a fluffy pillow to a tired head at nights. Mary became like a grandmother to Apple and a few whores in the place. She had wisdom and had experienced so many tragic incidents in her lifetime. She was able to relate with many of the girls' stories, not just Apple's.

Mary reminded Apple of the pain she felt when her first newborn child was ripped away from her and sold. "There were many pregnancies, and many painful tears that followed behind seeing my children carried out of my life," she said sadly.

"I can't go through this anymore," Apple said.

Mary took Apple's hand gently. Mary already knew the truth; it wouldn't be Apple's last pregnancy. There would be more heartbreaks and hard, stained tears to follow. "It is our life now," Mary said.

"It's not mine!" Apple spat. "I can't live here anymore. I can't do this, Mary. I hate that muthafucka! I hate him so much, that—"Apple stopped her final words, her mind suddenly slipping into a dark place.

"What you plan to do? Escape?"

"I need to do something."

"He will then hunt you down and find you. Shaun has power and connections everywhere, and you are a marked woman and far away from home."

"This will never be my home!"

"You still believe that this man will find you, huh?"

"Chico will come for me, Mary. I know he will. And when he do, I will make that muthafucka pay dearly for what he's done to me."

Mary started to reply, but she began to let out an aggressive cough. She hooked over with her hand to her mouth and continued to cough. It was bad. The cancer was eating away at her.

"You OK, Mary?" Apple asked with concern.

Mary nodded. She coughed harshly a few more times, and then there was blood spewing from her mouth.

"Oh my God!"

Mary reached for something to wipe away the blood. "I'm fine, Apple."

Apple stared at her with much concern. She knew Mary was dying. And with no proper medication to take and Mary not visiting a hospital or seeking treatment for her condition not once, the disease was becoming more aggressive inside of her.

The coughing soon subsided, and Mary was back to her old self again, talking to Apple like nothing had happened.

"This place done drained me, Apple, physically and mentally," Mary said.

"It ain't gonna drain me, Mary."

Mary respected the fight in Apple. She was once like that, but after years of neglect and abuse, she had given up hope.

The two women talked for an hour. It gave Apple some comfort. Mary made her smile a few times, and then their session was interrupted by Mary's deathly and recurring coughing. Mary had to excuse herself and rush toward the bathroom. Apple just sat there with a worried gaze about her friend.

※

Apple awoke naked and hungry. She didn't know what day of the week it was. The past couple days she was doped up on drugs and unaware of her surroundings. She hadn't turned a trick since she'd given birth, but Shaun was ready to put that to an end.

She got out of bed and exited the room. The hallway was starting to fill with awakened whores coming out of their rooms to get ready for the day and a few tricks that lingered overnight. The scantily clad women laughed and talked for a moment. But Apple had to go pee. She felt her high fading. The dope was dissipating from her system, and she was becoming conscious of her surroundings.

Shaun was nowhere around, and Apple was relieved. She stumbled toward the bathroom and rushed to the stall to pee. She squatted over the dirty toilet and sighed as she drained her unwanted fluids. After her talk with Mary last night, she felt a little better, but she was still suffering from some depression.

Apple continued to pee, and when she was done, she stood up and pulled up her panties. But something suddenly caught her peripheral vision. It was peeking from underneath the second stall. She looked down and noticed that it was part of an arm—Someone was sprawled out on the floor.

Apple became startled. It was a woman. She exited the stall she was in and swung open the door to the neighboring stall. "Oh my gosh!" she uttered. "No! No!"

Mary was sprawled out unconscious on the floor in her underwear, blood seeping from her mouth.

Apple scooped Mary's body into her arms and tried to shake her awake. "Mary, get up! Get up, Mary! Get up! Get up!" Apple screamed, but it was to no avail. Mary remained motionless. "Help! Somebody help me! Help her!"

Moments later, other whores rushed into the bathroom and came across the stunning situation. They were all shocked to see Mary across the bathroom floor in her underwear and in the arms of Apple. A few girls rushed over to aid Apple with trying to revive Mary, but she was already dead.

Apple had to let go of the body, and a few girls were trying to console her from the grief.

A half hour later, Shaun stepped into the bathroom with a few of his goons. He peered at Mary's body. He was expressionless. He shook his head and said, "She was old anyway and wasn't profiting shit. Move outta my way. I gotta get her the fuck out of here!"

Apple snapped. She rushed toward Shaun, screaming, "You fuckin' bastard!" She snatched him by his collar and caught him with a quick, right-hand hook.

Shaun stumbled, caught completely off guard by the attack. But he promptly returned with a hit of his own. He punched Apple so hard, she slid across the bathroom floor and landed against the wall.

"Bitch, don't you ever put ya fuckin' hands on me again! I'll kill you!" Shaun ranted. "When I'm done cleaning this shit up, you gonna pay for that, you stupid bitch!"

Apple's lip was bleeding, and she was in a momentary daze. The other whores around didn't intervene. They were all scared of Shaun and his goons. Some went over to help Apple to her feet, and a few other girls didn't want to leave Mary.

Shaun shouted, "Y'all bitches get the fuck back to work! This ain't ya business in here!"

The women scrambled out of the bathroom, leaving Mary's body on the cold, dirty floor and Apple looking shaky in the corner.

Shaun stared at her. "Yo, bitch, you heard what the fuck I said? Get the fuck outta here before I give you more of a hurting!"

Apple locked eyes with Shaun. She didn't flinch. She wiped the blood from her lips, glanced down at Mary's lifeless body and held back the tears. But she was moving too slow for Shaun, which made him even more frustrated.

"You think I'm fuckin' playin' wit' you, Apple? That's it? You think I'm a joke. This ain't Harlem, bitch. I run shit here, and you better understand that."

Shaun removed a .45 from his waist as he glared intensely at Apple. "You still mad because I snatched that little bitch from your arms? She was my property to sell off, 'cuz I can do whatever the fuck I wanna do out this bitch."

Hearing Shaun disrespect her newborn daughter was starting to cause Apple to get emotional. But she fought the tears back and slowly made her exit, but not before hearing Shaun say to his goons, "Wrap that bitch up and dump her somewhere."

Shaun's goons wrapped Mary in a dirty sheet and then moved her out of the bathroom and dumped her into the back of a dusty pickup truck like she was a piece of trash. It was like they were moving furniture, not a body. The women were all saddened by Mary's demise. It showed in their faces and work. To them, Mary became a surrogate mother. She was tough and honest. And she was caring. She was going to be missed greatly.

Apple sat in her still room. She lay curled up on the mattress, constantly drying her tears. Even though they had developed a short friendship, Apple knew she would miss Mary. It was a strange friendship that developed, but it was still a friendship. Time was becoming a blur to her. She felt hopeless.

Shaun had left for a few hours, giving Apple momentary peace.

The echoes of whores turning tricks seeped through her walls, and the activity and traffic outside her door looked like the red light district in Amsterdam.

There was a knock at Apple's door. She refused to answer it. The knocking continued, but she just sat on the stained mattress, looking lost to the world around her.

The door opened, and a young Mexican whore named Alba eased her way into Apple's room. She spoke little English. She looked at Apple, showing that she cared about her condition. She wanted to know what was wrong.

"¿Apple, estás bien?" Alba asked.

Apple looked up at Alba. The girl was petite, only standing five-two, with small breasts and long, curly hair. Her face showed the age of a fifteen-year-old, but her eyes showed a well-experienced woman. She was clad in a tattered nightgown, soiled from past customers.

"¿Necesitas algo?" Alba asked.

Apple shook her head.

"He...soon...back, no?" Alba said.

"I don't care," Apple stated.

Alba moved closer to Apple. She took Apple's hand into hers and did what Mary would have done. She spoke Spanish to Apple.

Apple only listened, but like with Mary, she felt comforted.

Alba was one of the youngest whores working for Shaun. She'd been on the streets since she was thirteen and had linked up with Shaun a year earlier. It was the closest thing to a home that Alba had.

The two girls spent a quality moment with each other.

Suddenly, the room door flung open, and Shaun and a few of his goons appeared in the doorway.

Alba looked scared. She avoided eye contact with him and stood to her feet.

Shaun glared at Alba. "Get the fuck outta here, Alba!"

The girl didn't ask any questions. She rushed past Shaun and his men, and bolted to her room a few doors down.

Shaun stepped closer to Apple, his eyes fixed on her. "I told you that you was gonna pay from that incident this morning. You thought I was lying?"

Apple held his gaze. She stood from her seated position and looked around her. Three men flanked Shaun, and they all had a devilish smile focused at her. She knew what was about to take place. It wouldn't be the first time.

Shaun shut the door and marched toward Apple. He forcefully grabbed her by the wrist and hurled her across the room. Apple landed on her side and was hurt.

"It's a new day for you, you dumb fuckin' bitch! You defy me in front of my hoes," Shaun shouted.

Apple looked up as Shaun towered over her. He removed his belt from around his waist and struck her repeatedly, across her back, arms, and chest. She began to cry out from the assault. She tried to run, but Shaun kicked her back down to the floor and shouted, "You don't fuckin' move unless I tell you to!"

He then lunged for Apple, grabbing her with her hair wrapped around his fist, and dragged her back to the bed.

She kicked and screamed, but Shaun was too strong for her to break free. He pushed her on the bed and ripped away her shirt and tore off her panties. The welts from the beating showed on her skin.

"I told you, I'm about fuckin' business, and you're big business to me, Apple. Now, we get to have fun." Shaun turned to look at his goons and nodded.

All three men began to unbuckle their jeans and stepped toward Apple with a lustful look.

Shaun took a few steps back from her. "Y'all niggas do what ya need to do to break this bitch in again."

"No problemo," one of the men replied with a smile, his swollen dick in his hand.

Apple knew she was about to get gang raped. It was nothing new to her, but it always hurt. The men shifted closer to her while she curled up into the fetal position. They swarmed on top of her like ants over something sweet. They pinned her to the mattress and forced her legs open, grabbing her breasts roughly and began penetrating her.

Shaun stood by and watched. He smiled. "Yeah, y'all niggas fuck that bitch right," he said sharply. "'Cuz I want that bitch pregnant by tonight. I got money to make off of her wit' that pregnant pussy and the next child she births." He walked toward the door, making his exit, leaving the wolves to feast on Apple.

Chapter 13

The line to get into the Playa's Lounge on Twenty-Fifth Street stretched half way down the block. The Playa's Lounge was a popular midtown club that was frequented by a lot of celebrities, athletes, drug dealers, beautiful women, and wannabes. It was situated in the middle of the block, and high-end cars lined the city block with the city's elite moving about.

The night was cool. Business was booming. The ladies were dressed in short dresses and skirts and tight jeans, highlighting their thick hips and curves, and some of the finest women in New York City were standing on line outside of the club waiting to get inside. The waiting crowd outside watched as luxury cars and limos pulled up and a few of the city's top-notch got out of their vehicles and were rushed in the club, bypassing the long line and security.

Around midnight, a black Infiniti QX56 sitting on 22-inch chrome rims and tinted windows pulled up in front of the club. The crowd outside quickly took notice of the magnificent-looking truck that came to a stop. Edge stepped out of the passenger side looking sharp in a pair of stylish denim jeans, beige Timberlands, a fitted black T-shirt that was adorned with a long, platinum chain with a diamond-encrusted Jesus face pendant swinging at the end of it. He was bejeweled in diamond rings and earrings, and a bracelet that screamed "hood wealth."

The driver and a third passenger seated in the backseat stepped out from the Infiniti truck and followed behind Edge. They strutted toward the front entrance of the club and bypassed the long line.

Edge slipped one of the bouncers a C-note, made it clear to them that he only wanted bottle service and walked inside. He was greeted by blaring rap music and sweaty revelers crammed on the dance floor. Edge moved through the energetic, body-hugging crowd, following behind one of the female employees who led him toward an elevated lounge/VIP area.

The men took seats and peered out at the massive crowd.

Edge nodded his head in approval. "Yeah, I'm lovin' this shit."

"Word! So many fuckin' bitches is lookin' nice out there tonight," Gamma said. "Shit, you know a nigga gotta leave wit' somethin'."

Edge agreed.

The three men sat like kings on thrones, and had the privilege to be seated amongst a few rap celebrities that recognized Edge because of his street credibility, and they showed him respect. The groupies about took notice of the men and activity going on in the VIP area. They smiled and flirted with the ballers, hoping to snatch up the cream of the crop in the place.

Moments later, a few booty shorts and tight-shirt-wearing female employees hurried to where Edge sat, with bottle service on the way—steeply marked-up Grey Goose, Moët, and Cristal—sparkling like a lit firecracker, along with ice buckets and glasses.

Edge handed one of the girls $5,000 in cash, along with a serious tip. She thanked him with a wide smile. The men were pampered with whatever they desired, even if it was pussy, as a string of scantily clad women came to join the men in their section.

Glasses were filled with liquor. And there was laughter and flirting, and groping and drinking.

It was nearing three in the morning, and Edge's section wasn't about to slow down anytime soon. More high-profile rappers joined them, and a lot more women flooded their area. They caught almost everyone's attention. Some of the male revelers looked up at the private party going on and could only wish it was them.

Edge was tipsy. He clutched a half-empty bottle of Goose and threw his arm around a well-known rapper from his hood, a tall and nimble rapper named C-Black.

"This my fuckin' nigga right here. Y'all muthafuckas hear me? Ain't no muthafucka in the game fuckin' wit' C-Black." Edge hugged C-Black tight. "Yo, C, spit somethin' for these muthafuckas sleepin' on you."

C-Black smiled.

The ladies were crowded around them smiling, their short, tight skirt or dress riding up their thighs, or seated on a baller's lap as niggas' hands slipped between their legs for a quick feel, which the majority of the ladies didn't mind.

C-Black stood tall in his sagging jeans, fresh white Nike's, a designer T-shirt and decked off in diamonds and white gold. He was ready to rap for the group. The DJ was blaring a Lil Wayne track, and C-Black nodded.

After C-Black's rhyme, the group loved him and praised his rhyming technique. Edge was the most hyped. He jumped up and down, spilling the bottle of Goose he clutched on everyone near. "See, what I told y'all—My nigga C-Black is fuckin' nice. This rap game ain't ready for him," Edge took a swig from the Goose.

The club was jumping. It was a quarter to four, and it was still packed. The DJ was mixing Jay-Z and Kanye West.

The VIP section was thinning out, as some of the ladies left with a few rap stars, and both of Edge's goons went to dance and mingle with a few ladies on the dance floor.

Edge sat slouched against the plush, leather chaise longue. He still gripped the bottle and nodded to the music playing. He looked up, and the most beautiful woman he'd ever seen immediately captured his attention. He was stunned for a moment.

"Damn!" he mumbled.

She smiled at him.

Edge perked up and gazed at the woman from head to toe. She was looking stunning, wearing a revealing red low-cut, V-neck mini dress with a low back that gathered in the middle and cinched at the sides with ties. Her long, defined legs were stretched out in a pair of black stilettos. Her skin had a slight tan to it, and there was plenty of it showing.

"Yo, ma, what's good? Damn! You in that dress is making red my favorite color," Edge joked. He stood up and staggered a bit. "What's ya name, ma?"

"You OK?" she asked.

"I'm good, love. I'll even be better if you come and chill wit' a nigga."

She smiled.

Edge gestured for her to sit, and she agreed. She sat next to Edge, crossing her legs in his direction.

Edge smiled. "You drink?"

She nodded.

"That's what's up. I like that."

Edge poured her a shot of Goose. She downed that quickly, and he was impressed. He took another swig from the bottle and finished it. And then he focused his attention on the woman with the curvy figure in the tight red dress and legs that stretched to the heavens.

"What's ya name again, ma?" he asked.

She smiled. "I never gave it the first time."

"Oh, so you teasin' a nigga?" Edge placed his hand

against her exposed thigh. She didn't push it off, but let his hand rest there with comfort.

"Elise."

"Elise, huh? Damn, ya fuckin' beautiful. You here alone, ma?"

"I'm wit' my girlfriends."

"Damn! Where the fuck are they? Shit! I got niggas up in here too. You see how we do it, big and shit."

"I see that."

"So, what you about, ma? 'Cuz the night is still young. And I'm tryin' to get it poppin'!"

Elise shrugged.

"You smoke?"

"Shit! Who don't?" she returned.

"A'ight, a'ight, that's what's up. Shit, where the fuck was you hiding at all night?"

Elise chuckled.

Edge poured her another shot, and the two began to converse. As the club began unwinding, Edge's talk with Elise grew stronger. And soon his boys joined him again, and it so happened that the two beautiful ladies they were with were Elise's girlfriends.

"Oh shit! That's what I'm talking about. We like one big happy family now." Edge pulled Elise closer to him with his left arm and groped her breast. "Y'all ready to leave. We got the trees and y'all bitches know we got the fuckin' ends. Shit, the night ain't over."

The ladies agreed to leave with Edge and his group. They strutted out of the club as security and NYPD officers were trying to keep order outside with a mob lingering on the city block. Edge and his entourage hurried by the chaotic crowd and jumped into the truck and drove away. But the girls had their own vehicle, an Audi Q7, and decided to follow behind the men to their destination.

The group made it back to Edge's West Side apartment on Riverside Drive. He had a phenomenal view of the George Washington Bridge and the Hudson River. Dawn was about to break when the groups stepped out of their vehicles after finding parking.

Edge went up to Elise with a smile and placed his arms around the five-star, video vixen-looking woman. His boys followed suit. They hugged the woman of their choice and crossed the street headed toward the towering bricked building with balconies overlooking the Hudson River.

The men were excited being with such exquisite-looking ladies. They laughed and joked around, and thought about sexual fantasies, smoking good weed, and doing what they usually did best—which was switch partners when one was finished fucking with the next.

It had become routine with Edge and his goons. After club hours, they would bring a few women back to the apartment and have their way with them. And if they weren't down with it, then they were kicked out and had to walk home if they didn't have cab money.

The streets were calm, the sky gradually coming to light. Edge and Elise were the first to walk into the quiet lobby, his arm around her. They were only a few steps from the elevator, when he heard a sudden explosion.

Bam! Bam!

He spun around and saw his friend on the floor, shot—two holes in his chest. The woman his friend was holding had the smoking gun in her hand.

Edge suddenly realized that they'd been set up. He quickly pushed Elise away from him, shouting, "Y'all fuckin' bitches!" and moved for cover behind one of the pillars as shots rang out.

The second goon quickly snatched the .380 from his hip and returned fire. An intense shootout ensued, with one of the girls jumping the gun and firing too quickly.

Elise had her girls covered, removing a .45 from her purse. She let it ring out.

The lobby sounded like the O.K. Corral, as dozens of rounds tore into the walls and structure of the building.

Pop! Pop! Pop! Pop!

Boom! Boom! Boom! Boom!

The sudden gunfire had awakened and startled residents. Bullets went whizzing by everywhere. The girls went from vixens to killers in a mere moment.

But Edge was determined not to die by a females hands. He had his gun clutched tightly as he took cover. He took a quick glance and saw his foes by the front door. They were ready to retreat.

His other goon was shot in the side, but he was still functional somewhat, being able to return fire.

"Y'all bitches wanna fuck wit' me, come for it then!" he screamed. "You know who the fuck I am?" When he glanced back to see where they were at, he saw that they had fled.

Edge slowly removed himself from behind the pillar. He peered down at his dead goon, J. Rock, and shook his head. He then looked for C-Black and saw him slumped against the elevator door, bleeding profusely, grasping his wound with one hand and a 9 mm with the other.

"Yo, C-Black, hold on, man, just fuckin' hold on," Edge exclaimed.

"I'ma be good, yo. It's just a flesh wound," C-Black said, trying to sound confident. "Damn, those bitches set us up. Fucked us up, huh!" C-Black tried to laugh.

Edge repeatedly pushed for the elevator to release, and when the doors opened, he pulled his friend inside and held him close as the doors shut. He didn't want to be seen in the lobby with guns and a shot suspect when the police showed up. The elevator stopped on the fourth floor, and Edge rushed C-Black into his apartment.

Downstairs in the lobby, residents slowly emerged from their apartments and were shocked to come across a dead body and to see their entrance shot up with bullet holes and shell casings lying everywhere.

"Oh my God! Somebody call nine-one-one!" a female screamed.

Police were there in less than five minutes after receiving the 9-1-1 call. They sealed off the crime scene and began asking questions.

Two detectives soon noticed a small blood trail leading toward the elevator, so they checked every floor and found that it continued on the fourth floor. A group of uniformed cops and the detectives followed the blood trail to an open doorway down the hall. They entered cautiously with their guns drawn and moved throughout the apartment, shouting, "NYPD!" but after their thorough search, they found the place empty, except for some bloody clothing, wet bloody rags, and guns sprawled out on the kitchen table. Whoever was in the apartment had made a hasty escape.

Chapter 14

Kola stormed into the Yonkers stash house and shouted, "What the fuck happened? How did y'all fuck it up?"

Candace's crew had no words for her. They just stood around feeling dumbfounded.

Kola glared at Candace. She wanted answers right away. They had the chance to kill Edge, but somehow he'd gotten away. They'd fucked up the hit. Kola knew that window of opportunity was now closed. "Explain it to me, Candace," she said.

"Jennifer jumped the gun and shot one of 'em too fuckin' early," Candace said.

Kola cut her eyes at Jennifer. "What the fuck happened, Jennifer?"

Jennifer stared back at Kola. "He was on us, Kola. He recognized one of us. I saw him reach for his gun, so I pulled out and just shot him."

Kola continued to stare at Jennifer and clenched her fist. She was seething. "We fuckin' missed our shot."

"We gonna get that muthafucka, Kola," Candace assured.

"It's gonna be hard now, Candace. Now he's gonna be on alert, heavily armed and gonna be lookin' at everyone suspicious," Kola explained. "Damn! Fuckin' bitches!"

Kola was harsh with her crew, but she didn't care. She was stressed beyond belief by all the shit going on. The storm clouds were forming, and the ground was trembling underneath her feet. It'd been months since she'd heard from Eduardo, and her supply had all but dried up.

She had driven to Jersey City unannounced to see Eduardo one evening, but when she arrived, the place was shut down, and there were a few FBI agents asking questions and unmarked cop cars lingering around. Kola didn't want to be questioned or suspected and linked to the drug cartel, so she raced back to the city thinking that Eduardo's spot had been raided.

Kola paced back and forth in front of her female crew and spat venom at them.

Candace figured there was something else wrong. To Candace, Kola was her boss, but she was also a friend.

Kola shouted, "Y'all bitches get the fuck outta my sight! I'm done with y'all!"

The ladies rushed out of the room and collected in other areas of the house. Candace stayed behind.

Kola walked toward the window and peered outside. She let out a heavy sigh and tried to fight back the tears. She didn't want to cry in front of the girls, but the emotions from feeling betrayed, put down, hoodwinked and not knowing what to do about her connect were starting to get to her bit by bit.

Candace remained quiet.

Kola almost forgot that she was in the room. She didn't turn around, but only continued to look out the window and subtly dry her tears. She was thinking about Eduardo, but sometimes her mind drifted to Cross.

"What's really goin' on, Kola? Just holla at me. I've been by ya side for a while now," Candace said. "I can correct that mistake with Edge. I promise you that."

Kola sighed again. "We might have a problem."

"Like what?"

"I think Eduardo just got busted."

"Feds?"

"I drove by there, and the feds were sniffing all throughout that building. I didn't even get out of the car. I got scared, thinking they might be lookin' for me too."

"So we fucked?"

"I don't know."

"We're running out soon, and with the streets that we have on lock, we can't dry out now, Kola," Candace said.

"You think I don't know that, Candace!"

"I'm just sayin'—"

"Save your opinions to yourself. I'll handle this. I always do."

A cell phone was ringing. It was Kola's. She stared at the number and hesitated to answer it. But she did anyway. "What do you want?" she barked.

"Kola, we need to talk."

"I have nothing to say to you. Why the fuck are you calling me?"

"It's about Apple," Denise exclaimed.

"And? You got some nerves to call me about that bitch! She's dead to me, ma!"

"She's still your sister, Kola. Your twin fuckin' sister! And you need to come see me."

"What? Ma, you must be high. I ain't got no time for you."

"Kola, we need to talk . . . now! And it's about something serious!" Denise shouted. She was stern and wasn't taking no for an answer. "I know you hate me, but I'm trying to be useful to you."

Kola paused on the phone. She thought about it, and another stressful sigh escaped from her mouth. "A'ight, ma, I'll be right over." She hung up. "She's a stupid fuckin' bitch!"

"You cool, Kola?"

"No, I'm not cool!"

"You need me to handle something?"

Kola turned to look at Candace. Candace was a lethal warrior that killed like the best of them, but was packaged as a beautiful, curvy and voluptuous woman that could fool any man with her sultry appearance. She knew guns, drugs, and the streets. She was still wearing the red, low-cut mini dress from the club, a black wig, and had been Elise to Edge.

"I'm sorry, Kola. We fucked it up," Candace apologized. "But I'll fix it."

Kola didn't respond right away. She walked toward Candace, locking eyes with her female enforcer, and unexpectedly pulled Candace closer in her grasp, and the two began tongue-kissing.

Kola wiped her lips and said, "I gotta go see this bitch I call my mother. But you handle things here, Candace. I'll be right back."

"I always got your back, Kola."

"I know you do."

Kola made her exit and jumped into a black Audi. She sped back to Harlem to meet with her mother for a moment.

✳

Ten minutes after Kola's departure, two black SUVs came to a stop on the block near the stash house. A half-dozen men clad in all black stepped out, heavily armed with assault rifles and guns with silencers. They charged for the door like an invasion, moving like a tactical unit. Their mission—in and out, kill everything that moved.

Three men rushed for the front door, while the next three moved toward the back. They had the house surrounded, but security cameras caught their every movement.

The girls inside were slipping. They weren't monitoring the cameras like they should have been. They still were sulking about the failed hit on Edge, getting high, and listening to loud rap music blaring throughout the house from the high-end stereo system. Candace was undressing in one of the bedrooms. She couldn't wait to come out of the dress she wore and slip into a pair of jeans and a T-shirt.

On the porch, the door was rapidly kicked in, and three armed men rushed inside with their weapons raised, and they went searching.

The crashing sound of the front door alerted two of the girls in the kitchen, but only one picked up a gun to check on the sound. When she walked into the living room, her eyes grew wide and she found herself surrounded by goons armed with assault weapons. Before she could fire, she was cut down immediately, shot in the head and chest, the gunfire swallowed by the silencers and the loud music.

Soon, the back door came crashing in, and the girl in the kitchen was shot multiple times. The team then went searching throughout the house. The three men marched upstairs toward the bedrooms while the rest scattered throughout the rooms on the first floor and went down into the basement.

Poot! Poot! Poot! Poot! Poot!

It was the muffled sound of death spreading everywhere.

Candace was still in her bedroom, clad in her panties and bra. She was about ready to throw on some jeans when she heard a sudden sound outside her door.

She quickly looked out the window and saw two black trucks parked outside on the block. She instantly knew there was danger. The loud rap that blared throughout the house and the silencers shrouded what was going on, but she wasn't a fool.

Candace snatched up her gun, cocked it back and aimed it at the bedroom door. She was steady and waiting for the inevitable. "Fuck!" she uttered.

She looked around her bedroom with intensity and felt trapped like a pig in a slaughter. Before her enemies could charge into the room, Candace started firing into the door. The slugs from the Desert Eagle she gripped tore through the door madly and caught the men by surprise. She caught one in the chest and he fell back, but he wasn't dead, thanks to the bulletproof vest he wore.

The bedroom door was kicked in viciously.

Candace continued firing at them, shouting out, "Fuck y'all niggas! Fuck y'all! Fuck you!"

She was quickly overpowered by the intense barrage of bullets exploding from the high-end weapons. She caught two bullets in her shoulder, the force of which pushed her back into the window.

Candace went crashing through it and landed on the roof of the porch, her gun still in her hand. She was stunned for a moment but swiftly came back to her senses and returned fire at the bedroom window.

Boom! Boom! Boom! Boom!
Poot! Poot! Poot! Poot! Poot! Poot!

A third slug tore into Candace's side, and she bowled over from being hit. She then lost her footing and fell off the porch's roof and landed on her side with a hard thud, and the gun spilled from her hand.

Hurt and bleeding, Candace stumbled to get up. She staggered to escape, but two men came running out the front door. Before she could make it to the street, they gunned her down where she stood. She was left sprawled out against the concrete, her blood pooling underneath her.

The murderous goons then fled to their trucks and sped off with their mission accomplished. A total of five were dead.

Kola rushed toward her mother's apartment with an attitude. Her mother was the last person she wanted to see. It'd been a few months since they'd seen each other, and Kola didn't want to hear the foolishness that her mother wanted to tell her.

Kola strutted toward the building lobby. She made her way into the elevator and pushed for the fifth floor. The poverty-stricken projects with their urine-smelling stairways and trash-littered hallways were reminders of the way she used to live, and she refused to go back to that.

As the elevator ascended, Kola began to remember a time when things weren't all that bad with Apple. When they were kids, no one was able to separate them. Apple and Kola did almost everything together and were able to talk to each other about everything. But then as they got older and reached their pre-teens, things gradually began to change between them.

They began hanging around different crowds, and different roots were planted into each sister. Kola suddenly became the aggressor, while Apple was more docile and aloof from Kola's new world. Kola felt that Apple was the core of everything that went wrong between them, and that she was always selfish and envious of her.

Nichols' death had changed everything. Whatever love was left between the twins quickly dissolved after their youngest sister's murder.

Kola loved Nichols, and she still carried that pain in her heart after her murder. She couldn't let it go, and she blamed Apple for Nichols' death.

Kola clenched her fist thinking about her past, scowling as she remembered so many incidents with her mother and Apple within the past five years. Her life was never easy. Her father had killed himself on their birthday, abandoning his family, and her whoring, self-centered mother had neglected her children from day one.

She stepped off the elevator and walked down the narrow hallway to the last apartment. She paused when she reached her mother's door. There was a part of her that wanted to turn around and walk the other way. Kola took a deep breath and knocked rowdily to get her mother's attention.

The apartment door quickly swung open, and Denise at once exclaimed, "Bitch, why the fuck you bangin' down my door?"

"You wanted to see me. Now I'm here," Kola returned dryly.

Denise had a cigarette dangling from her lips and was wearing a pair of booty shorts and a cut-off T-shirt. She was still a stunning woman with her curves and raunchy attitude. She looked at her daughter.

"I see you still lookin' nice," Denise said.

Kola marched past her mother and entered the apartment. She did a once-over of the place. Denise was living well—leather furniture, a plasma flat-screen, polished floors, DVD player with top-notch sound system in the corner, and there was even an open Sony laptop displayed on the glass coffee table.

"I see you doin' nice."

"Not as nice as you doin'," Denise spat back.

Denise took a pull from her cigarette. She then closed her laptop and took a seat on the plush sofa. "You need to find your sister. 'Cuz I've been hearing these damn rumors about her."

Kola could care less about any rumors told about her sister. She stood in the room with a serious expression. "Ma, Apple is dead to me. Why the fuck did I even come to see you in the first place?"

"I've been hearing that she's selling her pussy at some whorehouse in Mexico." Denise shook her head. "My daughter selling pussy in some foreign country. You believe that shit, Kola?"

The news was even shocking for Kola to hear. "And you heard this from where, Ma?"

"I heard it on the streets. Muthafuckas is talking, and I'm the one looking bad, 'cuz she's my daughter, and they laughing behind my back about this shit. And I bet you it's that muthafucka Chico. I know he got somethin' to do wit' it, having Apple selling her ass."

"Apple's a big fuckin' girl, Ma! Whatever the fuck she's doing, I don't give a fuck! And, besides, scarred face or not, I doubt that bitch is in Mexico turning tricks. Apple never went anywhere, so how the fuck would she end up in Mexico, of all places?"

"I'm telling you, it's true, Kola. You need to find your sister."

"I don't need to do shit for that bitch! You can keep caring for her. I'm done wit' this fuckin' family!" Kola pivoted on her heels and was on her way to make her exit.

Denise jumped up from the sofa. Kola swung open the apartment door and walked out.

"You just gonna turn your back on your damn family, Kola? You that cold of a bitch?" Denise shouted from the doorway, watching Kola strut toward the elevator. "How fuckin' dare you! I gave birth to y'all. I'm your mother, Kola. You treat me wit' respect."

Kola spun to shoot a wicked glare at her mother. "You ain't shit to me no more! I'm tired of your shit and Apple's. And if you see that bitch, tell her I said, 'Fuck her too!'" Kola screamed.

The elevator doors slid open, and Kola stepped inside without giving her mother a second look. She could still hear her mother ranting and shouting as she descended to the lobby.

Kola rushed out of the building and jumped into the Audi, still cursing herself for agreeing to meet with her mother when she knew it would only stir up problems and emotions. She started the car, but she didn't pull out of the parking spot yet. She looked over and stared at the place where they'd found Nichols' battered body, and an irritated sigh spewed from her mouth. The memory of how they murdered her little sister still ate away at her. She had lost so much over a short period of time—so many friends dead or gone.

Kola snapped herself out of the painful memory and drove off toward the Major Deegan Expressway. She arrived in Yonkers shortly afterward and discovered a shocking crime scene. The block that her stash house was on was shut down from traffic and sealed with crime scene tape from corner to corner. The area was flooded with paramedics, uniformed officers, detectives, and onlookers.

"What the fuck?"

She had to stop a block away from her place. She rushed out of the car and strutted toward the police activity. She quickly moved through a crowd of people and was stopped from approaching the scene by a uniformed officer.

"You can't pass, ma'am."

Kola was about to shout to him that she lived there, but swallowed her words and looked on. "What happened?" she asked the cop as her voice quivered.

He ignored the question and continued to do his job of preventing anyone but law enforcement from passing through the area.

Kola looked beyond the cop and noticed a body sprawled out on the street, covered with a bloody sheet. She didn't know who it was. Her heart was beating like a dubstep song. She saw them removing bodies from her stash house. Kola's eyes widened with shock and worry.

Are they all dead? She turned to an onlooker and asked, "What happened here?"

"They killed everyone in that house, from my understanding," the lady explained to Kola. "Sad too. It was only women living there. Found drugs and guns too."

Kola felt weak and sick. Her entire crew, what was left of her drug supply, and her arsenal of weapons had been wiped out in the span of an hour.

Kola retreated from the area and walked back to her car in a fog. She felt so lost. She drove away and rushed back to Harlem.

The storm clouds were now producing rain and thunder, and the ground was shaking underneath her. Kola felt the planet was about to swallow her whole, the walls around her closing in. She didn't know where to go or who to turn to or trust.

As Kola drove aimlessly, she speculated that there was only one man behind the deaths—Edge. It had to be payback. They'd tried to take his life, but now he beat Kola to the punch and killed every single girl in her crew.

It was devastating for Kola, but she was determined to strike back. Edge had to go, and if Cross was involved with the killings, then he would be on her hit list too.

Chapter 15

Apple looked stunning in a sexy, satin dress with a low, open back and gold chain detail. The six-inch heels she wore made her long, lovely legs stretch to infinity. She was beautiful; shining like the sun on a summer day. She strutted toward her king, who was waiting patiently, but she stopped to look at her reflection in the mirror. Apple smiled—she was perfect. She felt good. She looked over her shoulder, and there he was, waiting for her with his golden smile, and looking sharp in his charcoal gray Tom Ford suit.

He reached out his hand to her, indicating that he wanted her to approach. He yearned for Apple's touch, her affection.

Apple smiled. She was happy. She was free.

Apple stared at her lovely image once again and didn't want to change a thing about herself. She pivoted on her stylish heels and approached her king. She was ready for him. She knew he would always come for her and rescue her from her prison and make things right. Apple never doubted him.

She approached her savior with the warmest smile and doting eyes. He extended his arms, and she fell into his grasp and wanted to melt in his hold. When her king wrapped his arms around her, she felt security and love. It blanketed her like the sky above the city.

"I love you," she proclaimed.

"I love you," he returned with his masculine tone. Every word he spoke was assuring.

She started to dance with him, and it felt like they were on clouds. Apple didn't want to look down from his eyes. She wanted to stay connected with him. She wanted that bond to become concrete. She fixed her eyes on her king and strengthened her grip around him.

"I got you, baby," he said.

She nodded.

They continued to dance. Then slowly her dress started to peel away from her skin. And then she found herself naked in his hold. Apple didn't mind; she wanted him to stare at her curvy waistline, succulent tits, and round, juicy ass. She knew her body would captivate his attention.

Her king squeezed her harder, indicating his approval, and they kissed passionately. His hands explored every curve of her body.

She moaned, savoring his touch, enjoying the warmth of his breath against hers and the way his strapping chest pressed against her breasts. Everything about it was pleasurable.

"Your face is so beautiful and angelic," her king spoke.

Apple blushed. She soon found herself floating on

her back, and he was naked. His manhood was hard and pulsating, and it was waiting to be pleased. She wanted to feel him inside of her, her pleasure box throbbing out of control.

He pushed himself inside Apple. She drifted into the rapturous thrusting, as his big dick filled her completely.

She gripped his shoulders, straddled her legs around her king, and panted like a winded runner. It was so good; she almost lost consciousness.

Apple closed her eyes and enjoyed the bliss of their naked flesh wrapped tightly together. Her king was a gorgeous specimen of a man, and he was devouring her sex as if he needed it to live.

Apple came, the pleasurable moment escaping her lips as her body rattled underneath his sweaty flesh.

Abruptly, her king stopped with his heated passion, and a look of shock registered on his face. He pulled himself away from Apple like she had the plague.

"What's wrong?" Apple questioned.

Her king looked speechless. "What are you?"

"I'm your queen?" she replied meekly.

"You're a fuckin' demon! That's what you are!"

Apple didn't understand what was happening. She went to touch her face and suddenly felt it melting away. She jumped up and ran toward the mirror. The reflection she once saw, the one that made her smile and feel perfect, was gone. She saw an image that horrified her. Her skin was melting and becoming loose and slacking, and it burned.

Apple screamed. She then looked back at her king and yelled, "Chico, don't leave me! Help me! Please! Help me!"

Chico began to fade away into the darkness, leaving Apple to bear the pain alone. She screamed out louder and then heard a big bang. The banging grew louder and louder.

Apple stirred from her sleep, oblivious to the chaotic noise outside her door. It sounded like a war in the hallway of the whorehouse. There was screaming and gunfire. The whores were yelling, and there was running and fighting.

She remained slumped against the mattress. The heroin that flowed through her bloodstream had her body listless, and the haze still lingered in her mind. She was in her own world.

Bak! Bak! Bak! Bak! Bak!

The sound of gunfire grew closer to Apple's room. The walls started to shake. There was loud rustling everywhere, but Apple still laid there, lifeless.

"Yo, check that fuckin' room!" a man yelled. "Check that fuckin' room!"

Apple's door was abruptly kicked open, and two masked men came rushing inside wielding heavy assault rifles. They looked around the room in a hurry and saw Apple lying on the mattress.

One of the men yelled, "In here!"

Another masked man walked into the room, and his

beady eyes zeroed in on Apple from behind the mask.

"Is this her?" one of the masked men asked.

He nodded.

Apple felt a pair of strong hands reach down to lift her up from the mattress. He cradled her in his arms and said, "Don't worry, I got you now. It's gonna be you and me again."

Apple heard the words, but she didn't know what was going on. It felt like she was floating on air. She couldn't see anyone's face clearly, even if they didn't wear masks. She was completely fucked up. Her mind was drifting and incoherent because of the drugs, and her body was weak, exhausted from everything that had happened to her.

Apple was carried out of the room. The hallway was scattered with bodies, mostly dead thugs on Shaun's end. The whores either ran for safety or cowered in their rooms or in the corner. No one wanted to fight, and no one wanted to die. The three masked men came heavily armed and were well prepared for a battle. But none of the bodies that lay in the pool of blood in the narrowed hallway were Shaun. He had been absent from the massacre of his goons.

Apple soon felt fresh air against her skin. She knew she was outdoors. It was dark out. She felt a gentle breeze. The man carrying her had strength and didn't grow tired with her in his arms. She felt herself being laid gently into a luxurious backseat. It had been too long since she'd been in a vehicle. She felt the rich interior against her skin and smelled the vivid aroma of expensive leather, and it suddenly became all too familiar to her.

"Chico," she uttered out. "Chico, I knew you would come for me. I knew you would, Chico. Chico. Chico . . ."

"I'm here now, Apple. I'm here now, and ya good," the man said.

The doors were shut, and the Escalade sped away from the scene.

Apple was spread out in the backseat still in her drug haze. She felt the truck speeding and repeated one last time, "I knew you would come for me, Chico. I knew you would." She then closed her eyes and dozed off.

Chapter 16

Kola stood like a ghost in Mt. Zion Cemetery, right off the Brooklyn-Queens Expressway, clad in a simple black dress and a pair of Fendi sunglasses to hide her teary eyes. Standing tall in her four-inch heels, she stared at Candace's casket. She couldn't believe her friend was dead.

She really couldn't believe that Edge had the audacity to show up to Candace's funeral. Kola plotted her revenge, glaring at that asshole from behind her large shades. The cemetery had too many witnesses for her to do anything to him—over two-dozen mourners had shown up to the burial—so she held her rage and continued to stare at the roses on the stainless steel casket.

Kola stood opposite Cross and Edge, who were both clad in dark suits and shades. Kola didn't know if Cross was involved with the massacre, but she didn't trust him.

She didn't trust anyone. She felt alone. She felt angry. Candace was dead, her crew was dead, and somebody had to pay.

Everything pointed back to Edge, and probably Cross. Kola knew there was no way one man could get the drop on Candace. She was too good. It had to be a team of men that invaded her stash house.

When Cross tried to console Kola, she refused to accept his help or tell him her worries. She'd heard rumors that he was living in Brooklyn with Cynthia. She started to hate everything about Cross. Her love for him had changed into contempt and anger, and she felt caught in a web of betrayal and death.

Kola looked around the cemetery. Pastor Jones was saying a few words about the deceased, but she wasn't listening. Her mind was too focused on revenge. She continued to glare at Edge from behind her shades. He had to go. She'd already devised a plan to kill him once and for all, and maybe find out if Cross was involved with Candace's death. Pastor Jones was a stout, black man. Kola remembered him from his church in Harlem. When she was eight, the mother of one of the twins' friends from her building took her and Apple to a few church services. They went for a month and had gotten to know him to some extent. He would always say to them, "Such beautiful twin girls. Keep the Lord close to your heart, and everything will always be OK."

Then years went by, and Pastor Jones, his words, the twins' mutual friend Tina, and everything else became a memory. The streets became more important.

Pastor Jones stood over the casket in his gray suit. He said solemnly, "Ashes to ashes, dust to dust . . . dust thou art, and unto dust thou shall return. I will bring thee to ashes upon the earth in the sight of all them that behold thee." He then sprinkled a little bit of dirt onto Candace's casket, concluding the service.

The crowd began to leave the burial site, but Kola lingered around near the casket. She let out a heavy sigh. She knew death was part of playing the game, but it was still painful to endure when it was a close friend.

Pastor Jones walked up to her. "It's been a long time, Kola."

Kola was surprised he still remembered her. "Thank you, Pastor, for everything you've done."

Pastor Jones stared at her, making her a bit uncomfortable. He told her, "Don't let it be you in that casket without you finding your way soon."

"I have found my way, Pastor, and once I make things right, you'll have plenty of business coming your way."

"Revenge is not the way to salvation."

"You need to preach that somewhere else, Pastor Jones, but not here, not now. No disrespect to you, but stay the hell out of my business!" She walked away, leaving him dumbfounded by her comment.

Kola noticed that Edge had been eyeing her hard throughout the burial service. *He got balls*, she thought. As she walked toward the parking lot, she heard someone behind her. She turned and saw Edge approaching. She glanced around to look for Cross and saw that he was already gone. *It figures,* she thought.

"Hold on a minute, Kola!" Edge called out.

Kola continued walking.

"We need to talk."

Kola stopped in her tracks and turned to face him, her murderous look hidden behind Fendi. "What the fuck do you want, Edge?"

"Listen, I know we had our differences over the past months, and my condolences to your girl. She was cool peoples. But I'm here to help. You family, Kola, and whoever did this, they gonna fuckin' pay."

Kola thought he had some nerve, but she kept her feelings to herself and went along with the program. "Thanks. And you're right, they will pay. Painfully too."

"You look really nice, though."

"Whatever!" She turned away from him and headed back to her car.

Edge quickly took a hold of her arm. "Wait a minute, Kola. We need to talk."

"About what? We have nothing in common, and we never will."

"You know how I always felt about you, Kola. He ain't never deserved you."

"And you think you could do better, Edge?"

"I'm not him."

"You definitely aren't."

Edge frowned.

Kola softened up her attitude. "What do you need to talk about?"

"Not here, Kola. Someplace more comfortable."

"Like where?"

"Let me take you out to dinner, and I'll explain everything that's going on. I promise, you gonna want to know what I have to say to you," he said calmly.

She thought about it for a moment. "OK, I'll go out wit' you, and we'll talk."

"Cool."

Edge gave Kola his new number. She saved it into her phone and watched him walk away. He moved like everything was cool between them, but they were far from cool.

Kola knew that pussy always made niggas weak and stupid, and Edge had been craving for a piece of her pie for the longest. She was ready to use her sexuality to get with him and carry out what needed to be done. Desperate for payback, and with her crew murdered, she had to take matters in her own hands.

Kola parked her black Audi a few blocks from the projects and took a taxi to her mom's crib. She had no choice but to return home and try to rekindle some semblance of a relationship with her mother. She swallowed her pride and decided to make things work, since she had few options left. She had a little over a hundred and fifty thousand dollars in cash and a few ki's stashed somewhere safe; her bailout money that no one knew about.

Eduardo was still MIA. The uncertainty of his whereabouts put a hollow feeling in her stomach. Each day she wished he would call and tell her what the fuck was going on. Instead, all she had was the ominous threat. Kola didn't know if he had been detained by the feds or if he had escaped to Colombia. She was worried that she was on the feds' radar, so she tried to keep a low profile, or planned to, after dealing with Edge.

She strutted into her mother's apartment and heard New Edition blaring from the stereo. It was hard to return home after the harsh words she'd said to her mother. Denise constantly gave her a look like, *I knew you would be back home sooner or later*. So Kola put five thousand dollars in her mother's hand to ease the tension.

For Kola, staying in the projects was a risk. She had enemies and haters, so she didn't go out much, mostly at night, if ever, and she always carried a gun. She hoped that she was strategically hiding in plain sight, moving like pieces on a chessboard. Everyone knew how she felt about Denise, so it would be the last place anyone would think to look.

She passed her mother's bedroom and heard loud moaning. Her mother was fucking some young nigga. She paid it no mind and went into the bedroom and locked the door.

Once she was situated, the tears started to flow. The pain and hurt of losing Candace became fresh for her once again. She couldn't show weakness, so she masked her grief behind the four walls in her mother's apartment.

The young girl in her began to show. She had grown up way too quickly, and didn't know what it was like to have a childhood. At thirteen, she was fucking. At fourteen, she was hustling. By the time she was sixteen, she was seasoned in the street life, and became a "queenpin" before her twenty-first birthday.

Kola didn't cry for too long. She quickly dried her tears and walked over to the window. She peered down at her Audi. Everything appeared normal. She needed to make moves. Kola knew she wasn't going to last too long in the projects, and in her mother's apartment. The two clashed like plaid and polka dots. She didn't like that her mother had wild parties and niggas coming and going from her bedroom. Strangers were dangerous in Kola's line of work.

Kola picked up her cell phone. She thought about Edge and Cross, but she focused on Edge more. She needed to flirt with him and get as much information from him as possible. She dialed his number, and it rang a few times before he picked up.

"Who this calling?"

"It's Kola."

"Oh, what up, love? You good?"

"I just needed to talk."

"Shit, you know that's what I'm here for. I know ya goin' through it after losing ya girls. That shit is hard. You know I understand."

Edge tried to be sincere, but Kola knew it was all bullshit. "What you doing?" she asked.

"I'm chillin' right now. Why you ask?"

"I just asked."

"Why you ain't call Cross, though?"

"'Cuz he hurt me, and I don't trust him right now."

"I know, that's my dude and all, but he can be a foul nigga sometimes. I don't trust that nigga most times myself. He's starting to act funny on a nigga too."

"What you mean?"

"He doin' you dirty, Kola. I'm just keepin' it real. Nigga got all that work and cash now, and he keepin' shit on lockdown from a nigga, probably in Brooklyn wit' shorty."

"What the hell you talkin' about, Edge? What work and cash? And what bitch?"

"It ain't my place to tell you, but he be spending most his time in Brooklyn now. He shacked up wit' his baby mama. They, like, tryin' to get married."

"Are you serious?"

Edge sucked his teeth. "I was there when he bought that bitch the ring."

The news was a serious blow to Kola. She was distraught.

"I just thought you should know about it, since the nigga is into keepin' secrets from muthafuckas. But I can keep secrets too."

"I can't fuckin' believe him!"

"He ain't worth tears, ma. It's how that nigga can be sometimes. I mean, that's my dude and all, but he doin' you *and* me dirty."

"Muthafucka!"

"I'm sayin', Kola, I know you and me had our serious differences back then, but let's just let bygones be bygones and start over. You feel me?"

Kola felt black and colder inside. Edge had only added more fuel to her burning hatred. She was done crying over Cross, and she was done feeling betrayed. It was time to implement her next move.

"I'm saying, Kola, let me take you out. I got you, ma."

Kola was silent for a moment. She was thinking. "OK. But when?"

"Fuck that! Tonight, ma. Let me get things off ya mind, and we can talk."

"A'ight, I'm down. But keep this between you and me, Edge. If Cross finds—"

"Kola, he ain't gonna find out shit, and he don't need to know what goes on between you and me. It ain't his business anymore. This is our fuckin' business. You just make sure you show up. Let me worry about Cross, and believe me when I say, he ain't gonna be a problem to us anymore."

After the two established a time and place, Kola hung up the phone and shouted, "Shady muthafuckas!"

She was going to be ready tonight.

It was a quarter to ten at night when Kola stepped out of her mother's apartment looking stunning in an ultra-short, halter-style mini dress with scrunched sides and low neckline—no panties. She wore six-inch heels that highlighted her well-defined legs, and carried a small Gucci purse. A loaded .22 Magnum was concealed inside.

Kola turned heads walking to her parked Audi. The

neighborhood knew her name, and about her scandalous reputation, and the locals stayed away from her, fearing that she was trouble. Kola was the talk of the hood, but she didn't care at all. Everything was about business and a come-up for her. If you got in her way, then she was ready to cut you down.

Kola got into her car and was ready to meet Edge at Junior's Restaurant in downtown Brooklyn. Anywhere in Harlem or the city would've been too dangerous for them to link up, and she didn't want anyone in her business.

She arrived at Junior's shortly after ten-thirty and parked down the block. She strutted toward the restaurant and looked around for Edge. She soon spotted his truck parked on the corner and walked over cautiously. She kept her gun close, not knowing what to expect.

Edge stepped out of his truck with a broad smile. He muttered, "Damn!" his eyes absorbing Kola's sexy attire, from her tight dress to her sexy walk.

"I'm here," Kola said. "So let's talk."

"You lookin' good, Kola," Edge said, lust showing across his face. "Damn! Really fuckin' good. I love that dress you got on."

Kola knew Edge was a horny hound dog who thought more with his dick than his head. The way he looked at her gave her the creeps, but she knew how to use his eagerness to her advantage.

Edge was wearing a wife-beater, dark jeans, Timberlands, and a thick, long chain. He was constantly showing off, flexing his muscles, but Kola was far from impressed.

"Let's talk in private, Kola," he suggested.

"How private?"

"Damn! Very private."

"You got a cigarette?"

"I got one left in my truck."

"Then let's go for a ride."

Edge smiled, and they began to walk in the direction of his dark green Yukon.

He got behind the wheel and passed Kola his last Newport.

She quickly lit it, took a few drags, then looked at him.

"Just drive. I need to clear my head."

"A'ight. But you cool wit' leaving ya shit parked here in Brooklyn?"

"I'm good."

Edge started the ignition and slowly pulled out of his spot. He was excited. Cross had fucked up his chance with her, so he was going to take advantage of the situation.

"Where you wanna go to?"

"Back to Harlem?" Kola said.

"For what?"

"I know a place where we can go."

"So why you have me drive out here to meet you at Junior's? I coulda met you somewhere out there."

"Think, Edge—My car is known, me and Cross are known. They see me get out of my car and get into your truck, and you think muthafuckas ain't gonna speculate some shit going on? Us three, we're too fuckin' known in Harlem not to have eyes watching."

"True!"

"A'ight, just drive," she spat, "before I change my fuckin' mind."

Kola rolled her eyes. She figured Edge wasn't as stupid as he looked, but she was smarter and fiercer. She continued to lead him on, lifting her dress slightly and exposing her smooth, thick legs.

He smiled. "I like that."

"I bet you do."

Edge clutched the steering wheel with his left hand, leaned closer to Kola, and moved his right hand between her slightly opened legs. His touch alone made Kola cringe, but she let him massage her thigh as he crossed over the Brooklyn Bridge.

"Um, you feel so soft."

"I do, huh? You like that?"

"Hells yeah."

"I love the way you touch me," Kola lied. She then took his hand and slowly slid it between the depths of her legs.

"You ain't got no fuckin' panties on," he uttered excitedly.

"I knew you would like that."

Edge began to finger Kola's love box gently, pushing two of his fingers into her shaved pussy and playing with her clit.

Kola began to moan from his touch, clamping her

thighs around his hand when she felt his touch digging into her.

"Ooh, I can't wait to fuck you, Kola."

"I bet you can't."

Edge continued to finger-fuck Kola as he drove his truck into the city. He grew hard as he stroked her pussy, and was ready to pull over for a quickie with his friend's chick.

He navigated through the nightly traffic and raced north on the FDR, while still fingering Kola's wet pussy. He was about to go crazy if he didn't have it soon. They made some small talk, but Edge's main concern was sex. He even went down on Kola briefly while stopped at a red light, pulling up her dress and snaking his tongue inside of her, causing her to squirm and moan.

The two soon made it into Harlem, where the street traffic and nightly activity wasn't too thick in certain areas of the hood. Edge was determined to find a desolate block so he could fuck Kola in the backseat of his truck.

"You got condoms?" she asked.

"Nah."

"We gonna need some . . . and some cigarettes too."

"A'ight, I'll stop by the store."

Edge soon found a twenty-four-hour bodega on Seventh Avenue and double-parked on the street.

"I'll go get 'em," Kola volunteered, pulling down her dress, collecting herself from their brief sexual encounter.

"A'ight, get me somethin' to drink too 'cuz I'm gonna be thirsty after I finish waxing that ass." Edge smiled.

Kola returned a counterfeit smile and walked into the bodega. Once inside, she took out her phone and started to dial a cab service.

"Uptown Cab," a lady answered.

"Yes, I need a cab," Kola said.

"Where are you?"

"I'm on the corner of West One Hundred and Forty-Seventh Street and Malcolm X Boulevard. How long?"

"Fifteen minutes," the dispatcher said.

"OK. I'll be waiting."

Kola hung up and got everything she needed out of the bodega, except for a pack of Newports. She strutted toward the truck and jumped inside.

"We cool?" Edge asked.

"Yeah, we cool."

Edge then parked around the corner on 146th Street, a narrow, quiet block with hardly any parking. He was fortunate to find a spot near an abandoned building in the shadow of the block. They had enough privacy to fuck uninterrupted. He turned off the ignition and grabbed for Kola.

Kola flinched. "Damn, nigga! Be fuckin' easy."

"I want this, Kola. You don't understand how long I wanted to fuck you. Fuck Cross! He ain't know what to do wit' you."

"A'ight, just take my pussy slow and shit."

Edge began unbuttoning his jeans, ready to pull out his throbbing dick. The hunger in his eyes was like a famished lion watching antelopes graze in an open field.

"Oh shit!"

"What the fuck!"

"I fuckin' forgot the cigarettes in the store."

"What?"

"I forgot the pack of Newports."

"Get them shits later!"

"They're about to close, and I like to smoke right after I fuck."

"That's a fuckin' cliché!"

Kola was surprised that he knew what the word meant. Edge looked frustrated. He had his dick exposed, his jeans around his ankles, and the condom already torn open. Kola was surprised by his size and thickness. *What a waste!* she thought.

"It'll be only a minute," she said, opening the passenger door to step out.

"Hurry up, 'cuz I'm about to explode."

Kola feigned a smile.

She began to walk toward the bodega on Seventh Avenue and then stopped. She reached into her purse, gripped the .22 Magnum, and removed it. She then spun around and started walking back to the Yukon.

On the block where they were parked, only a closed school and a few abandoned buildings about to be demolished lined the street, so Kola didn't have to worry about any eyewitnesses peeking from windows above.

She strutted toward the truck and crept to the driver's side. She had the gun ready and hidden from Edge's view. She knocked on the driver's window delicately and startled

Edge, who was still exposed and waiting.

Edge quickly turned and saw Kola. He rolled down his window. "What the fuck, Kola! You scared the shit outta me! You got the fuckin' cigarettes? 'Cuz I'm ready to fuck, and you—"

Kola swiftly raised the gun and aimed it at Edge.

His eyes widened with shock. "What the fuck is this?"

Bam! Bam! Bam! Bam!

Kola put four hot slugs into his frame—three in the chest and one in the head— leaving him slumped over the steering wheel, his brain leaking on the dashboard and the front seats a bloody mess. She then shoved the gun back into her purse and strutted toward Malcolm X Boulevard and 147th Street, confident that no one was around, the cover of night protecting her identity.

When she arrived on the corner of 147th and Malcolm X, a black Lincoln town car pulled up and came to a stop where she stood. She jumped into the backseat and said to the driver, "Take me to downtown Brooklyn."

The driver nodded.

She passed him a fifty-dollar bill. "If you get me there fast enough, you can keep the change."

The driver smiled and drove off.

Kola arrived in downtown Brooklyn right before midnight. She got out on Flatbush Avenue and thanked the driver. When he drove away, she looked around for her car. Flatbush Avenue was almost empty. There were only a few cars left parked on the block, and every store was closed.

When Kola got to her car, she noticed she had been ticketed for parking next to a fire hydrant. She smiled. She removed the ticket from the windshield and opened it up. The ticket was written at eleven p.m., giving her the perfect alibi—Junior's Restaurant.

Chapter 17

Chico tried to find comfort in Blythe's arms in their master bedroom, but he constantly stirred, and he couldn't sleep. His mind was constantly on Apple. Ever since Two-Face had slipped up and mentioned that Apple might be whoring in Mexico, he'd been restless. He wanted to know where she was. He believed that Dario would find her. He was ready to fly into Mexico and look for her himself, but it was too big of a country, and he didn't know where to start. It had been a week since he'd hired Dario, a week too long in waiting. If he didn't hear from Dario soon, then he was prepared to risk the trip.

Chico looked at the time illuminated on the clock on the nightstand, and it was after midnight. He stared up at the ceiling, his mind spinning with thoughts. Blythe lay naked next to him in the dark, silent room. She had been asleep for hours.

Chico had been sleepless for days. He had a lot going on. Business was still booming, but the heat on him and his crew was escalating. He felt safe in his new home in Great Neck, but some days and nights it was just too still and boring for him. He missed the bustling sounds of Harlem and the city, and being closer to his business. But with the war with Cross, his presence in Harlem was always a risk.

Chico decided that sleeping wasn't an option tonight. He rose up out of bed and sat at the edge of it in his boxers. He peered at the four walls around him. He lit a cigarette and began smoking. He glanced back at Blythe and admired the way she slept. Wrapped snugly in the silk sheets, she looked beautiful and peaceful. He continued to smoke and thought about random things in the shadows of his bedroom.

Chico then got up and walked toward the window. He pulled back the blinds and stared out at the quiet suburban street. There wasn't a soul in sight. There were no unmarked police cars looking to harass young black males, and the corners weren't inundated with gamblers, drunks, and hood rats. The still, peaceful night was almost frightening for him.

Blythe called out to him, as she noticed him by the window, "Baby, you OK?"

"I'm good. Go back to sleep."

"What's wrong?"

"Can't sleep," he said.

"You aren't able to sleep for almost a week now. You sure everything's OK?"

"Yeah."

Blythe removed her naked body from the bed and walked toward Chico. She slipped her arms around him caringly and kissed him softly on the back of his neck. Her bare tits pressed into his back and the strong texture of his skin against hers made her pussy tingle. "You can talk to me, baby," she said. "I'm always here for you."

"I'm thinking about business, that's all." Chico couldn't tell her that he had been thinking about his ex-girlfriend for the past week, and that he still had feelings for her, despite everything that had gone down with them.

"Well, you need to get your mind off the streets just for tonight. You need to rest, baby. You got everything on lock, and it's your world. You need to relax. Here, let me help you."

Blythe's voice was soothing in Chico's ear. She massaged his chest, nibbling at his ear. She reached around his waist again and began to stroke his dick with a soft touch. She felt him growing harder as she had him clutched in her fist.

"You like that, baby?"

"Damn!" he moaned.

Blythe started grinding against his body, and her fingers stroked him to the height of his lust, each caress the most sensuous Chico could imagine, and then some. Blythe was really good with her hands and exploring her sexuality. It was one of the things Chico loved about her. She was able to take her man places that most women didn't know existed. Chico's mind instantly went from stressing about Apple and his business in the streets to pussy.

He turned to face Blythe, and the two soon found themselves positioned near the bed. She pushed Chico onto his back and situated herself between his thighs, underneath the sheets.

"I'm gonna give you something nice to get your mind off the stress." Blythe took a tight hold of his hard-on and moved her lips to the mushroom tip and teased it with her tongue. She then took his dick into her mouth and slid her lips down to the base, deep-throating him.

Chico moaned and squirmed a little. "Shit!" he uttered.

Blythe released his dick from her mouth but not her hand and looked up at her lover. She smiled. And then she continued.

Her suction and salivating mouth continued to bring Chico closer to an orgasm. She cupped his balls, her nails tickling the back of his scrotum, her other hand gripping the base of his cock like a vise. She sucked him harder.

Blythe moaned while she gave Chico head. The vibrations flowed along his shaft, went past her fingers, and traveled into his balls. "Oh shit!" he cried out. He moaned and moved with her.

"I'm gonna suck you dry, baby." Blythe began to suck on his dick harder as her hand gripped his dick, stroking it nicely, using her saliva as a lubricant. It went easily down her throat.

Chico felt her suction pulling his come out of him. The sexual endeavor successfully took his mind from the worries he had earlier.

Blythe continued to please him for a long while, until he could no longer take feeling vulnerable in her grasp. He placed Blythe on her back and slid his tremendous erection into her awaiting cave.

Chico grunted as the two entwined effortlessly from position to position. Soon, he released the pent-up sexual energy, and the two lay spent against each other.

"That should put you to sleep," Blythe joked.

Chico didn't respond, lost in a haze of bliss, but he was able to fall asleep not long after.

✳

Chico's cell phone ringing on the nightstand interrupted him from the hours of sleep that he was finally able to have. It was a little after nine in the morning. Blythe was asleep next to him. He sluggishly moved to answer his phone. It was Jason calling.

Jason had been Chico's ally on the streets for years. The two grew strong together during street wars, police investigations, and violence. Jason maintained a low profile throughout the years and didn't need to conduct himself in street violence and murder. He was well known through networking with the city's influential citizens, and the profitable business he had set up.

Jason was book-smart as well as street-smart, and knew how to make legitimate investments to wash his dirty money.

Jason had set up shell companies and trusts, along with real estate and "black salaries," or cash salaries to unregistered employees. Jason was known as a financial genius in his hood, and was sitting on millions in capital, stocks, and business, and he was only twenty-nine. He had so much legitimate income coming in through his smart business dealings; it was almost impossible to detect any illegal income or straw purchases in his name.

Chico answered his phone.

Jason said, "We need to talk."

"About what, Jason?"

"Not on the phone. Meet me in two hours. Bakersfield." Jason then hung up.

Chico looked over at Blythe and had a flashback about the previous night. His woman was a freak. But he wasn't complaining. He got out of bed and headed into the bathroom.

It only took him a few minutes to shower and get himself ready. When he walked back into the bedroom, Blythe was awakening from her sleep.

She looked over at him, surprised he was up early and already dressed. "Where you going, baby?"

"I gotta go out."

"I was gonna make you breakfast."

"I ain't got time. I gotta meet someone. It's important."

Blythe sighed. "Whatever." She rolled over and tried to go back to sleep.

Chico removed his gun from the drawer, stuffed it into his waistband, and then rushed for the door. He jumped into his white Porsche, one of his three cars parked in the circular driveway. He rushed onto the Cross

Island Parkway, where traffic was light, and then crossed over the Throgs Neck Bridge, entering the Bronx.

He arrived at Bakersfield, Inwood an hour after his departure from home. He drove by the security gate without difficulty, parked in one of the many empty spots in the lot, and waited for Jason's arrival.

Ten minutes later, a pearl colored Bentley GT drove into the parking lot and parked two spaces from Chico's Porsche. Jason stepped out of his swanky GT. Tall and handsome, and looking suave in a dark-blue Karl Lagerfeld tailored suit and Italian wingtips, his style screamed wealth and class. His pale-bronze skin exaggerated the depth of his ink-black eyes. And a pencil-thin mustache and goatee framed the corners of his pearly-white smile.

Jason walked toward Chico with confidence and assurance. He was alone. He had no need for security at the moment. His reputation was all he needed. He handed Chico an envelope. "Merry Christmas."

"For what?" Chico asked.

"For that account you invested in. You remember the shell company I told you to invest into a year ago? I told you to be smart about it. Well, there's fifty *K* in there for you. Make it matter."

Chico nodded.

"But, on other important matters, you heard what happened to Edge?" Jason asked.

"Nah."

"He's a memory. My peoples say they found him last night, shot four times, three in the chest, one in the head."

"It wasn't me," Chico said.

"It don't matter. I told you before, separate yourself from the violence. I got a call from my source. They say your name is coming up in the investigation."

"Man, fuck their investigation!" Chico barked. "But one less to fuckin' worry about, right?"

"You need to wise up, Chico. You're doing well for yourself, but the people in your corner, they're bad news, especially that new kid you have, Two-Face. I got a bad feeling about him. You need to let go of him. I hear disturbing things about him on the streets."

"Like what?"

"With a name like Two-Face, it's self-explanatory. But he's too much heat for you, and then I hear things. He might be plotting against you. How well do you know this young fool?"

"About a few months."

"He was useful to you for a moment, but do you still need his hand around your arm?"

"He got me my connect wit' the Mexicans. His uncle is part of a major cartel. I kill that nigga off, and I might be biting off more than I can chew."

"You need to think, Chico. Look around you and take advantage of the situation that is happening. Edge was a major figure in Harlem, so there will be people looking to retaliate for his death."

Chico smiled at the thought.

"You keep that little Mexican muthafucka around longer than needed, and he'll bring upon more trouble to you than he's worth. You understand this?"

"Yeah, I get you."

"Then start turning the wheels and make it happen. I don't want to see you get caught up, Chico. You and me came a long way from the block. Cross and Kola are becoming shaky, and when they crumble apart, we'll be there to collect the pieces. You work smarter, not harder."

"I feel you."

"I'll keep in touch."

Jason walked to his GT and got inside. The car purred with power when he revved the engine and sped out of the lot, leaving Chico standing in the parking lot pondering his next move.

Chapter 18

Cross held his son in his arms and smiled. His boy was his heart, his only light to the darkness surrounding him. It was the one thing that he felt he'd done right. Jeremy had just turned one, and Cross had showered his only child with gifts from Toys "R" Us—teddy bears, clothes, toys, and so many other things. He had spent a small fortune.

As he held and played with Jeremy, he looked over at Cynthia, who stood by the window of her apartment with vacant eyes in a pair of cut-up jeans, a T-shirt, and tube socks. Cross hated what Kola and Candace had done to his baby's mama. The incident created a rift between them, but he was determined to fix it and be with his family. Brooklyn had become his temporary safe haven from the volatile activity going on in Harlem and Washington Heights.

In Brooklyn, Cross wasn't known too well, but uptown, he felt like he had enemies even within his own circle. Ever since they'd hit Eduardo, killing a few of his men and stealing over a million dollars in drugs and cash, Cross had sense to lay low and play his cards right. Eduardo was a major figure, so a hit on him was always going to have repercussions for everyone involved. When Cross heard about the massacre of Kola's crew in Yonkers, he immediately knew the order had come from Eduardo. It was payback.

The Colombians were ruthless, but Cross was ready to fight back. If Eduardo was going to be looking for him, then he would also be hunting for Eduardo. Cross put out the word for his goons—fifty gunmen on the street at top dollar—to be on the hunt for Eduardo night and day. Cross was still upset Eduardo had fucked Kola. He knew that Eduardo could only get at Kola because he, himself, was unfaithful. That was the only reason Kola was still breathing. Kola could get a pass; Eduardo could not.

When Cross saw Kola at the funeral, he'd tried to console her, but she'd made it clear that she wanted nothing to do with him. That upset him. He went on his way, but not before he noticed Edge talking to her. Cross suspected something was going on. His instincts were telling him that Edge was plotting something, so he knew he had to keep a close eye on his once best friend and right-hand man.

But when Cross had gotten the phone call about Edge, he was still devastated. An associate of theirs had called him in the early morning and said, "Yo, they got your boy a few hours ago. Shot four times."

"What?"

"Edge is dead, Cross," the voice said.

As soon as Cross heard about Edge, he thought about Eduardo. He thought that Edge was caught slipping and got hit up easily.

Cross stood still with the cell phone clutched in his hand. Edge was gone. They had known each other for so many years, the two were inseparable and invincible around each other. They'd been through thick and thin— blood and tears—and dominated the streets and drug game. They'd had rifts and arguments, but they were like brothers. They always had each other's back, and each one trusted the other with his life. Now one of his driving forces was gone.

A sudden panic spread through him, but he kept his composure. His empire was crumbling, brick by brick. But he had a safety net set up to prevent his financial collapse.

Cross knew that if he was going down, he was going down fighting and not alone. If Eduardo wanted a war, then he was going to get one. Cross had power and reach in certain areas too.

Cross continued to hold and play with, his son. Jeremy was a pleasant distraction from his problems in the streets. His son's smiling face and gentle form put him in a world at ease. He loved being a father. He had planned on spending the day with his family, but business and Edge's murder were constantly playing in his head.

He looked over at Cynthia. "I gotta make a run back into Harlem tonight," he said.

"For what?"

"I gotta pick up some money, and I gotta see what went down."

Cynthia heaved a sigh. "I want you to stay home tonight, Cross. You need to be here with us, not on them streets."

"I gotta take care of some business, Cynthia. Understand that."

"Doesn't your friend's murder tell you something, Cross? It's not safe for you in Harlem."

"I'ma be good. I always watch my back, and I'll be back. I promise."

Cynthia was tired of hearing it.

"Give me my baby," she said, reaching for her son.

"Why you actin' like a bitch?"

"'Cuz you stupid, Cross!"

"You like the way you live, Cynthia?" he asked with frustration. "Well, if you wanna continue living like this, then I gotta go out there and grind and make myself known. I can't allow Edge's death to make me look weak. It ain't fuckin' happening."

"I'm not planning your funeral, Cross."

Cross sighed. He went into the bedroom to change clothes and make a few phone calls. He really didn't like her last remark. The one thing you never say to a street nigga is you're not going to plan his funeral. That was a bad omen Cross didn't want any part of. He hated to compare Cynthia to Kola, but Kola would've never said stupid shit like that. She knew better.

Cynthia sat on the couch holding her son, looking worried about Cross leaving. But she knew that there was nothing she could do to stop him.

Cross stepped out of the bedroom clad in dark attire—black jeans along with a black shirt, and a do-rag on his head. Cynthia noticed the butt of a gun peeking from underneath his shirt, tucked snugly in his waistband.

He observed her eyes and pulled his shirt down to better conceal the 9 mm.

"Look, I'll be right back. I promise you, Cynthia," Cross assured.

Cynthia remained silent and frustrated, her body language and attitude obvious.

Cross walked over to her, crouched down in front of her, and stared into her worried eyes. "You gonna be OK. But I gotta go out there and see what went down, and handle my business."

"You ain't gotta do shit!"

"You so fuckin' ignorant, Cynthia! I swear."

Cross calmed his temper. He then stood up and placed a key on the coffee table. Cynthia looked down at it. She didn't ask any questions about the key, but he wanted to let her know about it.

"That's a key to a storage locker on Atlantic Avenue—512. If something was to happen to me, you take that key, go to the storage locker, and everything in it belongs to you. You take what you can, and leave with my son. Go somewhere far."

Cynthia remained quiet. She didn't want to hear it.

"You understand me? You leave here immediately."

Cross then made his exit, and when the door shut behind him, Cynthia's tears began to fall as she held Jeremy in her arms. She had a bad feeling about tonight, and in her heart, she knew Cross wasn't coming back.

Cross drove his truck across the Brooklyn Bridge and made it into the bowels of Harlem late in the night. Cross wanted to be cautious. He wanted to keep a low profile, nothing flashy. He'd removed the chrome rims from his truck and replaced them with regular factory tires. His windows were tinted slightly, but not so dark as to attract the attention of the police. He carried the 9 mm and a .38 in his ride as he navigated through Harlem slowly, doing the speed limit.

He pulled up in front of a dilapidated bodega on Eighth Avenue. Before Cross got out, he checked his surroundings and got out his truck with the gun tucked snugly in his jeans. He entered the empty bodega. The young boy behind the counter noticed Cross and nodded.

"He in the back?" Cross asked.

The young boy nodded.

NISA SANTIAGO

Cross was about to go into the back room when he heard the boy from the counter say, "Yo, Cross, I heard what happened to Edge. Yo, I'm sorry about that."

Cross didn't acknowledge the boy's statement. He continued walking toward the back, passing piles of boxes and milk crates, and other stocked store goods. He came across a black steel door. He glanced up at the camera to show his face, and he was buzzed in.

An armed, muscled goon greeted him when he stepped inside. The man nodded, showing Cross respect. "Yo, sorry about Edge," the goon said.

Cross didn't say a word. He moved deeper into the illegal room, where dozens of guns were displayed in large crates to be either shipped or sold. It wasn't his business.

Cross spotted Tiko seated in a leather recliner chair behind his large oak desk with the phone to his ear. Tiko motioned for Cross to come closer and take a seat, and he did.

The discreet back room was windowless and had brick walls, but it was decorated stylishly with state-of-the-art surveillance equipment, posh furniture, and a flat-screen catty-cornered near Tiko's desk.

Cross took a seat across from Tiko and waited patiently for him to end his phone call.

Tiko's deep, raspy voice boomed through the phone. His graying beard was trimmed neatly, and he was clad in a chic brown suit. Tiko was a wise, handsome, aging hustler, and his fifty years didn't show.

Tiko was finally done with his phone call and focused

his undivided attention on Cross, who he'd always looked at like a son. "What brings you here, Cross? Is this about Edge?"

"We fucked up, Tiko."

"With what?"

"I let my emotions run wild for this bitch."

"Kola?"

"Yeah, and I did a stupid a thing. Really stupid," Cross quickly said.

"How stupid?"

"We got at Eduardo, killed a few of his men, and stole money and weight from his Jersey City operation."

"You did what?"

"I was caught up, Tiko. I had Edge in my ear talking and shit. I thought Eduardo was fuckin' my bitch."

"Was he?"

"I don't know, but she was spending too much time at his place."

"So you didn't know for sure, but you still acted. You a fool, Cross. You allowed pussy to fuck with your head, made you do a stupid thing. So you think Edge's death is retaliation?"

"Most likely, but I'm not sure. I've been keeping a low profile, staying in Brooklyn with Cynthia and my son."

Tiko exhaled noisily, his dark eyes fixed on Cross. "You stay in Brooklyn then and continue laying low. But what do you need from me, youngblood?"

"I need more soldiers . . . some thorough muthafuckas to join forces with my crew, just in case. And some guns.

High powered shit that will blow a nigga's brain from here to hell."

"Consider it done," Tiko said.

"I got goons hunting for that bean-and-rice-eating muthafucka, Tiko."

"Eduardo will not be killed by some Harlem Street thugs. He's too smart and advanced for that."

"Whatever. I know if any of his soldiers set foot uptown, I'm gonna be on them."

"And then what? I told you about the violence, Cross. I told you to work things out with Chico. But you don't listen to me. You are a hardheaded muthafucka, and now you got yourself backed into a corner. And you're ready to shoot your way out, thinking it's gonna solve your situation."

"I gotta do what I gotta do, Tiko. You sell guns. How you preach about no violence when the business you in is about violence?"

Cross thought that Tiko was being hypocritical. After all, Tiko ran an illegal gun operation that stretched all the way into Miami.

"Let me tell you something, youngblood. You think I'm contradicting myself, but one thing you need to get straight—I don't shit where I eat. Two, I'm a businessman, and I sell a product, not death. You niggas gonna continue to kill each other no matter what I say, so I might as well get paid from it. But I don't want that heat around me. Murder is always a major headline."

Cross couldn't argue with Tiko. Tiko had been his mentor for years, and the aging hustler had looked out for him plenty of times.

"But I got your guns for you," Tiko said.

Cross thanked him.

"But, Cross, this is the last favor you'll get from me. No more. You're too hot right now, and I'm not trying to get caught up in your war or bullshit. So you take these guns from me and a couple soldiers who wanna ride on your team, and we part ways from here. Your beef with Eduardo, I don't want any part of."

Cross nodded and understood.

They made arrangements for Tiko to drop off some guns for Cross' soldiers on the streets. Cross walked out the bodega and was very cautious about his surroundings. The corners were calm—no drunks, no gamblers, or hustlers about. But Cross knew that sometimes things weren't what they appeared to be. He kept his reach near his gun and walked toward his truck. He hopped in and started the ignition. He wanted to be in and out of Harlem ASAP. One more stop to make and then it was back over the bridge and into Brooklyn.

He slowly pulled off and made a right onto 145th Street. He looked through his rearview mirrors and noticed he was being tailed by a black Maxima with tinted windows. He couldn't tell how many occupants were inside the car.

"Fuck!" he uttered.

Not knowing what to expect, Cross placed the 9 mm in his lap and had it ready for action if needed. He drove his vehicle to a crawl and came to a stop at a red light, his heart rate tripling from anxiety. He constantly glanced at his rearview mirror. The car had been on him since he'd left the bodega.

When the light changed to green, he sped out. The Maxima raced behind him, and then suddenly Cross noticed the police lights flashing behind him, pulling him over to the curb.

"Fuck!" Cross shouted. He stopped the truck and threw the 9 mm into the center console and tried to act normal.

Three plainclothes officers approached his truck, their hands on their holstered weapons, and their eyes fixed on the driver and his ride.

"License and registration," one of the cops said as he flashed his badge. He had his eyes steadied on Cross and his movements.

The other two officers shined their lights into his truck, looking for anything suspicious.

"What's wrong, officer?" Cross asked.

"License and registration," the officer repeated.

Cross calmly reached across to the glove compartment, unhooked it open, pulled out the things he needed, and then handed the information to the cop.

The cop took a glance at everything, and then said to Cross, "Step out of the car, please."

"Officer, did I do something wrong?"

"Step out of the car!" the officer said sternly.

Cross looked defeated. He knew he was done. He glared at the officer and slowly complied. When he put both feet onto the pavement, the officer began reading him his rights, pushing him face first into the side of his truck before cuffing him.

"What the fuck did I do?"

"You have a warrant out for your arrest."

"Nah, that's fuckin' bullshit!"

The other two officers searched Cross' truck, and then one soon shouted out, "Gun!" They removed the 9 mm from the center console and then found the .38 under the passenger seat.

An hour after his arrest, Cross sat tired and hungry in a dull, gray interrogation room handcuffed to an iron bar that lined the wall. It had been a long day for him. Two detectives entered the interrogation room and sat opposite him behind the long table.

Cross glared at them.

"I know you heard about Edge," one said.

"What the fuck you want from me?" Cross barked. "My friend is murdered, and y'all muthafuckas picked me up. You must be fuckin' crazy!"

"You're a damn menace, Cross," Detective Rice exclaimed. "You're pretty much fucked right now, so you have two options—You cooperate with us, or you go down to the pokey pen and take your chances with the courts."

Cross sighed. "Call my lawyer, and we'll work this shit out."

"Fine with us," the second detective said.

The shit hit the fan when Cross got the news that Edge had sworn on affidavit to their involvement in organized crime, and was planning to turn state's witness. Cross couldn't believe it, but the proof was clearly in his face. The betrayal had him feeling a wreck. The detectives figured that Cross, after finding out about Edge's betrayal, had set him up to be murdered.

Cross was taken down to Central Booking—the tombs—located in Lower Manhattan, where he was booked and processed. He sat on the hard, cold benches attached to the graffiti-covered walls in the filthy bullpens of the courts, jammed with prisoners. The first thing Cross wanted to do was contact his lawyer and find out what was going on. He couldn't rest. His mind was spinning, and he wanted out of jail by any means necessary.

✳

Hours later, Cross heard a corrections officer shouting his name.

"You got a visit from your lawyer! Let's go!"

Cross didn't hesitate to exit the cell, pushing his way past the hooligans, bums, and troublemakers crowding the small holding cell. He was escorted into another holding cell, a bit larger and less rowdy than the one he'd just left. On the other side of the cell was a thick partition for inmates to meet with their attorneys.

Cross was called up and sat behind the partition on a hard bench.

His lawyer approached, looking sharp in his three-button, navy pinstripe Italian suit. Meyers Mitchell was the best at what he did, but when he sat down, the gloomy look in his eyes already spoke to Cross.

"Talk to me, Meyers. What the fuck is goin' on?" Cross spat.

"You fucked up, Cross. Two guns?"

"It was a bad night. But I need this shit to go away."

"How, Cross? I can't work miracles. I got the first gun charge postponed for a year, pushed the trial back as long as I could, but now you pull this. I warned you, stay out of trouble and relax. And then the murder charge that they're trying to pin on—"

"I ain't do it."

"I know. They don't have enough evidence to indict you. It's bullshit! But my hands are tied when it comes to the revoked bail."

"I need to get outta here, Meyers. You need to make it happen."

"How? I'm not a genie. I can't grant wishes."

"You got a seventy-five thousand dollar retainer from me last year and that shit ain't nearly used up, so do ya fuckin' job, Meyers, or I'll get someone else to do it for you!"

Meyers sighed. "The most I can do for you right now is maybe get the charges reduced, but the courts fear you as a flight risk, so there will be no more bail. It will get ugly, Cross, really ugly."

"I can't be in here, Meyers! Don't you fuckin' understand

me? I'm marked, and they can easily get me on the inside."

"Listen, I'll fight for you, like I always do, but these charges are not going to go away. I can talk to the DA, maybe have you take a plea—"

Cross jumped up from his seat. "Fuck you, Meyers! If you can't fuckin' do the job, then I'll find somewhere to take care of business for me. You're fuckin' fired!"

Chapter 19

Kola needed to release her stress. She wanted to free her mind from the chaos and murders swamping her world in the past weeks. She felt relieved to have finally gunned down Edge. The deed gave her a rush to the point where it almost felt better than sex. The streets were talking about his murder, with rumors and gossip about who did it and why. Kola had no time for the foolishness. She remained in her home for a moment right after the murder, not wanting to take any chances.

Kola lay naked on her back, her legs cocked back, while the young boy's tongue invaded deep into her pussy, instantly finding her G-spot. Her moans echoed off the bedroom walls as the young face buried between her legs twisted his tongue hungrily.

"Aaah! Right there! Do that shit right there!" Her mind spiraled into a touch of bliss as the orgasm rocked her into screams for more. "Shit! Ooooh! I so needed this! Ooooh! Ooooh!"

Nineteen-year-old Keno was one of Kola's young

workers. He was cute with his thin mustache, dark brown sleepy eyes, high-yellow skin, and a low-cut Caesar. Kola had had her eyes on him since noticing him on the block. She wasn't much older than him herself, beating the young boy by one year.

She was squirming, with Keno's tongue digging inside of her, when the phone rang. She ignored it, and let it go to her voice mail. But then it rang again.

Kola snatched up her phone. "What?" she shouted.

"You have a collect call from Cross. To accept, please press—"

Kola quickly hung up, pissed that she'd answered her phone in the first place. She looked down at her young stud.

"Continue, baby."

Keno dove back into her pussy.

Kola's phone started to ring again. "What the fuck!" she screamed out. Then it stopped.

Ten minutes later, the phone rang again.

Kola snatched up her phone and screamed, "I don't accept the fuckin' call!"

"Who the fuck you screaming at, bitch?" Cross shouted.

"Cross, what the fuck you doin' callin' me collect?"

"Why I gotta get my man to three-way you for me to talk to you?"

"'Cuz I'm not tryin' to be bothered right now. I'm busy."

"Look, I'm locked down in Rikers right now, and I need you to come see me."

"What? Nigga, is you serious?"

"Like the national deficit, hells yeah, I'm fuckin' serious. I need you to collect some information from me and gather up these papers. I need you to get at this new attorney for me. He's licensed in New York and Miami."

Kola chuckled at his orders. "You is a funny muthafucka, Cross. You need to be callin' that other bitch, Cynthia, to handle ya fuckin' business 'cuz I'm through wit' you."

"You think so, Kola?"

"I'm about to hang up now, so don't let the dial tone hit you—And don't drop the soap."

"Bitch, you hang up on me, and I guarantee you that you won't be fuckin' alive tomorrow morning," Cross said through clenched teeth.

Kola chuckled. Cross was no longer a threat to her. Edge was dead, and he was incarcerated. Her problem was already solved.

"I think I've already proven I can handle myself, so you can take your little threats and shove them up your ass!" she began. "It seems I'm smarter than you and your right-hand man. You both are memories while my name is still ringing bells. I'm the baddest chick these streets have ever seen—"

"You think that massacre at your stash house was the end of it? Bitch, that was only the beginning. You really don't fuckin' know, do you?"

"Was you a part of that, Cross?" Kola asked heatedly. "'Cuz I swear, you will pay."

"Come see me tomorrow, and we'll talk," he said. "And don't bullshit me, bitch! I got news that you need to hear."

Cross and the third party he'd connected through hung up, leaving Kola outraged and speculating about what he'd just said.

Keno tried to restart what Kola had put on pause, but she was no longer in the mood. She pushed Keno away from her, hissing, "Just get the fuck away from me!"

Keno shrugged. He knew not to push. He got out the bed and began collecting his clothing.

Kola just sat on her bed, worry, speculation, and anger mixed in with her emotions. She didn't want to visit Cross. However, she felt she didn't have a choice.

Her eyes followed Keno as he left the bedroom. It was a waste of good dick. Cross' phone call had soured the mood and had her pussy drying up like sand.

✳

Early the next morning, Kola was on the long and growing visiting line to see Cross. Rikers Island was bustling with guards doing thorough searches of incoming visitors. Streams of people passed through the metal detectors, and then were directed to their destinations. Visitors scrambled about, some with young children, to make sure their papers were in order.

Kola hated the putrid smell of the jail, the sight of bars caging so many men and women, and the heavy security presence that surrounded her. She thought about her own fate, being on the wrong side of the law.

She moved slowly behind a woman dealing with two small children. The woman looked too young to be a mother. She seemed poor and frustrated. She fumbled with the children's belongings as well as her own, as she moved through the metal detector and then was checked by a C.O. waving a wand across her body, and her children's.

Kola sighed. She could never see herself being someone's baby mama, and bringing kids into a harsh environment like Rikers Island. Kola shook her head at the shameful-looking mother and slowly followed behind her. She went through the search easily and proceeded into the larger room to register for her visit with Cross. The room was packed with people, young and old, and there were proportionately more blacks and Hispanics than whites.

Kola looked around the registration area and knew it was going to be a long day. She noticed the fleeting looks her way and some gawking by different groups of people she'd passed, both men and women. They had to be stuck on her tight, trendy jeans that highlighted her shapely curves, black sequined top with the peek-a-boo bodice, open back and sequined hemline, and six-inch heels that made her tower over some of the ladies.

A few guards tried to flirt with her, but she paid them no attention. Her main concern was seeing Cross and then leaving. She didn't want to stay longer than she needed to. At one of the many reception desks, Kola had to produce her driver's license or a form of identification, and the name of the person she was visiting. She gave the pudgy, soft-spoken redbone lady her license. The lady then typed Cross' government name into the system, and then she gave Kola a white piece of paper and told her the housing unit he was placed in. Kola had to sit in the waiting area with the other ladies and wait for the next bus to transport them. She looked around and took a seat and felt like she was in hell.

Twenty minutes later, Kola followed behind a group of ladies into the visiting area. They moved past a giant steel door that hummed a short alarm every time it was opened, and they entered the massive room with dozens of visitors and inmates seated at selected locations. Kola handed the lady guard by the door her white paper, and she said to Kola, "Table fifteen," pointing in the direction where she was to be seated.

Kola strutted to the area and once again felt the eyes of many upon her. She kept walking and remained nonchalant. She took a seat at the small plastic round table and waited.

Cross entered the visiting room shortly after Kola's arrival. He looked around for Kola, handed the guard his ID, and walked toward her with a confident stride and swag that appealed to a few of the ladies he passed.

Kola didn't smile when Cross came her way. She felt nothing but anger and hostility toward him. She once loved him, but now it made her uncomfortable just to see him. There were no hugs or kisses when he took a seat opposite her, his back facing the corrections officers and their elevated platform.

Cross was clad in the bright orange prison jumpsuit with "DOC" printed on the back in bold black letters. He sat upright and focused on Kola. "Good to see you, Kola," he greeted matter-of-factly. "You look good, baby. Got all these niggas sweating you in here and shit."

"Why am I here, Cross?"

"Were you fuckin' that nigga?"

"What? Who?" Kola looked befuddled.

"Don't play stupid wit' me, Kola—I'm talkin' about Eduardo."

"We were just about business."

"Business, huh? Then why a couple months ago, it took you over an hour to complete ya business wit' that muthafucka?"

"What are you talkin' about?"

"You know what the fuck I'm talkin' about."

"You followed me there?"

"I trusted you, Kola."

"You wanna talk about fuckin' trust? How 'bout you and Cynthia having a fuckin' baby? Making me feel like a stupid bitch. How dare you bring that trust shit up!"

"Well, ain't no worry about that nigga now. He's MIA since we ran up on him. And I had my peoples lookin' for that muthafucka."

"What?"

"Shit was on the news, but ya young ass is too caught up in the streets and yourself to change the channel from BET or MTV once in a while and see what's goin' on in the world. We ran up on him right after you left, shot up his goons, and took what we could."

"You're crazy, Cross. Why?"

"'Cuz you and him were fuckin' playin' me, so I did what I had to do. I wanted to take that muthafucka out, and we came close."

It finally made sense to Kola—the threatening phone call she'd received from Eduardo, then her calls being rejected, the feds lingering outside of the building, Eduardo suddenly becoming MIA, and then the hit at her Yonkers stash house. Only Eduardo had the power to pull off a massacre of that magnitude.

Kola knew she was fucked. She glared at Cross. "What the fuck have you done to me?"

"You fucked him, so now I fucked you. Let's just call it even."

"I didn't fuck him!" Kola screamed, catching everyone's attention in the room. "Fuck you!"

The guards turned and stared at her and Cross, keeping alert.

Cross glared at a few inmates with a menacing look, reminding them to mind their business. His fierce reputation was well known in his housing unit, where he had some allies and some enemies.

Kola pushed her chair back and walked away. She was done with her visit. She was done with Cross. She wanted to get as far away from him as possible. He had to pay for what he'd done.

"Where the fuck you goin', Kola? We ain't done yet! Get the fuck over here, bitch!" Cross screamed, jumping from his chair, ready to chase after her. "You don't fuckin' walk away from me!"

A few guards rushed over, restraining Cross and grabbing Kola, trying to defuse the situation. Cross was sent back to lock-up, and Kola left the area, feeling sick to her stomach. She had never been so angry.

When Kola made it out of Rikers, stepping off the bus and to her car in the parking lot, she was wishing she'd shot Cross that night instead of Edge. After she got into her car, she thought, *If they robbed Eduardo, then what did Cross do with the money and drugs they took from him?* Then she remembered Edge mentioning cash and weight before he told her about Cross buying that Brooklyn bitch a ring. Everything had to be with Cynthia in Brooklyn. Which meant Cynthia's life was now in danger.

Kola had held her tears in for too long. Once she was in the privacy of her own car, she felt faint and started to cry. It was a brief moment of weakness. She didn't know what to do or who to turn to. Everybody she'd once trusted was either dead or had betrayed her.

Kola felt that it was time for her to leave home and break away from what she knew best—the drugs, the sex parties, and the streets of Harlem—and regroup in a different city. She needed to travel to someplace and lay low for a moment. Eduardo was a dangerous and resourceful man. She knew he wouldn't stop coming for her and everyone else involved with the robbery and murder of his men. Kola was scared. It was the first time she felt the need to run from anyone or anything.

A few hours after her visit with Cross, she went to her mother's apartment and began packing her things. Then she sped to her home and got the money and guns she needed. She had enough money saved to go anywhere she wanted in the country.

Kola decided on Miami. She had some peoples out there she needed to see. She took what she could, and threw everything into the trunk of her Audi, along with her hundred and fifty thousand dollars in cash, and got on the I-95 South for the twenty-four-hour trip to Miami.

Chapter 20

Two-Face sat slouched in the backseat of the faded black Ford Taurus on 188th Street gripping an Uzi submachine gun. His two cohorts, Narco and Rage, two of New York's most ruthless thugs, sat in the car with him, waiting and plotting. New York City and Harlem weren't ready for the murderous Two-Face in their backyard. He had given a violent wake-up call to so many who'd doubted his brutality and murderous ways because of his youthful appearance, people were now afraid to speak his name.

Two-Face killed viciously with anything he could get his hands on: guns, knives, a brick. He even had a man twice his age mauled to death by a ferocious pit bull. The man, accused of being a snitch, was forced into a concrete basement in the gut of the hood and stripped naked in front of his peers.

✳

The tall, lanky victim was shaking like a leaf on a windy day. "Please, Two-Face," he said, "I ain't do nothin'.

C'mon, man, it ain't gotta be like this. I ain't say shit to any police!"

"You a snitch, homes. You fucked up, big time!"

The dog barked wildly, its echoing bark sending chills into the man, and its demonic eyes trained on its potential target. The powerful beast was eager to be released.

The other thugs surrounding Two-Face jeered at the snitch and spat on him, each of them looking to gain Two-Face's respect and approval.

"Fuck him up, Two-Face!" one of them shouted. "Fuck that snitch up!"

The terrier was confident, robust, and bursting with energy. Two-Face gripped the ferocious pit bull by its chain leash. He had a hard time restraining the dog, which constantly yanked him forward, ready to attack.

"Two-Face, please . . . I didn't do anything! I swear to you, man! I didn't say shit. I didn't say shit!" he screamed.

Two-Face locked eyes with the man, his gaze as deadly and intimidating as the dog's. The black of Two-Face's eyes showed a cruel, treacherous being that lived for the violence; a man without a soul.

Another thug shouted, "Do that shit, Two-Face! Do that shit!"

The naked man was cowered into the corner with his hands outstretched in front of him. The whites of his eyes dimmed with fear.

Two-Face sneered at the man. Without warning, he let go of the leash, and the dog rushed forward, slamming its victim into the wall as it tore its teeth into the man's flesh, ripping apart skin and his fingers.

The victim's blood-curdling scream brought the basement alive with laughter. The thugs stood around and watched pieces of the man fly in the air, and thick crimson blood began pooling on the floor. The assault went on for fifteen minutes, until the victim was left lifeless and his body contorted like a pretzel.

Two-Face smiled at his method of killing. It felt like Christmas day for him.

Two-Face's violent killings had placed him on the police and task force radar. When the cops were finally able to attach a face to the name, they were stunned at how young and innocent he looked. They understood why he had gotten the name Two-Face. The precincts made it their priority to bring the young killer and his violent organization, along with Chico, to justice and try him for his inhumane crimes.

Word on the streets started to surface about Chico and Two-Face being at odds with each other. Two-Face began asking around about Chico. He wanted to know why his boss was so insistent about getting information about a prostitute and disfigured whore in Mexico. He wanted to know the connection.

Little by little, information started to come back to Two-Face about Chico and Apple. He learned of the events and incidents that took place before his arrival in the city. He learned about Chico's undying love for Apple and her sudden disappearance without a trace. He knew Kola was her twin, and that they were warring sisters.

People were willing to tell Two-Face anything out of fear. Whatever information he needed, it was given to him. The streets started to fear and respect Two-Face a little more than they did Chico. Two-Face was the one on the streets putting in work. He had the young killers at his beck and call, while Chico was playing house with a Brooklyn bitch and the streets were seeing less and less of him every week.

The plan to bring Two-Face in for muscle and control had backfired on Chico. A few soldiers were starting to turn against him. Jason had forewarned him about this.

Two-Face had gotten a taste of the action and power in New York City and wanted more of it. With his name ringing bells in the streets, and having plenty of young thugs ready to follow his lead, Two-Face planned on taking over. He had gotten Chico the connect with his uncle's Mexican cartel, and he was the one spilling blood on the streets, so he thought he should no longer be Chico's subordinate. He should be the one wearing the crown.

The streets soon started buzzing about the situation between Chico and Two-Face becoming rivals, and people started to take sides.

Two-Face made the first move against Chico, declaring that certain corners were his to control and take over. If you went against him, then you would be dealt with violently. A few soldiers and workers still had loyalty to Chico, so Two-Face decided to make an example of them.

Two-Face sat in the Taurus playing around with the Uzi while waiting for those loyal to Chico to enter the 188th Street building. He kept a keen eye on the block as they sat snug and obscured, parked between a dark van and a Ford truck. It was nearing eleven p.m., and foot traffic was light.

After the men sat for an hour waiting, Narco asked, "You sure about this, Two-Face?"

"What you mean, Narco? You tryin' to back out on me now?" Two-Face asked. "Huh, homes?" He leaned forward, the Uzi almost aimed at Narco in a threatening way. "You got doubts?"

"Nah, you know I'm down, one hundred and everything, but Chico . . . I known the nigga for years, and he ain't somebody to play wit'. We fuck this up, and he'll fuck us up."

"Fuck Chico! I'm tired of that muthafucka!" Two-Face spat. "He don't run the show no more."

Narco decided to remain silent. He knew Two-Face was a psychopath. Narco had killed before, but Two-Face took death and violence to a whole other level. He was the new terror, while Chico was becoming the old.

A short while later, a Dodge Magnum crept down the block and stopped in front of the building they'd been staking out. It doubled-parked, and two men stepped out and walked toward the building carrying book bags. Two-Face knew they were filled with money or coke.

The two men, Donny and Lennox, loyal workers for Chico for years, refused to go along with Two-Face's command. They weren't about to be bullied by some young, baby-faced thug, who wasn't even from Harlem.

Two-Face glared at Donny and Lennox, both men in their late twenties, and deadly figures in the underworld. They strutted toward the building, keeping a watchful eye on the block.

"Let's do this!" Two-Face said, opening the car door.

Donny and Lennox walked through a darkened area toward the lobby of the six-story building, its entranceway pushed back from the street and towered by walls. When the men were near the door, Donny pressed the call button for the apartment they were going to.

Two-Face and his goons slowly ran up near the front entrance. He peeked around the corner, the Uzi gripped firmly in his hands. Rage held a sawed-off shotgun, and Narco carried an Uzi also. They wanted the hit to be messy.

Two-Face looked at his goons and nodded. Before Donny and Lennox could enter the lobby, the trio charged from around the corner and opened fire. The shotgun exploded, pushing Donny back into the glass, and then the sound of the two Uzis exploded into the night, cutting down both men.

Two-Face ran up to the bloody bodies and snatched the book bags from their lifeless hands. He looked down at the bodies and smiled. He then ran back to the car and sped away. It was a clear "fuck-you" to Chico and his peoples.

Chico had had enough of Two-Face. He was back in Harlem with a full force, but his actions were subtle. The one actual advantage Chico had over the ruthless Two-Face was more money and influence in Harlem. Even though Two-Face was feared, many still considered him an outsider, and the enemies began to pile against him.

Chico offered fifty thousand dollars for word or information on Two-Face's whereabouts, knowing some greedy, desperate individual would take the bait, and one week later, he got word of where Two-Face was holed up. He knew he had to be careful coming at the young killer, because he was also cunning and deadly.

Two-Face was snatched from outside the Bronx apartment he was staying in when he walked out the lobby during the late hours of the night to get into the idling Taurus on the street with Narco waiting behind the wheel. Chico's men had been waiting for Two-Face's exit, and once he showed his face, they rushed him, throwing a sack over his head, beating him down viciously, and then tossing him into the trunk of a car. Narco had been part of the setup. He wanted the fifty thousand, and he wanted to show his loyalty to Chico.

Two-Face was taken to a remote location far from Harlem, where he was subdued with zip-ties around his wrists and his ankles chained to a chair, shirtless and barely conscious after the brutal beating. The sack was snatched from around his head, and Two-Face found himself in a basement.

Two-Face looked fiercely into the face of each man. "You fuckin' wit' the wrong *vato*, homes. You have a death wish?"

"Fuck you!" one of the thugs shouted. He struck Two-Face with the butt of his gun.

Two-Face didn't flinch from the blow. He quickly absorbed it with a grin. His mouth began to fill up with blood. "You touch me like that again, and I'll cut your throat, muthafucka!"

The thug scowled at Two-Face, but he didn't attack him again.

Two-Face squirmed in the chair, trying to free himself, but he was bonded tightly. The blood trickled from his mouth, and his teeth were stained red. Two-Face wasn't frightened. He was cursing and threatening everyone, promising them a gruesome death if they didn't let him go, but the half-dozen men in the basement looked unmoved by his threats.

Chico entered the room, and the two giants glared at each other for a moment. There was silence.

Two-Face suddenly shouted, "You a fool, homes. My uncle is gonna fuck you up!"

"Not before I kill you," Chico replied.

Two-Face fought to free himself from the restraints, but to no avail. His eyes burned with anger. He once again glared at the men he thought were his soldiers, including Narco. "I'ma kill you all! I swear."

Chico pistol-whipped him. "Where is she?"

"Who, homes? That bitch that me and my *cholos* fucked in Mexico? Yeah, we had a good time wit' that ugly bitch, homes. Wore that pussy out."

Chico struck him again, and then again.

Two-Face's face started to bruise and swell, but he took the beating without whining or begging for it to stop. He continued his defiant stare at Chico. "I can do this all night, homes. I'm built for this, pussy. I fuckin' come from this. You don't scare me."

Chico hit him one last time and then fell back.

Two-Face smirked, his face bloody and battered, a few teeth loose. He knew his fate was inevitable. "I shoulda killed you in D.C., muthafucka!"

"Yeah, you should have. I gave you a chance, but you choose to stab me in the back and fuck my girl."

"I ain't know she was ya woman, homes."

"That's irrelevant now. But know somethin', you little bitch—This is my town, my business. I've been in this game for too long to have a snake like you pull it from underneath me. You thought it would be that easy? But, hey, you proved your usefulness, and now your services are no longer required."

Chico raised the pistol to Two-Face's head. Two-Face didn't recoil, as he continued to stare at death boldly. Their eyes connected, and both men knew what was to come next. Chico knew that Two-Face was too stubborn and defiant to talk about Apple's whereabouts in Mexico. The only information he was able to get was, she was held captive in a border town.

"Fuck you, homes!" Two-Face screamed with his last breath.

Bam! Bam! Bam! Bam!

The force from the pistol sent Two-Face and the chair crashing to the floor with a thud.

Chico walked over and put three more rounds into the body. He then turned to one of his goons and said, "Dump that nigga's body back in Harlem and blame it on Cross."

The thugs dumped Two-Face's body near the projects on 155th Street with a bloody note attached: *You kill one of ours and we kill one of yours. For Edge.*

Two-Face's death was big news throughout Harlem. It stirred a lot of speculation. Many people in the area didn't buy that Cross was able to get at him so easily, and they believed that it was Chico who had punished him for his betrayal.

It was midnight when Chico stood alone on the rooftop of one of the project buildings in Harlem and peered at the vibrant neighborhood. The view was phenomenal from where he stood—the flowing traffic, the illuminated buildings that stretched from block to block for miles—not to mention the late-night sounds of the city.

Even though he had gotten rid of a threat, and was making tons of money, Chico felt empty. Apple was still on his mind.

Just then his phone rang. When he saw Dario's number on his caller ID, he thought it might be good news. "Speak to me."

"We had a problem."

"What the fuck you mean there was a problem?"

"We found her, but then lost her."

Chico barked, "What the fuck does that mean?"

"She was in a small town call Los Mochis, Mexico, about three hundred miles from the border on the west side. I had my peoples track her. It was perfect. But we arrived too late. The place was shot to shit, and the girls said she was already taken."

Chico was fuming. "By who?" he shouted.

"We don't know. They went in fast, killed a few men, and took Apple with them. But the place was run by a guy named Shaun. He's from your part of town. You familiar with that name?"

Chico thought long and hard about it. He vaguely remembered a Shaun. "I'm not too familiar wit' that name."

"Well, word is, she was abducted from up there and brought down here to become a sex slave. This Shaun, they say, had some kind of vendetta against her. He wasn't one of the men found dead, so that means he's still out there."

Chico was still upset that they hadn't found Apple, but the information was valuable to him.

"What you want me to do, Chico?"

"You keep looking, but I'm coming down there."

He was determined to find Apple and bring her

home. He needed her in his life again. Just knowing that she didn't leave on her own free will had reignited his true feelings for her. The thought that some nigga named Shaun had abducted her on some vendetta type shit had him questioning his own manhood. How could he have left her vulnerable? That wasn't what real niggas did. He vowed that when he got her back he'd do everything in his power to make it up to her.

"You sure?" Dario asked.

"Yeah, I'm sure."

Chapter 21

Due to heavy traffic, it took Kola a day and a half to arrive in Miami, her longest drive ever. New York was so far behind her; she felt secure once she crossed into the city limits of Miami.

The hot, humid city, the sun flaring above, lit up Kola's eyes. It was like a mini New York for her, but it was so much warmer and exotic. The traffic on the Dolphin Expressway reminded her of the FDR. She couldn't wait to explore every part of Miami.

Kola knew she had to get situated with her cousin and her peoples fast. With a hundred and fifty thousand dollars in the car trunk, cruising in a stylish black Audi with New York plates, she knew she was a magnet for attention. She felt fortunate to not get pulled over during the trip down.

Kola cruised through the city, peering from a distance at the towering skyline. The sun was slowly setting behind the horizon, with the night consuming the day, and it was almost time for everyone to come out and play. Kola knew that Miami was famous for its beaches, clubs, nightlife, and glamour.

She got on her phone and dialed Nikki, her cousin, who she hadn't seen in five years. She had forewarned her cousin of her arrival, so Nikki was anticipating her arrival.

✳

Nikki and Kola were like two peas in a pod. They loved the same things— making money, niggas, and being the flyest bitches wherever they went.

Nikki was three years older than Kola. She had made Miami her home after the trouble she'd caused in Harlem. She'd caught a drug charge and did two years in federal prison. When she got out, Harlem became a bore to her. She felt it was time for a change in scenery and business. Since her departure, she'd never bothered to return north.

Nikki was Kola's mentor while growing up. She'd introduced Kola to the street life when she was fourteen, linking her up with Mike-Mike and Cross' crew. Whatever Nikki did, Kola loved to follow. When Nikki left New York in search of bigger and better things, Kola followed in her cousin's footsteps and became that bitch not to fuck with in Harlem. The two rarely kept in contact, but Kola had made it her priority to locate her favorite cousin and put her on to what had been happening in Harlem.

✳

Kola drove west on the Dolphin Expressway and exited into a neighborhood called West Little Havana.

The sun had finally set, and the sky was littered with stars. She moved through the Cuban neighborhood searching for the address her cousin had texted her. Kola took in the one-story homes with stucco rooftops and the palm trees that lined the streets. It was a total contrast from the streets of Harlem. She knew she stood out among the many Cuban people that flooded the area, but they only glanced at her when she drove by them.

Kola turned onto her cousin's quiet, no-traffic street, close to a park. She pulled up in front of a bright orange, one-level home with shrubbery fencing, tall palm trees in the front yard, and a silver BMW parked in the driveway. Kola parked and stepped out onto the street, her Jimmy Choo's hitting the rocky pavement. She was tired and hungry, but excited to see Nikki after so many years.

She strutted toward the front entrance, walked onto the small porch, and knocked loudly. The house looked quiet and empty. Kola didn't see any lights or hear anything, but she assumed her cousin was home because of the flashy car parked in the driveway. She waited for a moment, but there was no answer.

She knocked again and waited. When no one answered, Kola sighed with frustration. "Where is this bitch?" she uttered to herself. She stepped off the porch and peered around the house. Everything looked empty and calm.

Kola began to wonder if she was at the right address. She exited the yard and looked around. The block was quiet like a cemetery. She reached into her purse and pulled out a pack of Newports. She lit up a cigarette, took a deep drag, and then exhaled.

Kola pulled out her cell phone and dialed Nikki's number. It rang a few times before she picked up.

"Hello?"

"Bitch, where you at?" Kola said lightheartedly. "I think I'm at the right address."

"Oh shit! Hey, Kola. You're early. I had to bounce for a minute, handle some business. I'll be there in like ten minutes."

"OK. I'm here."

Kola hung up and decided to sit in her car to wait. She took a few more pulls from the cigarette and flung it out the window.

As she sat back, she thought about everything that had transpired over the past week. Her mistakes and unawareness had forced her to leave Harlem in a hurry. Eduardo had constantly been on her mind, but she tried to push the worry to the back of her mind.

No one knew she was in Miami. It was her secret. No one but Apple and her mother even knew about their cousin being in Miami. She felt somewhat safe in South Florida. She wanted to recoup her sanity and business, and come up someplace different. Harlem was still her heart—her home, and she would always have love for it, but with Chico, Cross, Eduardo, Two-Face, and so many others betraying and hunting her, she would be a fool to stay. Sometimes it was better to run and live to fight another day.

Kola waited for her cousin for fifteen minutes. She had a lot of time on her hands and did a lot of thinking. Love had fucked her, so while in Miami, she decided she had no time for love. It would only be about business and her come-up.

Kola heard Rick Ross' "Hustlin'" blaring from up the block. She turned to see a truck coming her way; a luxurious black Escalade EXT with dark tints and sitting on 22-inch chrome rims. It stopped right next to her Audi.

The young, thuggish driver peered at Kola then turned to the passenger and asked, "That's your cousin?"

"Yeah."

"Damn! She's fuckin' cute!"

"Stop drooling, Rash."

Nikki stepped out of the truck and strutted around it to greet Kola. She was curvy and beautiful, and looked stunning in a yellow, ruffled-hem mini dress with a low-cut front, open back, and circle-ring detail. She had a long, black weave with blonde streaks and hypnotic dark eyes.

Kola quickly stepped out of her car and ran over to greet her cousin. "Nikki!" she screamed.

"Kola!" Nikki screamed back.

The cousins embraced each other lovingly. It had been a long time.

"Damn! That's sweet. Can I get in between that?"

Nikki turned to Rash. "Rash, get the fuck outta here, wit' your perverted self!"

Rash smiled. "I'll catch you around, Nikki, and you too, cousin." He then drove slowly away.

Kola and Nikki continued on with their moment, both excited to see each other.

"Damn, bitch! You lookin' good," Nikki said.

"You should talk, workin' them hips like you dancing on the pole."

"Shit, this is Miami. We do everything down here to get money. Come inside. See how a bitch lives."

Kola followed behind Nikki and entered the one-level home. When Kola stepped inside, she was taken aback by the décor. The home boasted high, textured stucco walls with terrazzo flooring and high ceilings—large bedrooms, and two bathrooms. The living room was decorated with top grain leather furniture, an elaborate aquarium, and a few framed pictures of Nikki scattered throughout. There was also a 60-inch LED TV with a surround sound stereo system.

"Damn, bitch! I like how you living. I see you queen bee down here."

"I do a'ight." Nikki smiled. "You thirsty?"

"Yeah."

Nikki walked into the kitchen and came back out with two cold Corona beers. She passed one to Kola and started downing the other. Kola sat back on the plush furniture and relaxed for a moment.

"So what brings you down here to Miami, little cousin?"

"Business . . . and I had to get away from the bullshit goin' on in Harlem."

"I hear you. Where's your twin?"

"She be around," Kola replied matter-of-factly.

"Damn, I missed y'all. How's Aunt Denise?"

"She a'ight."

"I see you styling now. I heard a little about you gettin' money in New York. And, looking at you, the truth speaks for itself."

Kola took a sip from her beer. She didn't want to speak about her family. She'd come to Miami for a reason. She needed a new connect and hoped her cousin had the influence in Miami.

"When you got a minute, Nikki, I need to talk some business wit' you."

"You know a bitch is always about her paper. Shit, you see the way I live. A bitch always gotta keep her ends up."

Kola nodded.

"I know you smoke," Nikki said.

"What you blowing?"

Nikki went into her bedroom and came back out with a swelled Ziploc full with weed. She dangled it in front of Kola. "This that straight Miami 'island lady,' AKA 'ganja dwarf.' Get a bitch twisted in no time."

"I like that." Kola smiled. "Start rolling that shit."

Nikki grabbed two Backwoods from the kitchen countertop and started prepping to smoke, splitting open the two cigars on her costly glass coffee table, and disposing of the guts.

Kola kicked off her shoes and lounged around with her older cousin. Each had her own blunt to smoke. They talked, joked and laughed, and reminisced about growing up in Harlem.

"You gonna love it down here, Kola. I mean, niggas get money down here, and they ain't cheap wit' it like niggas in New York. When I take your ass to South Beach, you gonna see that muthafuckin street lined up with nothing but Bentleys, Ferraris, Beamers, Benzes, Porsches, and all types of shit. Shit, a bitch like me comes every time I walk down that bitch."

Kola laughed. "That's what I need to hear."

Nikki took a long pull from the burning weed. She then sat back in her chair and looked at her cousin. "So, you trying to get money down here?"

"Of course."

"My little cousin came up. So what's the story? What you working with?"

Kola took a pull from the weed and coughed slightly. It was some potent shit. "I fucked up in New York, Nikki; really fucked up."

"What you mean?"

"I got caught up wit' Cross. We started fuckin' around wit' each other, but it ended badly. He did me dirty, Nikki."

"You were fuckin' wit' Cross?"

Kola nodded. "Yeah, we linked up. He had my heart. But when I started doing transactions wit' his connect, Cross started hatin'. Eduardo had a thang for me, and I almost got caught up wit' him—but I didn't go there. Business was lovely until Cross did some foul shit and now things for me are teetering between life and death, Nikki. Cross has put my life in danger and never tapped a bitch on the shoulder to warn me." Kola fought back tears as the gravity of the situation spewed from out of her mouth. "Do you have any idea what will happen to me if Eduardo and his crew gets their hands on me?"

Kola went on to explain everything that had happened to her in the past months. She told Nikki about the war with Chico, flirting with Eduardo, the killings, the sex clubs, Two-Face, Candace, and Nichols' murder.

The only thing Kola left out was her feud with Apple. She knew Nikki had love for the both of them and would want to add her two cents.

"Damn, bitch! You were banking like that?"

"I was doin' it big, Nikki, and then fucked it up. I need to re-group and make things right again."

"Well, you came to the right city. It's money down here, Kola. It ain't no nickel-and-dime shit in Miami. You either come down here big with some long paper or an extreme hustle, or you don't come at all."

"I got a hundred and fifty thousand dollars and two bricks stashed in my trunk right now."

"What?"

"New York is too hot for me, so I need to lay low, get my shit right and find me a new connect down here."

"You have all that money stashed in your car right now?" Nikki asked, looking at her in awe.

"I wasn't leaving all that in New York. I came down here to grind and network. I know I came to the right bitch to help me get started back on my feet again."

"Shit, you definitely came to the right bitch. I got

peoples in this city, and with what you bringing to the table? Shit, we can definitely make it happen."

It was what Kola wanted to hear. She took another pull of the "island lady" and felt the euphoric high seeping through her system.

"Fuck that! Tonight, we party, Kola, and I'll introduce you to some peoples of mines. Shit, you and me, we can run this fuckin' city. I definitely got your back. You under my wing, and ain't shit gonna happen to you while you in Miami. We about to fuckin' make it happen."

It was a quarter to eleven when the cousins strutted out of the house and got into Nikki's silver convertible M3 BMW. They were dressed strikingly with Nikki still wearing her yellow, ruffled-hem mini dress, and Kola in a black satin dress that hugged her curves.

Nikki started the car, and the engine hummed to life. She smiled at Kola, threw the top back, and said, "In Miami, you always gotta do it with a convertible, so muthafuckas can see you stunt."

"I'll have mines soon," Kola said.

Nikki backed out of the yard and drove toward South Beach for a night of fun and business. She did eighty miles per hour on the Dolphin Expressway. She was a speed demon, racing from lane to lane, flying by cars. She made it into South Beach in no time. She cruised down Ocean Drive, where the girls became the core of attention for a few guys lingering on the drive.

Kola looked around in wonderment at the scene. Ocean Drive was a busy and illuminated street, and the epicenter of cool. It ran right along with the Atlantic Ocean, with sandy beaches on one side of the street and high-end trendy bars, cars, restaurants, and hotels on the other. The people dressed classy and looked posh, with the thugs, greasers, posers, pretty boys, hoochies, and gang-bangers mixing into the scenery. It was an assortment of characters.

Nikki stopped in front of a club called The Twelve Lounge on Ocean, where there was a long line to get inside and a crowd loitered outside. Kola and Nikki stepped out of the convertible, and Nikki passed her keys to a valet. Nikki then sashayed toward the front entrance with no intentions of waiting on the long line, Kola following behind.

She walked toward the two bouncers standing out front, slipped one of the men a C-note, and smiled. He unhooked the velvet rope, and she and Kola passed through and skated into the club.

They moved through the club, pushing their way past the crowded dance floor, and walked up the stairs onto an elevated section overlooking the crowd below. They entered the VIP section, where mostly thugs, ballers, and shot callers were popping bottles, smoking cigars, and flirting with the beautiful women surrounding them. Kola was used to that scene. It was the same look in a different city.

Nikki glanced around and walked toward a man seated in the middle of it all. He was clutching a bottle of Moët, laughing with his peers. The man was colossal, wearing a crisp Calvin Klein white tee and black Prada jeans—six feet of portly tattooed excess. His drooping pecs flexed, and dark shades covered his menacing eyes. He had a diamond grill and a long, diamond chain. His distinctive voice boomed throughout the room.

The alpha male of the mob looked up and noticed Nikki and her cousin. He smiled and shouted, "There go my baby right there," and motioned for Nikki to come over.

The mob around him parted and made way for Nikki to pass through with Kola. Nikki hugged him tight, indicating respect and love for him. She then introduced Kola to the man.

"Kola, this is OMG, and this is my cousin, Kola."

OMG stood up, took Kola's small hand into his massive grip, and gently shook it. He stared at her with a slight grin. "I see beautiful women runs in the family."

OMG towered over the ladies by half a foot. Kola was impressed by his stature. She gazed at him for a moment and then took a seat next to him, while Nikki took a seat on his other side.

OMG placed his arms around the cousins. "Whatever y'all ladies want, do you. We're celebrating tonight."

Kola poured herself a shot of Patrón and took it to the head.

OMG was impressed. Kola didn't have a hard time fitting in with the crowd. She was eye-candy for the fellows, but witty and ruthless like a thug. OMG instantly took a liking to her. He started to make conversation with her and admired her New York accent.

But Kola was scarce with information. Though Nikki had vouched for the man, she didn't know him, and she was hesitant to tell him about her world.

OMG was one of Miami's most notorious in the underworld. He moved drugs, guns, and even women. Miami was his personal playground, and his name was infamous, from the poor, gritty pork 'n' beans section to the glamorous streets of South Beach. Sometimes, he was all smiles and laughs, but he had a dark side, and many had suffered from his deathly anger.

Nikki used to dance naked at one of his clubs, networking with a string of high- end players and socializing with them. Over the years, she'd befriended OMG, even having a brief sexual affair with him, and then later on she went into business with him.

During her time in Miami, Nikki had gotten to know OMG's world—it was prosperous and dangerous at the same time. She was one of the few he trusted. She sold drugs for him, handled business dealings, turned tricks, and even killed a man for him. But she wanted to start her own franchise and break free from his organization, and she saw Kola as the perfect opportunity. Her little cousin was a blessing from above.

OMG was somewhat smitten by Kola. He would constantly eye her, admiring her plump backside, curvy figure and the way she handled herself among his thugs.

Nikki leaned into OMG's ear and said, "When you get the chance, baby, I need to talk to you. It's about some business I want to pull your coat to."

"Not tonight, Nikki, no business tonight. Tonight, I'm trying to get drunk and fuck my brains out. Besides, you know I don't fuckin' discuss business in public."

"I'm sorry, baby. So when is a good time?"

OMG downed a cup of Hennessy. "Tomorrow, at my place."

Nikki nodded. "I'll be there."

"Bring your cousin too."

"I plan to." Nikki smiled at Kola, then winked.

The ladies closed the night out in VIP with OMG and his goons.

The next day, Nikki navigated her BMW farther south of Miami, toward Coral Gables, an impressive Miami suburb and gated community with soaring palm trees and posh homes.

She pulled up to a 4,000-square-foot mini mansion that stood on one acre of land, its driveway encircling a white porcelain fountain. The place sat far away from the quiet Mercedes- and Jaguar-lined street, and it was enclosed by sprawling manicured lawns, towering palm trees, shrubberies, and plants. Its rear exterior had a wraparound deck and large glass-enclosed patio. The scenic backyard boasted an in-ground swimming pool, basketball court, three-car garage, and a breathtaking view of the lake from a distance. The homes on either side of OMG's exclusive residence were spread at a more than respectable distance.

Nikki and Kola stepped out of the car looking nice; both ladies in tight shorts, white Nikes, and casual tops. They walked toward the front entrance with confidence and rang the bell.

One of OMG's young goons answered the door. He smiled at the ladies and eyed them from head to toe. "Whaddup sexy and sexy!"

"Where's OMG?" Nikki asked, ignoring his statement.

"He's in the back, by the pool. But I'm sayin, what's good with yo' cousin, Nikki? She single?"

"You're not her type."

They moved past the young hoodlum and entered the house. Nikki had been there dozens of times and knew her way toward the pool.

Kola observed the décor inside and admired how OMG was living in Miami—countless skylights, volume ceiling, sunroom, and floor-to-ceiling windows.

The girls stepped into the backyard and saw OMG seated on the patio in the swanky lawn furniture. He was shirtless, exposing the many tattoos that decorated his upper torso. A long canary yellow diamond chain and a colossal diamond crown pendant dangled from his thick neck. OMG puffed on a cigar while seated next to one of his female admirers, who was scantily clad in a bikini.

"Ladies," he called out. "Y'all are definitely looking fine. Glad you could make it."

"It's always a pleasure stopping by, especially when it concerns getting money," Nikki said.

"So true."

OMG removed his shades and placed them on the table in front of him. He peered at Nikki, and then at Kola, his attention lasting longer on her long and well-defined legs.

Kola knew his look all too well. Her beauty was a gift and a curse.

"You know you're a beautiful woman, Kola."

"Thank you."

OMG turned his attention to the bikini-clad groupie and said, "Go inside for minute. I need to talk business out here."

The young girl looked reluctant. She stood up and brushed by Kola, cutting her eyes at her.

Kola only tossed her eyes toward the sky, knowing the young bitch was far from her level. She could easily wipe the floor with her, but she was there on business, not to get into a catfight.

"Have a seat, ladies," OMG said.

Kola and Nikki sat opposite him, a small table with a few drinks on it between them.

OMG sat back. "So what's this business you need to discuss with me, Nikki?"

"We've known each other for a long time, OMG. And you know, over the years, I made a lot of money for you."

OMG nodded. "Indeed."

"I got nothing but love and respect for you, but I'm not getting any younger. I need some stability right now, OMG. I need to branch off, start my own thang."

"In Miami?"

"I'm not trying to step on any toes out here. As you know, ATL is wide open right now since that big drug bust a month ago, along with a few areas of the South. And further north, there's Fort Lauderdale. That area is wide open for business. And my cousin Kola is from New York. She's doing it big up there. We just need a connect."

OMG stared at the girls for a moment. "It's expensive out there, Nikki."

"You know me, OMG. I got expensive taste, and only fuck with the best. So it makes sense we only want to fuck with you."

OMG took another pull of his cigar, pondering the proposal. He knew Nikki was well known and had business savvy. His only gripe was, he didn't know Kola at all. He was wise enough to know trouble could come in any form—even in a young, beautiful woman.

"I can vouch for you, Nikki, but your cousin, she's a new face. You know how I feel about a new face in my organization."

"She's cool peoples, OMG. I can vouch for her."

OMG's eyes rested on Kola, whose stare never veered from him.

"What? I need to prove myself to you or somethin'?"

"You could be police."

"OMG, you think I would be stupid enough to bring a cop in here? You think I'm a snitch?" Nikki asked.

"Like I said, I know you, but I don't know her," he repeated firmly.

"So what do I have to do to gain your trust in me?" Kola asked. "And I'm not fuckin' you."

OMG chuckled. "I get plenty of pussy, little girl. The slit between your legs is nothing new, or anything to bargain with. I would take it if I wanted to. But I do like your assertiveness, and your eyes sing a rough tune. I'll tell you what. You do a favor for me, and I'll return the favor."

"I'm listening," Kola said.

"I'm having a problem with an individual in this city . . . a lingering problem that's becoming a fuckin' thorn in my ass. I need that problem to disappear. You make it happen for me, and then we're in business. You have my word on that."

Kola replied, "Cool. Consider it done."

"A friend of mines will fill you in with all the details necessary," OMG added. "Now y'all can go."

The ladies stood up and walked toward the front entrance.

The young hooligan continued to flirt with Kola during their exit, persistent with his approach. They ignored him a second time.

Before Nikki drove off, she looked at Kola. "You sure you're ready to do this?"

"Look, Nikki, I didn't come down here to fuckin' fail, so if I gotta snatch a nigga's life so I can get this connect goin' and get paid, then so be it. It won't be the first life I took."

Nikki smiled. "We are *definitely* family."

Chapter 22

Chico arrived in Los Mochis in the late evening. It was a tiresome trip having to deal with Customs agents, jet lag, and the traffic. He landed at General Roberto Fierro Villalobos International Airport in the city of Chihuahua, Mexico. Los Mochis was hours away from the airport, and there weren't any commercial flights in that direction. The trip to Los Mochis had to be completed either by bus, car, or a single-engine plane.

Los Mochis was a coastal city in northern Sinaloa, Mexico with a population a little over two hundred thousand. The climate in the dusty, rural town was hot and dry, with the summers extremely hot, and the winters dry with almost no rainfall.

When Chico finally arrived at Los Mochis, he linked up with Dario. They quickly greeted each other and got into a dusty Ford pickup truck.

Dario drove Chico to the whorehouse where Apple had been staying. It was located on the outskirts of the town, near a back road and land stretching for miles.

The road that led into the shaky, one-story compound with its crumbling structure was nothing but dirt and rocks, and seemed to be never-ending. The windows to the compound were boarded up, and there were no signs around indicating that it was a brothel.

Chico glared at the place and had no words for a moment. When the truck stopped, he right away stepped out and walked toward the building. It was now empty with evidence of recent violence.

"She was here?" Chico asked.

"Yeah, to my understanding. A few whores say some men rushed inside, killed a few of Shaun's men, and took her during the night."

"Who the fuck took her?"

"We're trying to find out now."

"I need to fuckin' find her," Chico stated, exasperated.

Dario nodded. He didn't understand what made Apple, a whore in his eyes, so important to Chico. But he wasn't paid to question Chico's motives. He was paid to kill or track people down.

Chico walked closer to the place. He entered the structure and started to look around. The smell was overwhelming. The horrid conditions inside made him wonder about Apple's treatment. He knew it had to be hell on earth. He explored everywhere, going from room to room, looking at the makeshift showers, dirty toilets, and filthy rooms that lined the narrow hallway. Dirty, stained mattresses lay across bug-ridden floors, and used condoms were scattered about next to tainted articles of women's clothing.

Dario entered the room where Chico stood.

"I don't know how people can live like this," Dario said. "Inhumane. And they call me an animal because I kill people. But to keep them alive and living like this . . . Shit, I'd rather be dead."

"Yo, Dario, you wanna shut the fuck up? I don't need your opinion right now."

Dario shrugged. He stepped out of the dilapidated bedroom and gave Chico a moment to himself.

Chico looked around the room, trying to find some evidence of Apple's existence in the place. He spent a short moment in the room. When he exited, Dario was in the hallway waiting.

"What you wanna do now?" Dario asked.

"Continue looking." Chico walked out the compound feeling disgusted and angry. The men got back into the truck and sped away from the horrid brothel.

As they sped toward the town, Chico said to Dario, "When we find Apple, I want you to find this Shaun muthafucka, and before you kill him, make that nigga suffer for hours. And I want his torture videotaped. I think it'll be something Apple would like to have as a memento. I'll pay you double for that shit."

Dario nodded. "You got it. It's your money."

That night, the men checked into the El Dorado motel. The rooms were simply decorated with a full bed, a shaky table, a few chairs, and a retro color TV.

Chico wasn't in the mood to watch TV. He stared out

the window and took in the town, thinking heavily. He now remembered Shaun, Memo's brother.

Dante had taken Memo out with a shotgun. Blew his head right off. Then they had thrown his sister Ayesha off the project rooftop. Dante and Chico had nearly wiped out Shaun's family in a brutal way. Chico figured kidnapping and brutalizing Apple was only payback. He was ready to hunt the last brother down and finish it.

Early the next morning, Chico and Dario were out on the road again, trying to find leads to Apple's whereabouts. They scoured the town of Los Mochis and Ahome, hitting up the local bars, motels, and underground establishments. Chico was willing to pay money for information on Shaun and "the whore with the burned face", as the men in town described her.

"*Sí*, I've seen her around, and then I haven't," one of the drunken locals said to Chico. "She pretty and ugly at the same time. Too bad though, that American chocha was some of the best."

It angered Chico how recklessly the man talked about Apple to his face. He glared at the drunken patron and clenched his fists.

The man went on, "And when she was pregnant, *sí*, the pussy was worth every peso I earned."

Immediately, Chico struck the drunk in the jaw, knocking him back into a few chairs. He stumbled and looked shocked.

Dario ran over to control the scene. He grabbed Chico and snatched him out of the bar.

"C'mon, we still got places to look into," Dario said. "I have a lead."

Chico walked away and got into the truck. When no one was looking, he shed a few tears but wiped them away as fast as they appeared. He couldn't look weak, and he couldn't look desperate.

He'd left a profitable drug organization in Harlem to come to Mexico to look for Apple. It was an outrageous thing to do for a man in his position. He'd told Blythe and others that he was leaving town for a few weeks to take care of business, but he didn't elaborate further. Chico knew that if his peers and Blythe found out that he'd planned on scouring Mexico to find an ex-girlfriend— one who'd become a whore—his reputation would be tarnished forever.

The following week, the men went searching through small towns like La Florida, Bachoco, Ohuira, and El Capulí, but they came up empty. Chico was willing to pay handsomely for any viable information, but he kept getting the same results or excuses from the locals.

"My friend, you just missed her, but I know where she *might* be."

It turned into a wild goose chase. Two weeks had passed, and they weren't any closer to finding Apple since the day he'd arrived. It was a tiresome search.

Chico was also aware that he was in the deadly cartel's

domain, and after what he had done to Two-Face, the last thing he needed was to run into them. Though he'd tried to pin Two-Face's death on Cross and Kola, Roman, might want to dead Chico just on GP.

✳

The men arrived in a town called Guamúchil, an ancient and pastoral town about a hundred miles south of Los Mochis. They walked into a local bar crowded with customers.

Chico quickly scanned the place, taking in the mixed crowd of elderly and young downing tequila like it was water. Chico didn't know any Spanish, but Dario was fluent in the language and was his interpreter in the country.

The duo immediately stood out, catching stares and fleeting looks from most people inside. Chico headed farther into the bar. He studied faces and remained cautious. He pulled out Apple's picture and began working the bubbly crowd inside. Dario was right behind him, .38 snug in his waist to ward off any possible trouble.

Chico approached the first individual by the bar. He raised the picture for the man to see, and Dario spoke for him.

"*¿Has visto a esta chica?*" Dario asked the man, asking if he had seen this woman around.

The man studied the picture for a moment and shook his head.

Chico moved on to the next individual and the next.

He received a collection of "no's" and confused stares from many of the locals. It frustrated him. He assumed that they were all lying, probably covering up for someone. He worked the bar for an hour, Dario following suit.

It was getting late, and the bar began thinning out. Only a few stragglers lingered behind, drinking their sorrows and paychecks away in the little bar.

Chico walked over to a short, round, cheery-looking man. He placed the picture in the man's face and asked in English, "You ever saw this girl around?"

"*Sí*," he answered.

"You said yes?" Chico questioned. "You speak English?"

"*Sí, amigo*, I know her."

Chico became alert. "From where?"

"She's a whore from my old town."

"I know that. But have you seen her recently?"

"No, not since I came here. But I have seen one of the other whores from there working here," he said.

"Where at?"

"At a brothel a mile from here, *amigo*. Her name is Alba."

It was news that Chico had been waiting for. He had gotten the address from his informer, and he and Dario rushed to the location.

A half hour later, they parked in front of a weathered two-story teal building with bars around the windows and an iron gate up at the front entrance. Chico knew it was the place the man had told him about.

They got out and proceeded into the building. There was no security. When they entered the building, there were over a dozen whores around.

Chico instantly began searching for Apple, hoping she was one of the girls in the place. The men went from room to room, sometimes interrupting a sex act of some kind, startling the whore and her trick.

The madam approached Chico and Dario and asked, "*¿Puedo ayudarte?*"

Dario looked at Chico and translated. "She's asking if we need help."

"Yeah, tell her we're looking for a girl." Chico showed her Apple's picture.

The madam looked at the picture and shook her head. "*No sé quién es,*" she replied.

"What?"

"She hasn't seen her," Dario explained.

"Fuck that! We close. I can feel it. Alba, ask about Alba," Chico said.

Dario began asking about Alba.

The madam knew the name but was leery about letting them know which girl it was.

Dario lifted his shirt to reveal the pistol tucked in his jeans, to give her some incentive.

Her eyes widened.

Dario calmly asked again in Spanish for Alba. The madam reluctantly pointed to a petite, young girl seated on the couch in the next room. "*No duele le,*" the madam stated, saying, "don't hurt her."

Dario assured the madam that they were only there to talk.

Chico and Dario walked over to Alba, who was dressed in a yellow sundress and barefoot. She became confused. She looked up at the men with frightened eyes.

"You speak English?" Chico asked.

She shook her head, so Dario took over. He showed her a picture of Apple, and the recognition immediately showed on her face.

She uttered, "Apple!"

"You know her?" Chico asked.

"*Sí.*"

"Where is she?" Chico asked, and Dario quickly translated.

Alba had no idea of Apple's recent whereabouts. She told Dario about the shootout and kidnapping at the old place in Los Mochis. She described the men to him as American and black. She then went on to give critical information about Shaun, telling them that he might be farther south in Culiacán, a city in northwestern Mexico, and the largest city and capital of the state of Sinaloa. She also told them that Apple always knew that '*Chico*' would come to rescue her. That last line nearly broke his heart in two.

They left for Culiacán the following hour. They were in the town a few hours later, pursuing Shaun and Apple.

Dario and Chico searched throughout the city with

their routine, but to no avail.

The third week was exhausting. Until, with enough cash spread throughout the city, Chico was led to an important acquaintance of Shaun's. A street prostitute pointed them in the direction of Rivera, one of Shaun's closest friends. He was a regular at a local bar in the rough, seedy section of town. The prostitute gave the two men a full description of Rivera, describing him as tall and lean with long braids, and having a birthmark on his right cheek.

They found Rivera in a bar called Rio Grails, a quaint bar with cheap drinks, a tough crowd, and shady activity. When Chico and Dario walked in, the interest was on them so hard, Dario kept his pistol close, alert to his surroundings.

Rivera was seated at the bar with a prostitute.

Both men approached Rivera and swiftly flanked him, one on either side.

"You Rivera, right?" Chico asked.

Rivera turned and glared at Chico then at Dario. "What the fuck y'all niggas want?"

"We lookin' for a Shaun, and Apple," Chico told him. "You probably know her, a young American girl wit' a disfiguring burn across her face. We know you seen them both recently. Just tell us where, and make it easy on yourself."

"Don't know who you talkin' about. I'm busy right now." Rivera turned his back to Chico. "Get the fuck outta here!"

Chico glanced at Dario.

Dario nodded and slowly removed the pistol from his waistband. He gripped it by its handle and watched Rivera ignore them as he continued to chat with the short, big-breasted prostitute.

Chico stepped closer to Rivera. He hooked his eyes into him, tightened his fist, and said, "I'm gonna ask you again—Shaun or Apple, have you seen either one of them?"

Rivera shouted, "Nigga, fuck—"

The blow came fast, like a strike of lightning, across the back of his head from the pistol in Dario's hand.

As Rivera wailed and stumbled from the bar, Dario hit him again in the same spot, and he dropped to the floor.

The regulars looked on, but no one intervened. The violence was a normal thing to them. The men and women around knew to mind their business.

Dario dragged Rivera outside unconscious. They placed him into the back of the pickup truck and sped away. Dario drove away from the city, into the night, en route to the countryside and then pulled off Route 15 going south. He drove for forty minutes.

Rivera was waking up when they stopped.

Dario removed him roughly from the truck and held him at gunpoint.

"What the fuck is this? You know who I am?" Rivera shouted madly. "This is my fuckin' town. You two won't make it a mile from this city alive when I get fuckin' done wit' y'all!"

The men were unmoved by his threatening rants. Rivera's wrists were bound, and he was placed on his knees against the rocks and dirt under a blanket of vast stars above, and nothing but miles of grassland around.

Chico stood over Rivera, determined to get the truth from him. "We gonna ask you this one more time—Apple or Shaun, where are they?" he asked coolly.

"Fuck you!" Rivera spat. "I ain't tellin' you shit!"

Dario scowled. He pressed the barrel of the pistol to Rivera's forehead and cocked back the hammer.

"You think this shit scares me? Do it, muthafucka! *¡Ir a joder gilipollas de tu mamá!*" he shouted.

Dario whacked him across the face with the pistol.

Rivera began to bleed, but he was still defiant. He glared up at his captors. "Yeah, you lookin' for that burnt bitch, I remember her. Yeah, we made some good money off that piece of trashy pussy. She was fuckin' every day and night. We had that pussy bleeding and shit. *¡Puta perra!*"

Chico was angry. "These muthafuckin' Mexicans! Just tell me where she's at!"

"Fuck you!"

Chico looked at Dario and nodded. Dario understood the signal. They weren't getting anywhere with Rivera. He had become a dead end. It was painful.

Rivera continued to curse and taunt Dario to pull the trigger.

Pop! Pop! Pop!

Dario put three into Rivera's head, leaving him sprawled out on the ground.

Looking at Rivera's dead body made Chico even angrier. He was his last hope in finding Apple.

"What now, Chico?" Dario asked.

Chico didn't know. He had no more resources, and he had been away from home and his business for too long. He didn't want to give up on his search, but reluctantly, he had to fly back home to take care of business. To keep looking was affecting his mental state. The guilt, the grief, was overwhelming. He couldn't listen to another muthafucka tell him how they'd fucked Apple, or call her a beast or a monster. It was all too much for him.

"We tried, Chico. If you want me to keep on looking, I can. But it will cost," Dario said.

Chico thought long and hard about it. "Nah, I'm done looking. Fuck it! She's ghost to me as of right now."

Chapter 23

Apple awoke slowly from her hazy dream, stirring and turning under a dimmed light. She started to regain consciousness. The room was quiet and still, except for the soft hum of a fan blowing. She opened her eyes and saw that she was someplace different—in a room, lying on a bed.

The bedroom was comfortable and modest. The bed was soft like clouds. She wasn't in hell anymore. She started to wonder where she was. The filth from the whorehouse had been washed away from her. The clothes that she had on were different. Someone had taken the time to place her in a clean cotton nightgown.

Apple remembered her nightmare. There was shooting and screaming. It felt like Armageddon. And then she felt herself floating in mid-air—like the wind or the hands of God had reached down and grabbed her soul.

Am I still dreaming? She looked around the room. It was clean.

Apple placed her feet on the engineered wood floor and stood up. She had strength in her body. She didn't feel sick or tired. *Was I eating?* she asked herself.

She walked toward the windows to look outside, curious about her location. She pulled back the blinds and gazed outside. The humongous yard she looked out at was grassy and stretched for acres. The trees were tall and plentiful with leaves, and the bright sun beamed across the land for miles.

"Is this heaven?" she asked herself.

She turned from the window and continued inspecting the room. There weren't any electronic items in the room, only the bare necessities. There was fruit in a bowl placed on a table, a few books on shelves, and the walls were bare of pictures or posters. There was a dresser and mirror set near the window.

Apple thought, *If it's heaven, then my wounds would heal.* She walked over to the mirror and stared at her reflection.

Nothing had changed—Her disfigured face was still there as a reminder of the horrors from her past. She touched her wounds and sighed.

Apple wondered if she was still in Mexico. There weren't any clocks or calendars in the room, so she had no idea what day or time it was.

She began to think about Chico. She smiled and said, "He came for me. He found me..." It was the only rational reason as to why she was suddenly free from her prison.

Apple had a quick flashback of the event. She briefly

remembered the masked men, and heard the violence, but one of those men was her savior.

She turned in the direction of the door when she heard someone entering. She smiled, walked toward the door, ready to jump into her man's arms and kiss him lovingly.

The bedroom door came open, and a man appeared in the doorway.

"Chico," she called out.

Apple fastened her eyes on the man entering the room. She froze. She couldn't believe her eyes. It had to be a dream. It couldn't be him.

"I see you're awake," he said.

"How is this even possible?"

"You don't look happy to see me."

"How did you find me?" Apple asked.

"I have my ways."

Fear crept up Apple's spine. She didn't know if he was a friend or foe. She slightly backed away from him and looked around the room, trying to find an object to grab in case she needed to defend herself.

He moved closer. He kept his eyes on her. He didn't smile, but looked relaxed and non-threatening to Apple.

"Why did you bring me here? For revenge, huh?"

Apple stared at his chiseled physique. He was shirtless and wearing relaxed jeans with sneakers. He looked the same, but his body had improved greatly. He had been working out. She locked eyes with him as he approached closer.

"I didn't bring you here to hurt you, Apple. I knew you needed help," he said.

"I don't need your help," she spat.

"If it wasn't for me, then you would still be turning tricks at that godforsaken place. You needed rescuing, Apple. And I needed to shut that place down. I knew you were dying in there, and I couldn't let that happen."

"Why?"

"Why not? We go way back, and I still love you."

"After what I did to you?"

"I forgive you. What happened between us was a long time ago. It's forgotten. I'm willing to let bygones be bygones and start something fresh. Harlem was a different life for me. But, here, I've become a different person; a better person."

Apple stared at him. She was wary about getting closer to him. His eyes showed a natural calm, a look she hadn't seen in a long time—since they were young.

She stood against the wall, nowhere to run, her heart racing like a thoroughbred's on a racetrack.

He lifted his hand to her face and touched her wound gently.

"Karma's a bitch, right. I'm ugly to you now, huh?" Apple sadly stated.

"No, you're still beautiful, like how I remembered you."

He began caressing her wound. They locked eyes. His gaze still showed the love he had for her.

Apple was confused.

"I'm the only one that came looking for you, Apple," Guy Tony said. "Not Chico, not your mother, sister, but me. And I found you because I still care. Despite what happened with us, I still love you."

It was a strange situation and outcome for Apple. The one man she'd manipulated and even tried to have killed had saved her from prison and probably death. She didn't know what Guy Tony's true motives were, but his actions and eyes said to her that he was sincere. She still didn't know how he'd found her.

"Where are we?" she asked.

"Texas."

"Texas?" Apple was befuddled. "How did you get me across the border?"

"Like I said, I have my ways. But you're back in the States now."

"What about Harlem?"

"We can let that be a memory for us. There's nothing for me in Harlem anymore. My life is here now," Guy Tony told her.

Apple was indecisive about living in Texas, but she was grateful on so many levels that Guy Tony came to her rescue. He looked at her and pressed his lips against hers. Apple didn't resist him.

They kissed for a moment, and Apple gradually began to trust him. Apple all of a sudden pulled herself from Guy Tony's passionate kiss. She looked at him.

"What's wrong?"

"Is he dead?" she asked.

"Who?"

"That bastard Shaun."

"Nah, he wasn't in the building when we came through, only his thugs," Guy Tony informed her. "He can't hurt you anymore. You're under my protection now. But I got peoples looking for him. He shows his face anywhere, and it will be the last time."

Apple was ready to return to Harlem when the opportunity came. She would stay in Texas for a moment to regain her sanity and well being, but she had too much unfinished business back in New York. She wasn't ready to forgive or forget what had happened to her in Harlem and in Mexico. The horrors she suffered in Mexico were unforgettable, and the pain and anguish she endured lingered in her mind like a growing cancer.

Kola, Shaun, Chico, and Cross had all betrayed Apple or done her harm. She felt it wasn't right to let them live on with their lives or completely forget about them. Her objective was to find each and every last one of them and make them pay for their sins against her.

Guy Tony was her sudden reassurance. He had come up in Texas with his deadly gun-for-hire operation—becoming an assassin—and also shipping guns across the border for certain drug cartels in Mexico. Since they'd last seen each other, he went from being someone's errand boy and flunky to a major heavyweight in Dallas, and some Mexican towns.

Apple was impressed with his sudden come-up. She figured being with Guy Tony again would have certain advantages. It was time for her to get back on her feet and regain what she once had. It was time for her to become that bitch again. It was war, and her foes had created a beast inside of her.

Each night she made love to Guy Tony she looked into his eyes as he professed his undying love for her and promised he would help her get revenge against all those who hurt and betrayed her, just as he had done with Supreme. He was convincing, and Apple's trust in him grew, day by day.

Chapter 24

Kola was getting to know the city very well. She started to remember places and people. It didn't take her long to catch on, knowing the hot spots and the city's elite. Miami was an exotic place to live, and Kola was falling in love with the city.

Kola sat in her Audi parked on Washington Avenue and watched Sao, a handsome, clean-cut Cuban, step out of his car on the busy avenue and walk into the upscale café. She had been following him for a week, trying to memorize his routine, but it was difficult. Sao was spontaneous and skillful with the way he moved. He switched cars often, and his entourage was always full of pistol-packing Cuban thugs.

He drove around Miami in a Bentley coupe, a red Ferrari 458, a Benz, and a Porsche Cayenne, always in a pair of shades. His bling was subtle, nothing extensive—a diamond ring and a Rolex. A club-hopper in his early thirties, he frequented three spots in South Beach: News Café on Ocean Drive; South Dreams on Ocean Boulevard;

and The Velvet Spot.

Kola didn't know why OMG wanted Sao dead, but she was determined to make it happen. OMG didn't care if the deed was clean or messy; he just wanted it done. He wanted to see how hardcore Kola was and was fanning her out, in case she was an undercover.

Killing was nothing new to Kola. The bodies piling up in Harlem between her and her crew was starting to look like a war memorial. She was ready to show OMG how gritty a bitch from Harlem could get to secure a Miami connect. She couldn't go back to New York without one, and OMG was a powerful force that she needed behind her. The streets were buzzing about how potent his supply was.

Kola sat outside the café watching everything and waiting, while the Miami sun scorched the city like it was giving it a bear hug.

She thought about home as she waited. She missed Harlem. She missed Candace and her crew. She briefly thought about her relationship with Cross. They were the Bonnie and Clyde in the game. They had everything on lock, until it got fucked up. She had gotten word that Cross was looking at a mandatory twenty-five years if convicted. She didn't care at all. It was his problem. Now it was her time to reign supreme over everything. With Edge dead, Cross incarcerated, and Apple missing, the only real threats Kola had to worry about came from Eduardo and Chico.

Kola waited for an hour outside the café before Sao

strutted out talking on his cell phone, flanked by an armed thug. She watched him get into his pearl-white Bentley continental GT and pull off. She followed behind him, making sure she wasn't obvious. Sao drove to the legendary oceanfront Eden Roc Hotel on the Collins Avenue strip.

Sao pulled up to the valet parking, got out, and handed the valet his keys. Soon after, Kola did the same. She hurried behind him into the hotel and followed him into the hotel's great room bar, a circular Venetian-style bar surrounded by gorgeous Brazilian rosewood columns. It was nestled just beneath the infinity edge pools, with an incomparable panoramic view of the Atlantic Ocean through the canopy of a rushing waterfall.

But Kola didn't have time to admire the spectacle. She kept a close eye on Sao as he took a seat in one of the chairs in the lounge and ordered a drink from a passing waitress.

Kola needed to get Sao's attention, so she strutted by him in her white cowl-neck cocktail dress. Kola moved casually, like she belonged among the elite with her golden smile and stunning beauty.

Sao looked up from the paper he was reading and gazed at her, his eyes following her to the bar. He smiled and uttered, "Nice."

Kola glanced over her shoulder and caught him staring at her near-perfect bubble in the dress. She took a seat at the bar and ordered a drink.

A short moment later, she heard him say, "Can I buy you a drink, beautiful?" coming from over her shoulder.

She turned to see Sao smiling, showing his row of pearly-white teeth and smelling nice from the cologne he wore.

Kola responded with, "I like to pay for my own."

"You're beautiful, you know that?"

Kola smiled. "Thanks."

"And what's your name?"

"Let me have yours."

"Sao."

"Nice name," Kola said.

"I'm a nice guy, but I'm yet to know your name."

"Candace," she lied.

"The name fits you well."

Kola chuckled.

The bartender set Kola's drink in front of her. When she attempted to pay for it, Sao intervened. He handed the bartender a fifty-dollar bill, ordered himself a drink, and told him to keep the change.

"You're a baller, huh."

"I'm a businessman. A very wealthy businessman," he replied smugly.

Kola looked him up and down, taking in his sharp attire—the black slacks, crisp collared shirt, and Ferragamo shoes. Sao had green eyes, smooth olive skin, and a warm smile. He oozed sex appeal, and his demeanor reminded her of Eduardo somewhat. The way he moved and talked, his style, it was like he was cut from the same cloth as Eduardo. Kola was attracted to him, but she had to remind herself that she couldn't get caught up with his smooth talking.

She and Sao spent an hour talking by the bar. He was fascinated by her beauty and intelligence. He invited her to a party later that night and promised her VIP status and more of his time. Kola feigned reluctance and accepted the invitation.

※

The Miami nightlife was magical. The streets lit up in a rainbow of colors that extended for blocks. Lavish cars flooded Collins Avenue, Ocean Boulevard, and Washington Avenue, their sound systems blaring. The women were dressed in short skirts, tight dresses, revealing tops, and skintight jeans as they strutted up and down South Beach in groups, the men lusting after them like savages.

Kola and Nikki cruised through South Beach in the jazzy convertible and drew looks from the men and women on the strip. They were on their way to one of Sao's nightclubs on the strip, so they'd made sure to look their best. Nikki was in an off-shoulder mini dress, and Kola in a sexy, tight-fitting black dress.

"You got this, Kola? 'Cuz you can't fuck it up," Nikki said. "We need this with OMG."

"I got this muthafucka, Nikki. He's on me hard. You should have seen the way he was lookin' at me today. I damn near had the nigga's eyes falling out of his head."

Nikki was well aware of Sao's reputation in Miami. He was charismatic, witty, and fun to be around if he liked you, but his dark side was deadly. He was a recurring headache for OMG, and the two feuded over everything from drugs, to business, to women. For months, the two men had kept a respectable distance from each other and seemed to be at peace. That was, until Sao broke the treaty by having his crew rob one of OMG's stash houses.

"This shit can't connect back to us, Kola. If it does, we're fucking dead. Sao has influences every gotdamn where. He has power in this city. And he's not stupid. I guarantee that he's already had you checked out."

"I got this under control."

"You better, if you ever wanna see New York again."

Kola was calm. She knew how to get close to men like Sao. She'd done it before. A sniff of pussy and beauty always attracted powerful men like Sao, which gave Kola the open window. Candace had taught her the art of killing, showing her some unconventional methods of taking life. Kola learned from her top enforcer that there were effective ways besides using a gun, to bring down a man.

Nikki pulled up to Club Versus on Ocean Drive, where hordes of people were standing outside the two-story megaclub. There was tons of eye candy outside—male and female. The ladies got out of the convertible and strutted toward the front entrance, where two tall men clad in tight-fitting black shirts stood.

They were very strict at the door and took no nonsense from anyone. Men and women were begging to get inside, but the stone-faced security ignored them like they were insects underneath their shoes. If you weren't on the list of VIPs or doing bottle service, which was a minimum of $1,200, then there wasn't a chance of entry.

They walked up to the security, and one of the men quickly asked, "Y'all on the list?"

"Yeah, I'm with Sao's party. Candace, party of two," Kola said.

The man quickly scanned for her name. He was strictly professional. He didn't attempt to flirt with the ladies or give them a second look. He nodded his approval when he saw the name on his list. "Y'all good to go," he said, unlatching the velvet rope and stepping to the side to allow the ladies entry into the club.

Kola and Nikki marched inside Versus. The music was loud, and it was packed with revelers. The club had a 1,200-person capacity and it was almost there. Versus boasted 40-foot ceilings, Brazilian walnut floors, and a ground-floor smoking lounge with fountains.

The ladies headed toward the VIP area, where Sao was seated among other men and women.

When he noticed Kola approaching, he stood up and smiled. "I'm glad you could make it." Sao greeted Kola with a kiss to her cheek and a hug.

"This is my cousin Danielle," Kola lied.

Sao greeted Nikki, aka Danielle, with the same kiss to the cheek and a hug. The ladies then sat amongst Sao's VIP guests and sipped champagne and mingled. Sao played Kola closely. He placed his hand against her thigh, and Kola smiled and played along, waiting for the right moment to strike.

The drinks kept flowing, and Sao and his people joked and acted like they ruled the world. It was his club, so he had the authority to do whatever he wanted. He boasted about his money and power to Kola, but she was far from impressed. She had money and power too.

Hours later, everyone in Sao's entourage was either drunk or tipsy. A few of Sao's goons were watching his every move and that of those around him.

Kola and Sao hit it off instantly, and he was willing to take her to his home, but Kola didn't want to prolong the inevitable. The deed had to be done right away and proficiently. Nikki looked at Kola and read her look.

The area where they were seated was overcrowded. Kola saw her opening. She subtly slipped her hand into her purse and removed a small capsule, which she hid in the palm of her hand, while conversing with Sao and a few other ladies. Just then, she felt Sao's hand move up her legs.

Kola was ready to poison his drink with cyanide. It was one of the alternatives to guns that Candace had taught her; how to slip poison into someone's drink, food, or onto their skin. Candace was a master at it. When they needed someone killed without suspicion, she used a small dose of cyanide. The chemical would essentially kill its victim from asphyxiation. It was quick and also hard to detect in a toxicology test.

One drop of the odorless poison into Sao's drink was all Kola needed to do the job. Once the poison took effect, it would appear he was having a stroke or wasn't able to breathe.

Kola felt Sao's hand sliding between her legs.

He smiled when he realized she had no panties on. He whispered in her ear, "You feel like butter below."

Kola glanced at Nikki and noticed her flirting with one of Sao's goons. She created a slight distraction by spilling her drink, and when everyone's eyes were averted, she swiftly slipped the cyanide into Sao's drink. She couldn't look desperate for him to take a sip, so she just had to wait for the moment. Which could be soon or never.

Kola asked for another drink, and the waitress hurried to fill her order. She nervously watched Sao's drink sit there half-filled and untouched. The waitress arrived with Kola's new drink, and she took it from her hand and started to take sips.

Sao took a break from fondling Kola and picked up his Grey Goose. He sat back with his arm around Kola and said, "Life is good."

"It is," Kola replied.

Sao started to down his drink, and Kola smiled inwardly. She finished her drink along with him and tried to act natural. She just had to wait for the poison to take effect.

Things seemed normal for a moment, but suddenly Sao pushed himself away from Kola and grasped at his neck. "I don't feel well," he muttered.

Sao stood up in a panic, and his men rushed to his aid. He was struggling to breathe; gasping for air. He collapsed against the table, twitching violently, his eyes rolling into the back of his head.

"What's wrong with him?" one of his men shouted.

Sao was having convulsions and vomiting.

A crowd started to gather around Sao, and the ladies started to panic, moving away from the troubling scene. Nikki and Kola were among the worried ladies and carried the same expression of concern.

By the time the EMTs rushed into the club fifteen minutes later, Sao was already dead, sprawled out across the floor.

Sao's men were furious. They glared around the room with their guns drawn, looking for an enemy, but they were only among the lovely ladies and themselves. They had no idea what to do. Some assumed foul play, while others thought it was a stroke or a heart attack.

Kola appeared emotional and started to shed tears. It was Oscar-worthy.

Nikki pretended to console her cousin. "Candace, just calm down. Calm down."

"I can't. I need some air. I need some fuckin' air," she spat. "I can't look at him!"

Nikki escorted her cousin outside, and a few other ladies followed, exiting the club for air and removing themselves from the chaotic scene.

Nikki and Kola exited club Versus playing the role of two distraught women who had seen a friend die. They didn't want to leave too quickly and raise suspicion, so they lingered outside, watching the cops rush inside the club to try to maintain order.

The ladies stayed around for an hour and gave their statement to detectives. When the coroner brought out Sao's body in a body bag on a gurney, Kola quickly turned her head away, feigning weakness. The detective she spoke to assured her that she would be OK, and then the girls left.

When they got a few blocks from the scene, they both smiled.

Nikki looked at Kola and exclaimed, "Oh my God! You are the fuckin' bitch, Kola! I can't believe we actually pulled that shit off!"

Nikki pulled out her cell phone and dialed OMG's number. It rang three times before he picked up.

"Speak, Nikki," he said.

"We good on that," she informed him. "We gonna be some happy bitches."

"Y'all are, huh? I see your cousin is about her business. I like that. Tell her to come see me tomorrow morning and we'll talk."

"Cool."

"Good work, though."

Nikki hung up, excited. She looked at Kola. "He wants us to come by tomorrow. We are in there."

Kola smiled, and the two raced home feeling a sense of accomplishment.

Epilogue

The Hamptons area of Long Island, with its pristine waterfront homes, picturesque beaches, and trendy shops and restaurants is one of the most prestigious places in all of New York. Celebrities and businessmen own million-dollar homes in the area. Just seventy miles from Manhattan, it is a legendary place for parties and events. Chico thought it was the perfect place to throw an extravagant all-white birthday party for Blythe.

Apple had become a memory to him, and he needed to focus on his future and his woman. Too much time, money, and energy was spent in Mexico searching for a ghost. And, reluctantly, he'd moved on from that chapter of his life.

The balmy evening was filled with joy and laughter as dozens of guests made their way into the secluded estate sitting on acres of land with a phenomenal view of the beach. Chico had spared no expense. It'd cost a fortune to rent the place, but it was well worth it. The entrance was decorated with a series of stylish Balinese statues along the wall, and a wooden gate led to the reception area. The ground floor was a marvelous sight with its alluring dining area and large bar. In the back of the estate sat a huge in-ground pool set amid the minimalist garden, along with a pool deck and a Balinese bale to relax on.

Blythe was at first overwhelmed by the beauty and size of the estate, which made the Great Neck home that Chico had bought for her look like a cottage.

Security for the event was tight, and guards were situated all around the property, while the waiters and waitress glided around the affair in their white tuxedos, carrying large silver platters of hors d'oeuvres.

Blythe was delighted. It was the best birthday she'd ever had. She looked stunning in her white open-back, rhinestone-studded coat with a low-cut front, matching rhinestone-studded boy shorts, and a pair of white stilettos. She was the most eye-catching woman in the place.

Chico wore a white three-button, single-breasted Perry Ellis tuxedo. He was the epitome of sharp, sporting a white gold, diamond Rolex and a diamond pinky ring. He stood in the distance watching his woman work the crowd.

Business was good for Chico, and life was even better. He had the streets on lockdown, and he had defeated his enemies. Cross was incarcerated, Edge was dead, and Kola had been MIA for a few weeks. Two-Face was put down, and any suspicion about him was diverted from his organization, and his deal with the Mexicans still stood. The murder of both Two-Face and Edge remained unsolved, and the detectives didn't have any new leads.

Jason stood tall in a white tuxedo similar to Chico's, wineglass in his hand. He looked over at his date, Ariel, who stood by the pool. She was Brazilian and had the looks and body of a movie star.

"You outdid yourself with this event," he told Chico.

"I'm glad you could make it, Jason."

"I couldn't miss this. This is a beautiful estate. I might have to invest in a home in the Hamptons myself."

"Yeah, we might need to." Chico smiled.

"But, on a side note, what's this I hear about you going to Mexico? Was it business or pleasure out there?"

Chico was reluctant to answer him. He didn't want him to know that he went looking for Apple. Jason would have called it a foolish move. Chico looked at Jason and said, "I just needed to take care of somethin'. That's all."

"You sure?" Jason said. "Because I hear different."

"You hear different from who?"

"Just stay on track with business, Chico. You don't need any distractions. We're making money, and plenty of it. Look around you. Years ago, did you ever think this would be us in the Hamptons mingling with celebrities and the elite? Shit, look at our women. Such fine creatures for us to enjoy. You don't want to end up like Cross. He's a stupid muthafucka. You keep washing your money long enough, and you won't have to hide a damn thing from the government anymore, because every piece of income will be legitimate.

"So, a foolish trip to Mexico with a hired gun only attracts unwanted attention to you, and then it will trickle down to me. I don't need the unwanted attention, Chico. I came too far to fall, and so did you."

Jason, a career criminal, had stayed off the feds' radar for a long time. He had become the new "Teflon Don."

The two men moved farther away from the crowd, where they had a little more privacy.

Jason took a sip of wine. "Any heat from Two-Face peoples?"

"Nah, nothing yet," Chico said. "And my cop on the inside says the investigation turned cold."

"Cool. I like to hear that. But you stay out of the limelight. We're where we want to be right now, on top and in control of things. There's no need for the boat to rock. That means let the past be the past. So you need to insulate yourself from that street shit, and the daily activity, and become more business-minded. You have soldiers for problems."

Chico nodded.

Jason continued to advise him on a few things, and then the two went to be with their ladies.

It was midnight now, and the party was in full swing. The DJ was playing hip-hop, that had the crowd moving its feet, and the food and liquor were flowing.

Chico was hugged up against Blythe, kissing her lovingly and wishing her a happy birthday in her ear. She smiled, eating up his affection and enjoying her birthday to the fullest. It was her time to shine and she loved her man greatly.

"After this, you and me gonna celebrate your birthday the right way, alone in one of these rooms and only in our birthday suits," Chico said, making her blush.

She smiled. "Oh, really?"

"Ya know it."

As the two stood by the pool, Chico continued to hold her in his arms, a side of him that people rarely saw. He could be caring and affectionate when he wanted to be.

It was almost time for Blythe to blow out the candles on her birthday cake. It was her favorite, an extravagant, foot-tall, red velvet cake decorated with edible jewelry and pearls.

The couple stood around the cake along with other guests, and they began to sing and wish Blythe a happy birthday. Glowing like a princess, loving friends and family surrounded her, and the celebrities in attendance recognized her like she was one of their own.

Blythe quickly blew out the candles and thanked everyone for coming, and then she began cutting into the cake, aching to sink her teeth into it.

Chico stood away from the cutting of the cake, sipping his wine and looking around the impressive party he had put together. Some faces he knew well, and some he didn't know at all. He stepped away from the pool and walked toward the patio.

As he stared into the sea of faces, someone caught his eye. He couldn't believe it. He was wide-eyed as he focused on the woman wearing a long ruffle trim gown with open back and low-cut crossover front that showed her ample cleavage. Her hair was long and black like a panther. A handsome gentleman in a sparkling cream suit escorted her.

Chico thought he was seeing things. He locked eyes with the woman approaching, and she smiled.

"Hello, Chico," she greeted.

"What the fuck?"

"Surprised to see me?" she asked coolly.

After numerous plastic surgeries by some of the finest surgeons in the world Apple was almost completely healed from her burns. It had cost a small fortune, but the money was well worth it. She felt rejuvenated and alive again.

Chico was almost speechless. "Apple . . . how did you find me?"

Apple smirked. "Easily. But I'm surprised *you* never found *me*."

"I tried. I looked all over for you."

"Oh, did you?"

"Yes, I did. I truly did. I swear on everything I love." Chico shifted nervously on his feet. His heart began to beat rapidly. He continued, "But you look good."

"I do, huh? Feeling good too. You remember Guy Tony?"

Both men nodded at each other. No need for words or a handshake.

Apple looked around. "Lovely setup. I see you went all out for your new woman for her birthday."

"I thought you were dead," Chico explained.

"Well, I'm not. I'm alive, looking good, and very aware of things now." She kept looking around the estate. "Very aware."

Chico was almost paralyzed from shock as they stood eye to eye. He glanced over at Blythe, who was standing by the pool and the birthday cake, entertaining a few people.

Apple leaned in near Chico and whispered in his ear, "Your reign on top will be short-lived. Enjoy it while you can, 'cuz I'm back. Checkmate, muthafucka."

TO BE CONTINUED

GUARD
THE THRONE

NISA
SANTIAGO